PAWAN

Sorabh Pant, according to *The Times of India*, is 'one of India's top comedians'. He does stand-up comedy for money and writes books to spend that money. *Pawan* is his third novel. As one of India's most popular stand-up comedians, he has done 1500 shows across 85 cities in 18 countries; but he claims he did them only for the frequent flyer miles. He is also the ex-founder of East India Comedy—and his videos for shows such as *Rant of the Pant*, *EIC: Outrage*, etc. have over 120 million views online.

Other books authored by him are *The Wednesday Sun* and *Under Delhi*, both of which received positive reviews.

PAWAN
THE FLYING ACCOUNTANT

SORABH PANT

RUPA

Published by
Rupa Publications India Pvt. Ltd 2017
7/16, Ansari Road, Daryaganj
New Delhi 110002

Sales centres:
Allahabad Bengaluru Chennai
Hyderabad Jaipur Kathmandu
Kolkata Mumbai

Copyright © Sorabh Pant, 2017

This is a work of fiction. Names, characters, places and incidents are either the product of the author's imagination or are used fictitiously and any resemblance to any actual person, living or dead, events or locales is entirely coincidental.

All rights reserved.
No part of this publication may be reproduced, transmitted, or stored in a retrieval system, in any form or by any means, electronic, mechanical, photocopying, recording or otherwise, without the prior permission of the publisher.

ISBN: 978-81-291-4930-5

Second impression 2018

10 9 8 7 6 5 4 3 2

The moral right of the author has been asserted.

Printed at Parksons Graphics Pvt. Ltd, Mumbai

This book is sold subject to the condition that it shall not, by way of trade or otherwise, be lent, resold, hired out, or otherwise circulated, without the publisher's prior consent, in any form of binding or cover other than that in which it is published.

Disclaimer

Any resemblance to any God, living or dead, is purely coincidental. All demigods in this book are merely "inspired" by the originals—they are flawed, ridiculous and human; and definitely not the Gods themselves. These are the relatives of those Gods.

If, however, you still choose to be offended by these Gods, just remember, the Gods have a better sense of humour than you do.

And all Gods were born out of words.

The following story unravels in a land that is nothing like India, yet it is exactly like her. It takes place in an India that is absolutely realistic, except for the parts that aren't. This unreality makes the story more authentic.

The same applies to the *almost* reality of China.

Contents

Prologue / xi

Legend #38 / 1
Legend #64 / 19
Legend #23 / 41
Legend #12 / 51
Legend #89 / 89
Legend #14 / 99
Legend #66 / 111
Legend #35 / 129
Legend #90 / 144
Legend #55 / 170
Legend #20 / 194
Legend #6 / 208
Legend #61 / 227
Legend #2 / 234
Legend #95 / 251

Acknowledgements / 283

'I say, Gods are born out of legends and folklore but often, those legends start with truth. And the truest legend I ever saw had a tail, the strength of a thousand men, a wicked sense of humour and a heart that bore the weight of a nation. He was not just a God, a monkey or a human being, he was a legend—a *real* legend.'

—Lord Mountbatten's Secret Journals,
The Chronicles Of Mounting Difficulty.

Prologue

The following extract is procured from the secret journals of Lord Mountbatten, the last Viceroy of India. The extract details an incident that apparently occurred on his trip with Prince Edward to India in 1921. Most critics and a large chunk of the British government dismiss this story as a figment of a drug-induced hangover, a possibility that cannot be ruled out given the proximity of Shimla to the world's best hashish and a shortage of much else to do at the time.

Prince Charles called it "the product of an imagination that had inhaled horseshit mixed with some Indian moonshine" as part of an improvised speech at the knighting of Lord Benedict Cumberbatch.

A negligible group of people, however, believe the story to be true.

An Extract from *The Chronicles Of Mounting Difficulty*

I could hardly believe my luck. There, in front of me, stood a man the Crown considered their biggest threat. A man, who the Company believed, could derail the best-laid plans of mice and honourable men. A man whose moral compass was so convincing, one could hardly believe it was working.

There, underneath the foliage of trees, stood Gandhi. In the bright moonlight, his white woven khadi and his bony figure gave him a sepulchral feel—he was the ghost of the British kingdom's past. Back then, I hardly knew how true that description would be. He stood smiling in the misty air with no baggage. He only carried a tiny, white rolled-up sack—the kind children carried when pretending to run away from home.

'I say, Mr Gandhi, aren't you chilly?' asked Prince Edward, ever the gentleman, as he stood beside me. Such a naïve question when we both knew that in a few moments, the chill would be the last of Gandhi's problems.

'Your Grace and Mr Mountbatten, I'm warmed by my struggle for the freedom of my motherland. And the walk uphill helped,' said the man with a smile, not moving from his spot.

What a remarkable opening dialogue! Here was a man who had trekked for a couple of hours after an arduous train journey from Delhi, surely his wits were affected. But nay, his beliefs were genuine; further evidence of how dangerous he could be.

A few pairs of feet shuffled close to him. Dragging feet—

feet that could not keep up with the man's pace in walking or in morals. A few stalled around Gandhi, huffing and puffing like smokeless dragons. There were six of them with four porters. I did some quick mathematics to figure out if we had enough manpower to deal with the unexpected load.

'What's the hold up, Mohan?' said one of them in Hindi.

I will not get into the specifics of Gandhi's companions. It would suffice to say that they were the top tier of the Majesty's Rogues Gallery or in the Indian context, "freedom" fighters.

'These gentlemen were having a little chat,' said Gandhi. 'A warm chat,' he added, with a smile.

'We've got all morning to chat, Mohan. Let's rest,' replied another man.

'It is not the time to be tired. We can do that in a few years,' replied Gandhi.

The Prince shuffled nervously in his place, 'Is that your entire party, what? Everyone accounted for? No surprises, I hope?'

I sighed. He had a tendency to allow his fragile nerves to get the better of his limited sense. Royalty! They really would never be able to rule if it weren't for men like me—their cousins.

'Yes, that is all of us,' said one of the men, his sweater glistening with dew. 'Now, please show us our quarters.'

The Prince hesitated and before he could speak, I held up my hand, 'Gentlemen and Lady,' I began, in my best voice, 'we have come to talk about peace with India's best minds. It is an honour that you have arrived,' and I followed the little speech with a bow, more out of mock reverence than anything else.

Everyone, except Gandhi, was confused. It made me want to pluck my hair out. I continued, 'We shall give you refreshments shortly and dessert as well. In fact, let's start the discussion right now.'

With that, I clapped my hands thrice.

Within moments, the battalion was out from their hiding spots. They surrounded the motley crew of India's almost-freedom fighters. The soldiers' muskets glinted in the moonlight.

Almost-freedom fighters, I thought. In retrospect, I think myself an utter fool.

'I knew it!' one of them cried out, 'I knew it was a setup! I told you we should have come with our guards. I told you!'

'Calm down, Subhas. I'm sure these gentlemen have a perfectly logical explanation for calling us into a sparsely populated area and surrounding us with a battalion of armed soldiers,' said Gandhi. He even smiled, damn him. He smiled in the face of it all. Deuce his impertinence! Well, the smile would fade shortly.

'No,' said the Prince, 'it is to kill you, I say. There's no other explanation, I'm afraid.'

I sighed again. If he hadn't been the Queen's son, he would have barely made it even as an ironmonger's apprentice!

I turned to the party, 'Well, it has been good knowing you all. But the Crown is exhausted and cannot deal with this nonsense anymore. The Prince and I will be off now. We don't really like the sight of blood, gore and all that. Cheerio!'

I pulled the Prince towards the mansion behind us.

'Don't walk away! Fight like a man!' screamed one of the fighters.

I turned, 'Sir, my manhood is hardly in doubt. The manhood of the man with a battalion of gun-wielding soldiers is usually beyond question. Cheerio, once again!'

The Prince and I turned to walk away. I heard the stamping of the soldiers pushing in, the sliding of their weapons, and I waited to hear the final knell before the end of India's freedom movement. I awaited the shots but the sounds behind me were not what I had expected.

There were thuds and groans and sounds of kicks and grunts of men. *Fine*, I thought, *they're doing it without guns. Kudos to that. Torture them for how they have tortured us.*

We walked on.

'Perhaps,' said the voice of that familiar man again, 'you would care to turn around, gentlemen.'

I swivelled on my toes and looked behind me. My entire battalion was incapacitated! Some were groaning on the floor, a few were tied up, while others happened to be nestled on the trees.

'What the deuce!' howled the Prince. 'Apologies for my…err…French, Ma'am,' he said to the lady in the group.

The group stood shaken, their mouths open with disbelief. Once again, I noticed that man standing in the middle of the mess with his mischievous smile. I would have gladly scalped the Queen's head, right there and then, to wipe that smile off his face.

'Shall we talk about peace now, gentlemen?'

He asked and moved towards us. I pushed the Prince's jaw back up as India's future father of the nation walked towards me without a single break in his stride. If he thought it was over, he was sadly mistaken.

'Well done. Good job,' I said, 'I don't know how you did it, but you did. However, it's not over till the man with the gun sings.'

I pulled my new revolver out from my waistcoat and shook it in front of Gandhi's smiling face. This time he looked worried. 'It may look tiny but it packs a punch. Our people have been working on it for a long time. It can blow a chap's brains clean off,' and without a pause, I pressed the trigger. There was a gasp from Gandhi—the end always came rather anticlimactically.

There was a rustle in the trees and before I knew what was happening, a large figure stood between Gandhi and me. The piercing bullet bounced off the figure's chest and dropped innocuously upon the browned leaves below.

'Ow,' grunted a voice in deep timbre, 'that one stings.' It bent down and picked up the bullet with interest. 'Ah, interesting,' it said, and crushed the bullet as if it were a sugar cube.

I saw the face of the figure in the moonlight. It had a human face except for a slight protrusion of the lip and jaw, which popped out like a swelling. Its eyes were brownish-red and it had a mane of dark hair waving in the slight breeze. Its broad chest had a mass of hair that resembled fur. Its built could only be compared to a military jeep. It was intimidating. It might also be important to mention at this point that the figure was roughly seven feet tall.

'You took your time with that one,' said Gandhi, who was standing behind the figure.

'Sorry, Bapu. Didn't think he'd have that on him,' said the figure.

'Almost gave me a heart attack,' said Gandhi and then smiled, 'are you alright?'

The big head rose and burst into a toothy expression, which was half-smile and half-snarl.

'Does a mountain ever feel a pebble crash against it, Bapu? Shall I kill him?'

Gandhi ignored this question and looked past him with a sigh, straight at the Prince who reacted to the incident rather eloquently.

'What the deuce! Yetis are real?'

Gandhi walked past the creature and approached us, ignoring the gun that was still in my hand. I pushed the trigger for another shot but a massive hand descended upon mine, crushing both my finger and my gun.

'Stop it! Now!' it bellowed, its mane flowing with the breeze.

Gandhi put a hand on the creature, 'Calm. No violence. Remember, no violence, only self-defence.'

The creature grunted and released my hand. I howled in pain. The rest of Gandhi's party stood at the back staring at the creature with obvious surprise. It was clear that its presence was as shocking for them as it was for us.

'It is okay, everyone. I apologize for not telling you about him. But we have to keep a hidden assurance for our motherland. I may be non-violent but I'm not naïve. He is my insurance,' he said and patted the creature's back.

I saw a massive tail swirl around the creature's figure and that is when it struck me, 'He is a God, he is *that* God!'

'No, he's not,' said Gandhi, decisively, 'if he were a God, he wouldn't be in front of us. He's more and less than that.'

'I'm afraid I don't understand,' I said.

'For once, Mr Mountbatten, we agree. It is a good place to talk about peace in my land,' said Gandhi and began walking towards the guest house behind him. 'Come on, everyone. I for one could use a night's rest before we talk about the future.'

The rest of his party joined him and as they passed the Prince and me, we stood frozen, too stunned to respond. The creature in front of us was gathering the guns of the fallen soldiers in its giant hands. His lithe movement was mesmerizing. He saw us staring at him and a glint passed his eyes before he snarled again.

Before I could blink, he was in front of my face. He bent his head down and spoke with a rumbling voice, his breath reeking of animalistic venom, 'I'll be awake. If I see any trouble…' and with a single movement, he smashed the entire collection of rifles on his knee, which snapped like twigs. The threat was clear—we would be the rifles.

He bounded away into the trees as I shivered in my boots. The Prince's curiosity, however, was still intact.

'Wha...wha...what's your name?' he screamed at the creature.

It stopped in its tracks and turned back to us as the moonlight reflected off his red eyes. It considered the question and then said, 'They call me Pawan. Pawan, the XXII.' Looking down at me with pity and curiosity, he added 'Or the XXXIV, depending on who is counting.'

'I... I...I say, Sir, I...don't understand. The XXII?' the Prince stuttered.

The creature looked at me and did something I hardly wanted to see —it smiled; its teeth gnashed into a wolfish expression of joviality.

'There have been Pawans before me and there will be Pawans after me. One is already on his way. My own,' he said. 'For as long as there is the wind, there will be a Pawan,' and without another word, he bounded up the tree with nimbleness impossible for a human being.

And as if to put me in my place, he flew between two trees. Yes, flew! Not jump, mind you! It *flew* in the air like a human with wings; floated upon the bark of a tree ahead and then disappeared into the darkness from which it had come and possibly belonged.

That is the last I saw of the creature on that trip. It was more than I had intended to see. Over the next few years, his presence would linger around Gandhi whenever there was a moment of crisis or, as it seemed to me, whenever I would question the reality of that fateful night in Shimla.

Chapter One

Legend #38

Lord Hanuman was not the first, nor the last of his lineage. He was one of the vanaras—a people rumoured to have lived in South India, North India or even Madhya Pradesh, depending on who wants to claim credit.

Many think that there were only some vanaras with special powers but there were a handful of his relatives who were almost as gifted. The vanaras were a race of humanoid monkeys who had the power to be shape-shifters, and more. After all, the vanaras were Indian; they could not but have a really large family.
Hence, it's not beyond reason that some of them carried on the vanaras' legacy, but with all their human faults and weaknesses. It is true; humanity can turn even the purest to perverse.

Today was going to be the day Arjun Singh died. And he could not have been happier. His face shone with radiance, his teeth bared in a glorious grin. Spiritualists have maintained that living life to the fullest is salvation, but for Arjun, the possibility of death was true nirvana. More people should have this feeling. When they go bungee jumping, they should cut the cord and they should pray for a bird to crash into their plane mid-flight because nothing makes you truly alive than the chance of dying.

He stood on the terrace, looking down at the crouched buildings surrounding him and realized there could be no better place for a murder than a terrace in Lucknow. This particular terrace was a laboratory of subcontinental insanity: red chillies dried on one end, green chillies on another, pickles marinated in a jar, papads sunbathed on a blanket, a chillum containing hashish smouldered on a khatiya and undergarments swayed in the breeze—Y-briefs large enough to work as circus tents, a bra that could be used as a slingshot for cannons, and multi-coloured panties that looked like stonewashed candies.

Arjun stood facing his would-be killers and beamed. Four goons, each of them only a few inches shorter than him—which was saying something—stood with an array of weapons. Despite their unusual size, he dwarfed them and though he could snap them like toothpicks, he had no such intention.

'Tonight, Arjun Singh,' said the shortest but the meanest of them. Shorter people were always meaner to Arjun as if his heightened verticality was a biological insult to them. 'You'll learn what it is like to mess with the wrong people. Today, you die.'

'Awesome,' replied Arjun, 'makes perfect sense. I'm with you guys on that. Let's do this!'

The man was surprised by this response. Arjun had that effect on people. His physicality itself was confounding to most. He was well over six and a half feet tall, broad as a truck and wore a cheap suit and tie that clung to his thick body like entitlement on a neta's son—and that was just half of it.

'This guy looks like Salman Khan and Ram Kapoor had a baby,' said one of the goons, 'he has Sallu's body with Ram's abs. What a truly secular fellow.'

The other three goons agreed to this assessment and let out a timorous laugh. They needed to release the pressure of facing the intimidating sight that was Arjun Singh. If his bulk wasn't enough to overawe him, his uncut nails—almost three inches long— looked like they could scythe through titanium. He wasn't hygienic and it was obvious. But it was his face that struck people the most.

'Is he wearing an oxygen mask?' asked one of the goons.

'No, John. I think that's his face.'

Arjun buckled under the insult but he had to admit: the protrusion on his lips and mouth gave an impression that he was following safety procedures on a turbulent aircraft. Anyway, he was way too excited at the thought of his death to be truly insulted.

'You screwed with the wrong people, man,' began the guy who had a muffler around his head.

'I just said that, Darius. At least listen before making a threat,' said the leader.

'Why do you have to be like that, Manoj? I'm trying, okay?' complained Darius and he whipped out a weapon. It was a three-bladed weapon with a sickle on one side and two daggers pointing in the opposite directions. It shone in the sunlight and he whirled it around his own face clumsily.

The other three goons gasped, 'What the hell is that, Darius?'

Darius whirled the weapon awkwardly again, in front of his face this time, 'It's a Njiga. Cool, na?'

'Dude, don't use the "n" word,' reprimanded John.

'No, *Nji-ga*. My great-grandfather got it while fighting in Chad in Africa.'

'How did he die?'

'Oh,' said Darius thoughtfully, 'I think he mishandled his weapon.'

'You're going to cut yourself,' replied Manoj, 'put that thing away. You are Parsi—your life is precious.'

'Yeah,' agreed the other goons, 'the rest of us can afford to act like that. You do it—that's half your population gone. Tata needs an heir, Darius.'

'Screw you, guys. Enough with the bloody Parsi jokes.'

'We're not being funny,' replied Manoj. 'Tell him, John.'

'The extinction of the Parsi community is no joke,' agreed John.

'Afzal, you have four brothers. Tell your mom to teach Darius' mom how to make babies,' said Manoj.

'Man, why you getting my mom into this?'

'Hey, don't take offence. She's the professional, bro.'

'Okay,' said Afzal, 'if we're talking about professionals,

let's talk about your dad. Three wives and six kids. He's got an AK-47 down there.'

'Bro, that's a private matter,' squealed Manoj, 'Afzal, you suck as a best friend.'

All four began bickering incessantly. Arjun wasn't enjoying this—it was all very unprofessional. Here he was at the cusp of death and to have it disrupted by arbitrary bickering was so typical. This was the problem with the country; even low-level goons could not maintain competence.

He stared at the city and with the setting sun, he could see an orb of pollution engulf Lucknow. If the goons didn't kill him, at least he would eventually die of lung infection. There were always positives to a situation, but he was impatient.

'Guys, guys,' he said, 'you were in the middle of killing me?'

'Right,' said Manoj, the leader. 'Jiyo Parsi can wait. Arjun Singh, our client lost a lot of money. Your goddamn firm screwed us over. We had to pay so much tax! You're a C.A., that's *your* job! You have to save our money, not make us lose it. We lost thirteen lakhs because of...'

'Actually, it was 13.76 lakhs, to be precise. Almost fourteen lakhs,' corrected Arjun.

He didn't correct Manoj's other error: Arjun had not handled the client in question. Clients audited by Arjun never lost money. He took great pride in his job. But pride in your job can't come in the way of your dreams—of dying.

'Whatever. 14 lakhs is a lot of money. So, it is time for you to die,' said Manoj and whipped out a large pistol from his pocket.

'Agreed!' said Arjun and directed the pistol to his head. 'I think the brain would be best? Or would the heart be? Oh, look at me coming in the way of professionals. How do you guys usually do this? My recommendation would be to go for the heart and then, the head. Three bullets each. Can't be too sure.'

Manoj pulled the gun away from Arjun's head, 'We usually threaten and push people around for a bit before we kill them.'

Arjun held up his hands, 'Oh, sorry. Guess that would be premature. Who hasn't shot in advance, right? Please proceed with the threats.'

'We will tie your intestines around your neck like a bowtie,' said Manoj, smacking Arjun hard on the head with the gun. Arjun squealed with pleasure.

'I'll take your face, pull it out and make you kiss your ass goodbye,' said John, brandishing his knife and kicking Arjun hard on the shins. More squeals from Arjun.

'I'll take out your liver and dip it in alcohol so that you die of alcohol poisoning from the outside,' threatened Afzal, smacking Arjun in the chest with his hockey stick. Arjun wheezed with joy.

'Bro, I'm going to like, you know, kill you and stuff,' said Darius, whipping his Njiga around his head. The weapon flew in the air and its blades, whirring in the fading sunlight, descended upon Darius' head.

Arjun extended his hand out and somehow managed to catch the knife before it sliced Darius' neck. 'Be careful, man. Don't kill yourself! That's my thing.'

He then handed the knife back to the curly-haired Parsi in front of him.

'The hell is wrong with you, Darius?' screamed Manoj and charged towards his friend.

'For fuck's sake, man!' howled Afzal. 'This is not a joke.'

'You know what, I'm confiscating the weapon,' said Manoj and pulled back the Njiga from Darius before keeping it in his backpack.

John froze, staring at Arjun's face, 'Did no one see what just happened?'

'Aside from Darius behaving like a dumbass?' asked Afzal.

John pointed at Arjun, 'He saved his life.'

All four goons stared at Arjun as if looking at him for the very first time. They patted him on the back, stroked his hair and gave him multiple high-fives. Arjun smiled uncomfortably, 'Pshaw! It was nothing, what's a little life and death here and there?'

'What have you always said about our gang, Afzal?' asked Manoj.

'We need to implement Six Sigma quality,' said Afzal.

'Dude, you pursued your MBA for three months. Get over it,' said John.

'No, the other thing,' said Manoj. 'We have a Hindu, Muslim, Christian, Parsi but we don't have a...'

'Sikh!' completed Afzal and pointed towards Arjun.

'Well, technically, I'm not a Sikh...' began Arjun.

Manoj looked up at Arjun and smiled, 'Arjun Singh, you just saved Darius' life. Do you want to be part of The

Secular Gang?'

'The *what* gang?' asked Arjun.

'The Secular Gang. Divided by religion, united by our love for violence; much like India,' explained John. 'All in favour, say: Aye!'

'Aye!' said everyone, unanimously.

'One second,' protested Arjun, 'you are still going to kill me, right?'

'Nope,' said Manoj, 'that's cannibalism. We don't kill our own.' He then proceeded to put the gun back in his pocket.

'I'd like nothing more than killing you,' said John, 'but to quote Vin Diesel bhaiya—Family!'

The rest followed Manoj's example and put their knives, hockey sticks and swords away.

'But...but, you promised to kill me,' said Arjun.

'Nah. Promises can be broken. You can die some other day.'

'But I don't want to die another day. I want to die today. I had scheduled it all,' said Arjun. 'I screwed you guys over, remember? Behenji Capital Mutual Funds.'

'You're right. BC MF. That's like a double insult. First to my sister, then to my mother. Those are the guys we should kill!' said John.

'Your boss should die.'

Arjun was exasperated. What kind of a world was he living in where even the lowest scums of the Earth refused to honour their word? He stomped his foot like a child, constantly repeating, 'But...you...promised!'

With a sudden lurch, he grabbed Manoj's belt and

pulled out his gun, 'Fine. If you won't do it, then I will!' He removed the safety and pointing the gun to his head, he pressed the trigger—to nothing.

'Sorry, man. It's not loaded. We were only supposed to threaten you. Send a message. Not kill,' said Manoj. '14 lakhs…'

'13.76 lakhs,' corrected Arjun.

'Whatever. It's really not enough to get someone killed.'

Arjun looked at the gun—the weapon that held so much promise—and then back at the apologetic goons. He took the gun in his palm, crushed it like it was made of foil and threw it back at Manoj.

The man grabbed his crushed gun with surprise, 'Did you just crush my… That was a Glock… How did you…'

Arjun adjusted his tie, 'You know what? When you want to get something done, you have to do it yourself.' And without another word to his former-captors, he ran to the edge of the terrace, leapt into the air and flew five storeys to his death—with a final squeal of delight.

∽

Mukesh Bakshi had been a great man; he had given his countrymen a balm to soothe themselves in every crisis—when the economy collapsed, when wars were announced, when reality shows infected TV screens—he had been there for his people: by selling them tankards and tankards of booze.

Indians had downed his cheap rum to save themselves *from* themselves. He was the seller of the greatest magic potion any country could ever need—cheap rum, The Old Baxter.

He had even been a philanthropist of the oddest kind—donating 10,000 cases of rum annually to India's armed forces. Soldiers swore that his rum had saved them in their darkest hours, warmed them in chilling border towns and reminded them of the reason they fought for.

Bakshi & Sons had forayed into other businesses as well, all of which were terrible—their biscuits were too soggy, their diapers were not, their restaurants had waiters that were too sober, their airlines had pilots that were too drunk, their hospitals had nurses who were too hot and their ready-to-eat soups were too cold. But they stayed afloat because of yo-ho-ho and a bottle of rum.

The bottles featured a grinning Mr Bakshi with an old English bowler hat as an ode to the Brit he had bought the company from. Every drunkard, alcoholic or social drinker knew and loved this face. Now, that face was no more. Mukesh Bakshi had died of liver failure, which epitomized his legacy. And the face had been replaced by another face—that of his son, Rakesh Bakshi; a man who many believed had the charm of a migraine.

At that very moment, Druk Lepcha, resident of Tawang, a border town in Arunachal Pradesh and the owner of the "Lucky" restaurant/bar/coffeehouse/general store/crèche/hotel/ medical store/ wine shop/ but no cigarettes was contemplating the new packaging. He almost regretted drinking his beloved rum and giving Rakesh Bakshi's face his hard-earned money.

He didn't like the face one bit.

Very few enjoyed Rakesh Bakshi's face or The Old Baxter's new packaging that also happened to feature his face. His bald head and cocky smirk poked out of the new bottle of rum—looking pleased to have taken your money.

Since his father's death, it was a face Lepcha and the country had gotten tired of. Rakesh had the habit of showing up wherever he was not invited: which was everywhere. He had gatecrashed Apple's first launch in India by kissing Tim Cook in the mouth, he had streaked through an India-Pakistan World Cup final in Delhi wearing only the rum's cover on his groin area and he had punched Suhel Seth in the face during an Arnab Goswami debate. This had led to an all-out physical assault on the show—which many felt was overdue—that had ended with Arnab choke slamming Robert Vadra against a teleprompter, which, for the record, Lepcha felt was more than fair.

Bakshi's latest adventure had been gatecrashing the Republic Day Parade with his own float where he had screamed allegations against India's five PMs. He had claimed they hadn't rewarded him defence contracts because of inadequate bribes. He had then proceeded to ruin the credibility of his allegations by awarding himself a Bravery Award for "Being too damn sexy".

These actions did not befit the CEO of one of India's biggest companies, or even a human being. *The Economic Times* defined Rakesh's tactics as "disruptive", which apparently meant a good thing in modern marketing. *Business Standard* called him "Richard Branson on cocaine," which Bakshi accepted as a compliment.

'Well,' said Lepcha to the gorgeous view of mountains and the misty valley in front of him, 'if this rum lets me have as much fun as Bakshi, I guess it wouldn't be that bad after all.'

He poured himself another peg and lit the mosquito coil on his terrace. As he turned back to the valley, he saw something move in the distance. There was a loud screech, bright lights and a dragon emerged from the mists beyond. It was flying towards Lepcha.

A dragon!

Lepcha looked at the bottle of The Old Baxter and shattered it against the wall. That was the moment he decided he would never drink again.

∞

Arjun sat on his hospital bed with his eyes closed. He hated this bed. Like a mother whose son had failed to clear IIT-JEE, it reminded him of his failure. He had failed at dying. What kind of a life was this in which one couldn't even die properly? The fact that he had survived a five-storey fall disappointed him. Fortunately, the medicines were getting to his brain which was the only benefit of the hospital—they had given him so many painkillers, he didn't even need cheap rum to forget his existence. When he eventually opened his eyes, he found himself wishing he had not.

The room was of a higher class than he was used to. No stains on the walls, no holes in the sheet, a bed with automated levers and an air of sterility. It was definitely not a government hospital. But the eyesore of the room was its inhabitants.

'He's awake. Thank Krishna,' squealed Manoj.

'And Allah. Our best friend is alive,' howled Afzal.

'And Jesus. We thought we'd lost you,' screamed John.

'And Rooney. Does anyone know how to make this stupid TV work?' asked Darius, smashing the remote control on his thigh. 'I need to watch the EPL.'

'Oh God,' said Arjun to the three and a half eager faces staring at him.

Darius managed to get the TV on. A loud voice broke through as a news anchor screamed in Hindi, 'A naked Rakesh Bakshi's latest allegation against our PMs—he calls them P.M.S. But wait, India is under attack!'

He continued, 'And this time, it is a dragon. *Ji haan, azgar, ji haan, badi chipkali!* Arunachal Pradesh has witnessed a dragon trying to attack them...'

'Turn it off,' protested Manoj. 'If I wanted fake news, I'd speak to my Mausi.'

Suddenly, the painkillers did not seem enough to Arjun. He needed more. He reached for the satchel next to him and pulled out a Swiss army bottle of booze. Why give reality even a modicum of chance to raise its ugly head on him?

But the bottle was empty, much like his soul.

'Friend, you tripped and fell. You were so drunk on the terrace,' said Manoj.

'I didn't trip and fall. I...I...' began Arjun.

'Haha,' said John, 'classic Arjun. Falling off drunk from a terrace when Jesus saved him.'

'Classic Arjun, really? You've known me for what, six hours?' said Arjun.

'Sometimes six hours is enough, best friend!' said John and gently stroked Arjun's fur-like hair.

'Stop doing that. I need my bloody booze.'

Afzal pointed to Arjun's bedside table, 'We got you a substitute!' he said.

On his bedside were juice boxes and tea bags.

'Yay,' mocked Arjun, 'that better be Long Island iced tea and pina colada.'

'Best friends look after each other,' said Manoj. 'If the mango juice is good for Katrina, it is jolly well good for you, dost.'

At that moment, the nurse peeped into the room, 'Oh good, you're awake. Gentlemen, it's past visiting hours. Please leave.'

Afzal took out a knife from his pocket and bared it at the nurse, 'Guess what, visiting hours just got extended.'

The nurse scampered off at the very unsubtle threat.

Arjun closed his eyes, hoping his new companions would disappear. The purpose of the suicide was to reinforce the isolation that had been forced upon him for so long. Years of rejection, unfriendliness and apathy could not be compensated for by a few minutes with a bunch of overenthusiastic psychos.

He decided to sleep. He loved to sleep; it allowed him eight hours when he could forget about his existence. He could lie in the hospital bed for as long as he wanted. He was busy in his thoughts when suddenly, his contemplation was interrupted.

The door slammed open and a woman walked into the room. Her make-up and jewellery overpowered even her dramatic entry. She didn't just enter the room—she decimated it, she overtook it, she consumed it; she became the room. She was led inside by a nurse and as soon as she looked at Arjun, she broke into hysterics.

Arjun sighed. He had wished this upon himself. He shoved some cotton balls in his ears, preparing himself for the decibel-shattering yelling that was to commence shortly.

'Why? Why? Why? Have I not fed you enough? Have I not loved you enough? Have I not given you my soul? Do you want to eat my soul? Take it! Take my soul with some aam ka aachaar!' the Punjabi lady screamed, her garish face brighter than the reindeer's nose on a Christmas night.

Arjun stared at her with indifferent eyes and picked up a juice box. The crushed hopes of a fruit were preferable to the hysterics.

The nurse held the woman's quivering shoulder with a mix of fear and compassion. 'See what you have done to your mother, beta? Why kill yourself when your own mother loves you so much?' asked the nurse, looking accusingly at Arjun, who was now pricking the juice box with a straw.

'She's not my mother. She's my legal guardian,' replied Arjun. 'Do you notice any similarities between us?' He stroked the bump on his face as evidence.

The four men present in the room suddenly looked very uncomfortable. Their eyes shifted from Arjun to the lady and then to the floor.

'I just remembered,' said Manoj, 'I have an appointment with my...err...barber.'

'Oh yes, me too. With your barber,' offered Afzal.

'Your barber is my best friend. After you, Arjun,' said John.

'We just went to the barber yesterday, guys!' said a confused Darius.

All four of them —with Darius being dragged out—left the room, muttering their apologies to the new entrant. Arjun couldn't decide if he was happy or sad to see them leave. The nurse sighed and turned to the woman, 'Some forms need to be filled out, Mrs. Kapoor. Urgently.'

'Later!' said Mrs. Kapoor, 'Can't you see I'm in the middle of my melodrama?'

The nurse considered this and excused herself from the room. The second she was gone, Mrs. Kapoor transitioned into a calm and composed woman.

'I can't keep doing this, Arjun,' she said nonchalantly and took out a cigarette from her massive purse. 'You got to stop trying to kill yourself.'

She lit the cigarette, violating around three hundred hospital rules in the process. She took a deep drag and blew in Arjun's face, as if cancer was something worth sharing. Arjun reached for another juice box and looked at her, expressionless.

'And this time, you have dragged these gundas into this. Jumping off a building? I mean, really? What about subtlety? We don't need this kind of attention on you. You know that,' she said, between annoyed puffs.

Arjun responded by slurping his juice.

'How did you get into this fancy hospital anyway?' asked Mrs. Kapoor.

Arjun shrugged, 'When I failed to die, I pretended to faint on the ground floor. Then, there was some chaos. To avoid the drama, I decided to go to sleep. The next thing I knew, I was here. Who cares? The bed is so comfortable. It has real cotton in it!'

Mrs. Kapoor puffed, 'I'm happy that your attempt to commit suicide has found you a cotton bed. When I agreed to take care of you Arjun, I didn't expect this. But…'

'…you made a promise,' completed Arjun, 'I know. I'm sorry…it's just that I feel like…'

'…you don't belong?' she completed for him and smiled. 'I know, I know. We've been through this, again and again.'

They looked at each other in silence—she, with her black mascara eyes and him, with his feral ones. And then, she looked away, like she always did. His eyes were set too deep in his head; brown, animalistic and full of some ancient curse. She got up, opened the window and flapped her arms to get rid of all the smoke. She ended up looking like a Punjabi penguin, now more than ever.

She tapped Arjun's hands and said, 'I'll fill out the forms.' With that, she walked out of the room without another glance.

It broke Arjun's heart to see her like this. It always did. He never knew what to do. Mrs. Kapoor had been his guardian for very long and she had given so much to him. But yet, somehow, there was no love. She treated him with distance, like he was someone from another world—a burden. The worst part was that she was right.

He grabbed another juice box and finished it in one big gulp. Finally, he would get some sleep. He yawned lazily and was about to doze off when he felt cold metal against his forehead.

He heard a man's voice next to him, 'God, I thought they'd never leave.'

The man clicked off the gun's safety and thrust it into Arjun's head.

Chapter Two

Legend #64

It is not unusual for religious folks to claim that they have seen their Gods. Some see them in their dreams, a few in their mirrors, some on mountains while others in their toasts (yes, really!). But a number of well-respected prophets have claimed that they saw "Hanuman" from the 13th century to the 20th century; notable amongst them being Tulsidas, Swami Ramdas and Madhvacharya.

Of course, as the case is usually with such God sightings, since there was no one else to validate them and no Instagram photos, they are shrouded in mystery.

It stands to reason that maybe it was not Vayu's avatar himself but one of his relative's sons, daughters or just a really distant relative.

The gun poked deeper into his forehead as Arjun tried to catch a glimpse of his attacker but the man did not relent.

'No peeking. Come on. No peeking,' said the man.

'I have little money, unless you want juice. I have lots of juice,' said Arjun. 'I wonder if Manoj kept the bill for them. I could claim it as expenses.'

The man laughed, 'Funny. That would be the worst hold up ever, right? Guns for Appy Fizz.'

Arjun observed that the voice was of a cocksure maniac, an eccentric person who was used to getting what he wanted.

'What do you want?' he asked his assailant.

'You. I love the shape of you. Oh, oh, oh,' said the voice, singing the last part.

Arjun sighed. Ordinarily, he would have accepted the assailant and welcomed him to blow up his brains but that wouldn't do. He wanted to die, but not at the beck and call of an egotistical lunatic.

'I know who you are, Arjun. Or at least what you are, even if you don't,' said the voice.

Arjun folded his hands, 'You know my name? Great. You want to shoot me, go ahead. But I'm not going to enjoy it. I'm just telling you.'

The man squealed with laughter, the gun's barrel scraping Arjun's head, 'This is a fine game we play. A gun held against someone unaffected. It is like playing "Call of Duty" with the Dalai Lama. Just stop the pretence and admit it.'

His arrogance made Arjun want to do exactly the opposite of what he was suggesting. If this voice would have told him the Earth was a sphere, Arjun would have gone out of his way to prove that it was in fact a rhombus.

'I have nothing to admit. I'm an…'

'Accountant, yes. I know,' said the voice.

'Chartered Accountant. Big difference. But, yes. That's what I do. I'm good at my job and I'm manic-depressive. I'm single. I love drinking. There, I admitted it. What else do you want?'

The gun was poked at Arjun's skull again, 'Oh, you're funny. But you must know that I will get you to admit what you…'

He didn't get a chance to finish his sentence because right behind him had crept up Mrs. Kapoor. Her hysterics had evaporated and she stood behind him with a scalpel close to his neck. Her eyes were focused, and her hand, unwavering—she had the air of a person who had been in such a situation before and had survived.

'Drop the gun or I'll slice your neck so deep no doctor will be able to attach your bloated head back,' she whispered into the man's ear.

Arjun turned his head slightly and saw that the man wore a monkey cap which was covering his face. Behind the cap, he stifled a laugh and answered, 'Mrs. Kapoor. Fantastic you joined us. You and I both know the truth, so let's not pretend that what you said is going to happen. This is not a Mexican stand-off, this is stupidity.'

'Leave my boy alone and drop the gun, now,' said Mrs. Kapoor with such protectiveness, Arjun almost wanted to live for her.

'Your boy?' said the man. 'He's not *your* anything. You're his legal guardian as sanctioned by his family—his *real* family.'

For a moment, Mrs. Kapoor's hand quivered; but fortunately for the assailant, it didn't quiver enough to cut him.

She said, 'Many people know this. Lower the weapon now.'

There was silence. The man in the monkey cap seemed to consider this, 'If I don't, you'll chop my neck off because I'm harming your ward?'

'Yes,' said Mrs. Kapoor, 'obviously.'

The assailant laughed at this, 'Mrs. Kapoor, you were part of a force to protect the people of this country. You won't do shit to me. We both know I can't harm your ward, no matter what I do. But I really want to find out.'

With that, he pressed the trigger and the gun fired into Arjun's forehead. The sound of the gunshot echoed inside the room despite its silencer. A loud crackle of glass shattering followed, along with a moment's pause and peals of laughter as the assailant bounced around in ecstasy.

Arjun stretched his hands out and yawned, 'I guess my secret is out.'

Mrs. Kapoor dropped the scalpel on a table by her side. 'We got to leave. If not the gunshot, they must have heard the TV shatter,' she said, pointing towards the small TV that now had a hole in its centre around which the news anchor was still screaming, as if he was the one who had been shot.

The assailant stopped bouncing, 'Shouldn't be a problem,' he said, and removed his mask, 'since, the hospital is mine.'

Rakesh Bakshi removed his monkey cap and stood by

Arjun's side with his twisted smile, 'Everything will be taken care of, Mrs. Kapoor, especially Arjun. You did a great job hiding him but I'm afraid he has now been found. And he will work for me. You can be rest assured. You will be mine.'

Arjun looked at the man's shining baldpate, 'This was a great job interview. But, no thanks.'

'Oh, you wait for our group discussion. There, I will get six people to shoot you at the same time and nothing will happen,' said Bakshi and laughed at his own joke. 'So, when do you want to start?'

'I'm not going to work for you,' said Arjun, 'your dad made great booze, but that was the last great thing he made. You're no Old Baxter.'

Bakshi smirked, 'You don't want to play with me, Arjun. I'm very good with threats. And let me make one now: Republic TV,' and he pointed at the TV screen.

Mrs. Kapoor and Arjun looked at each other; Arjun was the first one to speak, 'I don't watch TV, so if you're pitching me a DTH service…'

'I just recorded this whole thing. Wouldn't it be great? Invincible man takes a bullet in the head and still doesn't die. I can see the headlines—Invincible Monkey Man. Is that offensive?' asked Bakshi.

Mrs. Kapoor didn't seem amused and opened her purse to fish for her handkerchief. She dabbed her sweaty face, removing roughly six kilos of make-up in the process. She then turned to Rakesh Bakshi, 'Well done, Mr Bakshi. However, the video will also have you firing a gun at an innocent. So, you really have nothing. And you may want to sit down.'

'Sit down? Sit down? I'm never going to sit ever again. Ever. Sitting is for losers. I will stand forever! I now have Arjun with me.'

'You don't have me. The only thing you have is a bleeding neck,' said Arjun, reaching for another juice box.

Bakshi touched his neck gingerly and then looked at his hand, 'Eww,' he said, 'bloody stuff.'

'I told you I'd cut you,' said Mrs. Kapoor, offering him her handkerchief. 'Don't worry, it's a superficial wound, no major arteries. However, I would have gotten them if I wanted to.'

She didn't have the chance to finish as Bakshi had fainted at the sight of his own blood. He would have landed on his face if Arjun's hand had not stopped his rapid descent to the floor. He half-wished he hadn't.

Arjun and Mrs. Kapoor laid him on the hospital bed, tied a handkerchief around his neck and tried to erase any sign of their presence in the room, except for a stream of squashed juice boxes, a bullet hole and a smashed TV.

'He just needs a Band-Aid and he's behaving like he needs a brain transplant,' said an annoyed Arjun.

'I've cleaned up worse,' said Mrs. Kapoor from the corridor, 'you can leave the army, but the army does not leave you. Oh, also, I quit.'

Arjun turned to her, 'I'm sorry. You quit what?'

Mrs. Kapoor placed Bakshi flat on his back, 'You, Arjun. I quit you. My orders were to care for you till you were "discovered". Well, guess what? You've been discovered. I can't jeopardize the department I work for, just for you.'

'But you're my only guardian!' exclaimed Arjun, dropping Bakshi's head which slammed against the side of the bed without support.

'You're a grown man, Arjun Singh. You want me to change your diaper? Feed you milk? I'm dry, Arjun. I can't. Now, help me with this body. I got a retirement to look forward to.'

Arjun cursed Bakshi's head as he assisted his former guardian. He would curse him for the next few weeks.

∞

Arjun Singh always tried to like people. He truly did. It was not his fault that nobody liked him. And he hated them for it. People always judged him for his looks. As if he could control his huge size. As if he could control his swollen face. As if he could control that his nails were three inches long. Well, maybe he could control that but Arjun had stopped caring.

Nobody cared for him so he stopped trying. People feared him despite all his efforts so he stopped combing his hair, bathed once a week and grew out his nails like the beloved plants outside his door. This ensemble made people want to talk to him even less but by that time, he was beyond social norms.

It had been a week since his "suicide" attempt and Arjun was glad to be heading back to work. His only human contact had been Mrs. Kapoor and she had also extricated herself from him so fast, it hurt—a fifty-eight year old married woman had managed to break his heart.

The only thing Arjun now gave a toss about was his job. He was damn good at it and he knew it. He wished others knew it as well. He looked at the "C.A. of the month" gallery and his name was conspicuous because of its absence. Rajiv Mehta, Aditya Desai, Sonali Thakker, Nikhil Mehta and even that utter nitwit, Kunal Rao, had made it to the gallery. Kunal Rao—the man who needed a calculator to calculate how many calculators he had. *That* guy had also been employee of the month once. Arjun sighed. He loved his job but his job hated him—as was evident from his current meeting with the head of HR.

Arjun sat on the opposite side of a large conference room table, while a smiling woman sat at the head. She had insisted that he sat as far away from her as possible, as if his gigantism was a disease she didn't want to catch. She held up a long electronic gadget, pointed it at Arjun and zapped it. A burst of red, white and orange light flooded him briefly.

'Hey,' he protested.

'I'm Kiran Chopra,' said the woman, ignoring his protest. 'My friends call me KC, so you can call me Mrs. Chopra. Nice to meet you, Mr Singha,' she said. She wore a business suit and a bad attitude, disguised under a high-voltage fake smile.

'It's Singh, Arjun Singh.'

'Oh, so sorry, Mr Sinha...'

'It's Singh. Singh! It's the second most popular surname in the country!'

She continued smiling, her expression contrary to her tone, 'No reason to scream. It's just a typo, Mr Singham.'

'Okay, forget it. I'm Mr Singham. That topless hero guy on the poster. Great. Whatever.'

The lady didn't seem to hear him and instead pored over a sheaf of papers, 'So, Mr Singhchanna. It's been so nice to have you work for us. But of course, everything has its shelf life. So, we've decided to transfer you out of your current position.'

Arjun was glad there was distance between them. Because right then, he wanted to rip the stupid smile off her face. Instead, he did what he always did when he was stressed—he stroked the pieces of a wooden jigsaw puzzle in his pocket. It was weird for a grown man to carry a jigsaw puzzle but it alleviated his stress with less harm than a cigarette.

'Okay. Transfer me where?'

'Oh, you know, to a department outside this company.'

'What does that mean? You're firing me?'

'Oh, no. We would never fire you, Mr Sinhalese. It's a temporary transfer which is kind of permanent to a department that is outside this company.'

'That sounds like you're firing me.'

'Firing is such a harsh term, Mr Sinhal. We just want to take you from your current position and put you somewhere that is not your current position, outside this company.'

'That's exactly what firing someone is!' screamed Arjun.

'No, no. Mr Sinhagad. Think of it as a promotion to another company, without our help.'

Arjun could not believe what was happening. His job was the only thing he could spend hours doing, happily forgetting all his frustration. It was a small bonus that this job also gave him enough money to buy the essentials such as alcohol, booze and drinks.

'All we need you to do is put in your papers.'

'You just don't want to pay me any severance. I'm not going to. No.'

'Okay, no problem,' she smiled again. 'Then, we're renegotiating the terms for your employment. Your salary is 1 rupee; your medical is now one Disprin per month and your PF is 0. You know what they say; you can't spell poof without PF.'

There was something amiss about this. It couldn't be a coincidence that it had happened immediately after his meeting with Bakshi. Surely that man's manipulation was behind this. But Arjun had never been good at being bullied.

'Okay,' he said, getting up from his chair.

'Sorry, what?' her smile seemed shaken.

'Okay. I accept your terms. I'll get back to work now. Let me know whether my salary of 1 rupee will be in cash, cheque or do you prefer Paytm?'

He was about to reach for the door when he saw a figure appear behind the woman. He saw the figure flicker, rise and briefly turn into the laughing image of Rakesh Bakshi. The figure mocked him, screaming, 'You son of a bitch. Come, be a Baxtard!' In his rage, Arjun picked up a chair and threw it at the figure, which dodged it effortlessly.

'Mr Singhnature, it's my pleasure to fire you without

severance for violence in the workplace. Thanks for coming,' beamed Kiran Chopra and closed her file as if deleting his existence with the slam of the folder.

'If Modi can do it, so can I,' cackled Bakshi's hologram by her side.

∽

Rakesh Bakshi looked up from his Android at the experimental lab he had created. It was his pet project—the backbone of his vision of creating a small army of Übermen, men who were stronger, faster and more aggressive than any before them. They would protect the nation, fight its uncomfortable battles and most importantly, get the government to pay him a truckload of money.

Four test subjects stood in four different cubicles in front of him. Each cubicle was numbered, but designed the same; housed with a small table, a jug, a treadmill, large dumbbells and a punching bag.

'What are the results? How's my potion?' said Rakesh, not looking up from his phone. He was on the verge of conquering the eighth level of Candy Crush Saga 4, and we all have priorities.

A man in a pastel shirt and a clipboard spoke up, 'Sir, we've added a new mix of ginseng, animal protein and a sprinkle of petrol into their blood. And of course, some Old Baxter—all in different doses.'

Rakesh didn't question or find it strange that there were men with fossil fuels in their veins inside his lab. He was used to far more peculiar concoctions—both in his lab and in his private life.

'Test subject X69...' began the scientist.

'Hah! 69!' said a grinning Bakshi.

'Err...yes, Sir. We tried unleaded petrol, concentrated ginseng, eleven ounces protein and a peg of Old Baxter.'

'Small peg or large peg,' he asked.

'Small, Sir,' said the scientist.

'Meh, wussies. Results?' he asked.

'Sir, the anatomical exigencies have driven his body into cardiac...' began the scientist.

'The short version, buddy. I'm a busy man,' interrupted Bakshi, 'you have three minutes.'

The scientist sighed. Here he was changing the human genome and his so-called financier was more concerned about phone games. He wondered if Tesla had to deal with his financiers' obsession with Backgammon.

'We've tried different combinations on all of them. X69 and X70 have roughly 56% increase in speed, 34% in strength and 22% in aggression.'

Without looking up from his screen, Bakshi said, 'Anabolic steroids give a 30% increase. You're not discovering anything new here, Doc.'

The scientist was stung. Bakshi had a habit of doing that—seeming out of depth and suddenly, springing out with something important. He was a rattlesnake with an Android.

'X71 is the one you want to see,' he pointed at the last cubicle and paused for effect. It had the desired result. Bakshi finally looked up from his phone to rebuke him for wasting his time but the figure in front of him got his attention.

All subjects looked stronger than he remembered from last week. They were running at a furious speed on the treadmill, lifting dumbbells weighing 70 kilograms, or pummelling the punching bags assigned to them.

But the change in X71 was the most visible. The man had discernibly pumped up. His body bulged though his T-shirt and he alternated between the treadmill, the weights and the punching bag with alarming speed, muttering constantly.

'Wow, champ. Wow,' said Bakshi.

'104% increase in speed, 112% in strength and a whopping 212% rise in aggression. Plus, high endorphins. We added a dose of anabolic steroids,' said the scientist. 'There's a small problem though...'

X71, his eyes darting wildly and his brow furrowed in confusion, collapsed in a heap in the midst of lifting a 120 kilograms dumbbell. Fortunately, the dumbbell landed right on the floor, away from any damage.

'Cardiac freezing. His heart freezes for just one second because of cardiac overload,' said the scientist and as he said this, X71 got up from his temporary blackout and resumed pumping weights as if nothing had happened.

'Shortest heart attack I've ever seen,' said Bakshi.

'Yes, Sir. But it is very dangerous, especially in a battlefield.'

'Dangerous shmangerous,' Rakesh waved his hands dismissively, 'obviously, he'll have blackouts. You're adding fossil fuels and steroids to his body.' He clicked his fingers and his assistant emerged out of nowhere.

The scientist jumped in surprise; he had not seen Kelly

lurking in the shadows. The woman had an unnatural way of creeping up on him. Of course, he, of all people, should not have been surprised by what she had become. Kelly, Bakshi's mysterious assistant, stood with her brooding black eyes and a poncho covering her torso, along with something that wriggled beneath. Her appearance was more disconcerting than Bakshi's, which was saying something.

'Increase the dosage. Kelly, you oversee this,' he said.

The scientist gulped, 'That is not advisable. With great effort, I've ensured he doesn't err...expire or explode, like so many others. It could lead to massive coronary and skeletal failure later...'

'Hey,' said Rakesh, 'I'm not paying you to think.'

'Actually, you are. And you haven't paid me in months,' said the scientist.

'If he improves 50% more than this, you will get your money. And that too, with bonus. Early Diwali baksheesh. Or, Bakshi-sh. Do it,' said Rakesh.

The scientist had a mental battle with ethics and a paltry bank balance and like many before him, he chose in favour of the latter. He nodded in acquiescence. Bakshi and his assistant walked out, leaving behind a scientist contemplating his career decisions.

As soon as the scientist was out of earshot, Kelly said, 'We need to figure out how to pay the man.'

'Meh,' said Bakshi, summarizing his HR policy.

∽

The sun was Arjun's alarm clock. Every morning, he awoke

as the sun rose. He never pressed the snooze button and woke up daily with enthusiasm. Seeing his new house, one would think he had very little to be joyful about.

His house was a tree. But Arjun was glad he had been evicted from his real house. It hadn't surprised him when the landlord had informed him that his dilapidated flat with half a bedroom, no kitchen and one-fourth of a bathroom had been taken over by Baxter & Sons. Bakshi had taken his guardian, his job and now, his house. But in Arjun's opinion, a tree was a better home.

It was located in a park in Lucknow and due to the heat, nobody ventured in. Hence, his home came with one acre of garden. He glanced at the orange glow and thought about exercising. It was the perfect setting for a short jog and some push-ups.

But as he did every morning, Arjun chose sloth over movement. He reached the top branch of the tree and pulled out his bushel of bananas and rum. The bushel was down to just eighteen bananas and the rum was down to two bottles. That was barely enough for two square meals.

This was inhumane. He gobbled his bananas, drank his rum and then cried drunkenly toward the sun, 'They can take away my job, my house, my Mrs. Kapoor, but they can never take away my bananas and rum!'

He was homeless, jobless and *rum-less*. This was the worst birthday ever.

His depression would have driven him to his usual thoughts of committing suicide but this time, he only felt rage. Arjun knew what topping he wanted on his birthday cake: Rakesh Bakshi's head. In some cultures, that was called murder but Arjun was beyond such technicalities.

Once again though, he chose sloth over action. He was calm because he loved trees. Whenever he felt lonely—which was perpetual—he'd sit on the top of a tree and read. There was a beautiful irony in reading a book on a tree. Plus, his tree was air-conditioned by photosynthesis. He picked up three books from his pile: a book on Russian war tactics (don't do it), a book on the history of the Kama Sutra (do it) and an autobiography of Adolf Hitler (Jew it). The view from his natural library was odd. Beneath the tree were statues of India's five current prime ministers.

It was the first time the country had five prime ministers. That in itself was a freaky kind of coalition politics. Momathaji, Niteshji, Powaarji, Mayawaliji and Gandhi had combined forces to wield power, but none of them had been willing to give up their dreams of heading the nation. So, when their symbolic head, Niteshji had been sworn in as the prime minister, his first order of business had been to amend the constitution to ensure multiple heads of state. It took seven months of parliamentary deadlock and a complete policy freeze, but what were the nation's interests over the interest of political egos?

The statues symbolised everything: first there was PM Mayawali's statue standing over two feet, next to it was a larger statue of PM Gandhi riding a horse, along with that was an enormous statue of PM Powaar riding a tiger, by him was a statue of PM Nitesh riding an elephant and finally, a massive statue of PM Momatha towering over all the other statues. Arjun sighed. This was what India's politics was reduced to: fighting a Freudian war of "mine is bigger", and that too, through sculptures. As he was thinking this, a crow flew past the statues and with a plop, smeared faeces on all of them, echoing the sentiment of the entire country.

'Well done, crow. Well done. You are an anarchist,' Arjun screamed at the top of his voice. Great, now he was a raving lunatic. Not that it mattered. He was hidden on a tree and did not expect company.

Suddenly, there was a knock on his tree trunk and a woman's voice from below said, 'Mr Singh, are you free for a minute?' Arjun almost dropped his book in surprise. Birds dropped faeces from trees, he dropped books. Who the hell knew he was living on a tree? His dhobi could not be this persistent!

The woman's voice was raspy, 'Mr Singh, are you in? A word, please?'

Arjun peered down through the bushes and saw a striking woman below—dusky complexion, intelligent brown eyes and an almond face that was cut as if in stone. *Her* statue Arjun could admire. Women never spoke to him, let alone when he was stinking by himself on a tree. He suddenly realized he was wearing no pants.

'One second,' he said, as if instead of a branch, he was in the bathroom of his house. 'Give me a second,' added Arjun and attempted to wear his pants rather clumsily.

From his pants, eight pieces of a jigsaw puzzle fell on the ground. The woman looked up at him, 'Is that a jigsaw puzzle?' she asked, picking up a piece. It seemed like a child's jigsaw puzzle. Eight pieces carved on wood, with the sun as the background—a blurred landscape that could either be snow or sand or even a large trident-shaped rock. Arjun leapt to the ground without his pants and grabbed his precious jigsaw puzzle from the woman, screaming, 'That's mine. That's mine!'

She looked at his furry legs, took a step back nonchalantly and said, 'Okay. I'm sitting on this bench here.' She then disappeared from view to give him privacy.

Arjun felt embarrassed. He was living on a tree with no pants, grabbing jigsaw puzzles from strange women. Had he lost his mind? He smoothed down his hair only to discover that his beard (fur, more like it) had grown all over his face. He must have looked like a beast. He *had* to shave daily for office but without office, why would he care? He took out his shaving kit i.e. his long nails and began clipping off his fur as best as he could. He pruned it, wore his pants and finally walked to the bench.

The woman looked at him and smiled, pretending like it was commonplace to behave this way. 'Good morning,' she rasped. She wore a smart business suit while he wore his old pants and a filthy shirt. From a distance, the scene could have easily been confused as an NGO worker helping the homeless.

'Please take a seat,' she urged, and made place for him on the bench. Arjun shuffled towards the seat, inordinately conscious of how he looked. But as soon as she spoke her next words, his composure was replaced by anger.

'Mr Bakshi would like to...' she began.

Who was he kidding? What was he thinking? An attractive woman would talk to a creature on a tree because she wanted to date him?

'I don't want to know anything about it,' he said and was about to spring back to his tree when the lady spoke again.

'Rakesh is an idiot,' she added, 'he has no idea how to treat or even recruit people, for that matter.'

Arjun turned and looked at her suspiciously.

'You have exactly one minute,' he said and sat down on the bench again.

'Mr Singh,' she said, 'you're living on a tree. Let's get some perspective. I'm sure you don't have an appointment with a pigeon up there!'

'How dare you?' screamed Arjun, 'You people caused this and now you are mocking me? I didn't put on pants and get off my branch to be humiliated. I will not rest till Rakesh is living on a tree.'

'If Rakesh lived on a tree, a bird would try and hatch his head confusing it for a giant egg,' she said. Arjun looked at her and guffawed. What was he doing? He was laughing with the enemy. But he had spoken to her for almost two minutes. This was his longest interaction with a member of the opposite sex who was not Mrs. Kapoor.

'Who are you? How did you find me?' he said, getting back to the point.

'Kelly. You aren't exactly inconspicuous hiding inside a tree! Plus, you stole from Bakshi's wine store nearby. We have CCTV.'

'It's not stealing if it's payback. He took my job. I broke in and took some of his booze. I should have taken more. His life maybe,' said Arjun, 'I'm never going to work for that crook.'

Kelly sighed, 'Rakesh tends to be a little overzealous. I would know.'

Arjun thought about this and then noticed something odd about the woman. He always wore a loose shirt because he had something to hide in his stomach—an aberration of his genetics. A tail that curved around his torso, a tail he could not reveal. But as Kelly spoke, he realized she shared the same unusual situation. She wore a loose blazer despite the fact that there was not an ounce of fat on her body. He blushed at the thought but could not help himself, 'What are you hiding under your shirt?'

She seemed taken aback by his straightforwardness. Asking a woman why she had extra weight could be risky. It could either mean she was pregnant or that the questioner was an asshole. Obviously, Arjun had no iota of social deftness.

'I'm pregnant with a snake,' said Kelly.

'Explains the wriggling,' said Arjun.

She replied with indignation, 'I'll tell you what's under my shirt if you tell me what's under yours.'

'It's only our first date,' said Arjun before he could stop himself. He blushed; there was a war of hormones inside him. Her smell, skin and aura was driving him insane. He was a dog on heat. A bird, a squirrel, a dog—this woman was turning him into the entire animal kingdom. He immediately wished he hadn't said it because her face cringed as if the mere possibility of them being romantically involved was rancid.

'Get to the point, what the hell do you want?' he said, with sudden anger.

She maintained her composure, 'I don't want you to work for Bakshi. I want you to work for me.'

'Aren't you his employee?'

'Technically, yes. I work under him,' and this time, she blushed at the innuendo. The very thought of the Vinod Kambli replica made her blush. But the idea of being with him was so repugnant. This frenzied Arjun.

'Leave me alone,' he said and got up from the bench which creaked in relief. 'You left me homeless, jobless and alone. Don't pretend you give a shit.' With that, he dusted himself off as he made his way to the tree.

Kelly spoke to his back, 'You have a tail under your shirt. You're suicidal because you constantly feel like you're in a land where people speak a language you don't understand. You have fears of abandonment because you were abandoned. You have to shave daily because what you get on your face is not hair but fur. And, today you missed a spot,' she got up and continued, 'and you think I don't give a shit? No, Mr Singh—it's you. You could go up to that damn tree, take off your pants and feel miserable about yourself. Or you could follow me and let me help you give a shit about yourself.'

She began walking away. Arjun couldn't help but stare at her behind. He looked at his tree, then her. It was not a hard decision.

'Don't insult trees,' he muttered to himself.

It was his first proper interaction with women, but already, Arjun did not understand them.

Chapter Three

Legend #23

Hanuman did not remember what his powers were until someone reminded him. Possibly because with great power comes great amnesia. It was weird how no one ever told him to use the power of memory…permanently.

It was the oddest meeting of Arjun's life. He was first led to an SUV which because of his size felt like an autorickshaw. But it was still more comfortable than what he was used to. For the duration of the journey, Kelly preferred the company of her phone. Because why talk to the person next to you when you can talk to someone miles away?

'I hate those things,' said Arjun, pointing to her mobile phone.

'Huh?' replied Kelly.

'You guys are so consumed by them. Why charge those things? You should charge yourself and the mobile phone should run your life.'

'Hah?' replied Kelly, holding up her finger to him.

'No wonder cell phone radiation causes brain tumours. All those applications on your phone are actually trying to take over your brain and if you resist, you get a disease,' he said.

It was good banter and his first around the opposite sex. So, he went on, 'One day you'll all be mobile phones. You'll meet each other like, "Hey, I'm Samsung 2310. That's my boyfriend, iPhone 8B,"' and smiled at himself, proud of his sudden social aptitude.

Kelly held up her finger again, 'One second,' she said, 'huh? Sorry, I'm on the phone.'

Arjun retreated back into gloom. Minutes later, they were ushered into a private air space near Lucknow airport, and he followed Kelly into a small plane waiting at the tarmac. The plane quelled any thoughts of questioning this venture. It was the sleekest thing Arjun had ever seen.

The colour of oil and black as the night, it appeared as if it was carved in marble, not metal. It looked like a 10-seater, with enough swag to accommodate 2000. Arjun recollected seeing a similar design on a B2 Stealth plane but this could obviously not be that—those were exorbitant defence planes manufactured for and by the Americans.

'It's a scaled down model of a B2 Stealth plane,' said Kelly with pride, 'but obviously, that's not important to you.'

The condescension in the remark rankled Arjun. Kelly seemed to think he was a dimwit. The progression of the meeting only exacerbated his impression further.

'I hope you claim at least 50 per cent depreciation on it,' he muttered.

They entered the plane. Arjun had expected a no-nonsense military plane but inside was a first class cabin. Eleven seats lay comfortably, with one considerably larger seat at the back. Without an invitation, he plopped himself on it. It was the most glorious seat he had ever sat on.

'Whoa, this is a good seat. My butt feels like it is being kissed by a big medu vada!' he said, to no one in particular.

Kelly stood in the front of the plane and began what felt like a business pitch.

'Mr Singh. We, at Bakshi Group, think you're special. We've been following your exploits for a while and the conclusions might help you shed some light upon yourself.'

She began, holding the cue-cards close to her chest, 'According to your DNA and ECG...'

Arjun raised his hand, 'Is there an airhostess with snacks on this flight? Or do you have to wait for take-off?'

Kelly sighed and pointed at a compartment on the wall behind Arjun, 'There is also a packet with some snacks under your seat...'

Arjun hadn't thought that he could love the seat more but like any good relationship, his affection grew with time. It made his bum feel comfortable and it also gave him free snacks. He tore through the packet and discovered his favourite meal—a dozen bananas and a bottle of rum. It was as if the seat was made for him.

He smiled, 'You guys are terrible human beings but I can't find any faults with your hospitality,' he said, shoving a banana—peel and all—into his mouth. He chomped greedily, his mouth wide open, just like his wont.

'You don't want to peel that?' said Kelly, visibly disgusted.

'Meh,' said Arjun, between loud chewing. 'Who has time for peeling? Please go on.'

Kelly steeled herself and went on, 'When we scanned you at your office…'

'One second, when did you scan me?'

'The exit interviewer scanned you with an electronic wand? That is how,' said Kelly without any remorse for the subterfuge, 'we got your DNA. But we could not get your heart rate because your skin is too strong to look through! It's ridiculous. Are you familiar with the way DNA works, Mr Singh? Let me first explain. DNA is the building block of life…'

Arjun was severely disappointed in Kelly. She had made the same erroneous assumption about him that he had lived with for decades—his hulking figure implied that he was stupid. It was more upsetting because Kelly was good-looking. And attractive women suffered from the exact implication—the assumption that if your physicality was overpowering, your IQ was below Siachen's temperature.

He listened to Kelly as she droned on about the basics of DNA in a patronizing tone that was reserved for really young children and Salman fans.

'…it is the genetic code of all organisms. You understand? Like plants, animals and even bacteria have different genetic codes, okay?'

He didn't want to interrupt. Would it be wise to tell her that he had studied the evolution of DNA right from Miescher's 1869 theories to Crick's 1957 treatise? Or would it be easier to eat bananas and drink rum instead? Not a hard choice. He chomped and slurped.

'…despite lack of evidence, we assume your heart rate at rest is almost 100 bpm, other humans have it at about 50-60. Bpm, of course, is the measure of heartbeats per minute, which tells you how fast your heart beats, is that clear?' she went on and on.

Arjun felt insulted but he had an endless supply of F&B, the greatest seat on Earth and more importantly, he had the chance to listen to her talk. He could listen to her raspy voice for hours. She could have spoken about the sewage system in Dharavi, a detailed history of toothpicks or even read out names from the obituaries and Arjun would have been riveted.

'…Now, I don't think you understand that you are a special person. Do you know what that means? You have special powers. Have you heard about the Greeks? They had Gods much like us…' she said.

Did he know about the Greeks? No, of course not. Did he know they created the myths of their Gods purely to explain the workings of the world to their population? Or how olives had contributed to one-third of Greek export? Or how they invented the Olympics only to give soldiers something to do in peacetime?

No, of course, he didn't know all that because he was just a giant. And giants were stupid.

'The Greeks? The same guys who made the salads, right?' he said half-heartedly, his interest dwindling. Kelly sighed. It amused Arjun. He dug his long nails into his ears and let out a belch instead of a laugh. Kelly picked up the remote control and turned on the TV at the front of the cabin.

'Based on the scans we conducted, we assume you have a heart thrice the size of the heart of an average human being. You have skin so thick; it may as well be an exoskeleton. You know what an exoskeleton is? It's what some animals and many insects have…'

'Oh, I had no idea. Is cockroach an animal or an insect?' asked Arjun, 'Or is it a bird? I've seen some of them fly.'

'I…' began Kelly, not sure if he was being serious or sarcastic, 'anyway, even your hair is not normal, it almost forms a body of armour. Imagine you are Anil Kapoor,' she said and smiled.

Arjun assumed this meant that she had cracked a joke but he wasn't sure, 'I'm sorry, Anil who?'

'Anil Kapoor.'

This one Arjun genuinely didn't know. And if he didn't know it, it only meant one thing—it was a pop culture reference.

'Is he a singer or something?'

'He's a hairy Bollywood actor. How can you not know…' began Kelly, but soon gave up.

'I don't know much about movies, sorry,' he said.

'Do you know about anything? Honestly?' she asked.

Arjun was not embarrassed. He hated pop culture. Its consumption made people stupid. And he had no time for stupid people, except when he was pretending to act like them.

'Anyway, you are almost a demigod—an invincible superhuman. This combination of genes and DNA has never existed anywhere in recorded knowledge. Your footage proves it...' said Kelly and showed Arjun the footage of his fall from the terrace. Cameras had been placed on the terrace and at the parking lot below. It had all been a set-up and as Arjun saw himself hurl through the air, he felt a sudden rage.

'And of course, the gunshot at the hospital,' she said and showed him the footage of a gun being shot into his skull—again, cameras everywhere. It was as if Arjun was in a reality show where despite being the only contestant, he was the loser.

'You guys planned all this?' he asked.

'Yes. It had to be done. We had to know if you were what we thought you were,' said Kelly, pausing the frame on the TV screen.

Arjun sighed, audibly this time.

'I'm sorry, am I boring you?' asked Kelly, putting the remote down.

'No, you're wasting my time,' said Arjun and got up from the seat with visible reluctance. It was like parting from a loved one. 'You talk about me like an asset, not a living thing. The bananas were great. If you need to reach me, please don't knock on my tree.'

Suddenly, the remote smashed against his head and shattered. Kelly stood there, looking furious.

'I heard couples fight over remotes but this is ridiculous,' said Arjun, looking bemused.

Kelly, on the other hand, did not look the slightest bit cheery. Her dusky face was red. *She looks a bit like strawberry chocolate*, mused Arjun. But her raspy voice was now an angry shriek, 'We stand on the cusp of an outright war in this country and you act like a stubborn ass and watch this country tear herself apart.'

Arjun tapped his nails on the seat next to the one he had been sitting on, 'Eh, not a big fan of countries.'

She looked at him, 'What? What do you mean you're not a fan of countries?'

'Don't you humans have enough divisions already—colour, sex, religion, politics? Some of you are even ready to stab each other over Bollywood stars. Why do we need one more division based on country?'

Arjun was enjoying himself. Kelly's face was about to explode, 'So, you want no countries and people to roam freely from place to place?'

Arjun considered this and leaned on the door of the plane, 'Sure, that at least means I won't need a visa. Just because I'm supposed to be "Indian", I need a visa to travel. A visa is racist. The Americans and Brits can travel anywhere because they were the conquerors of the world in the past. A visa basically says, "Hey you, your army was weak, why didn't you kill more people and steal more land?" That's what countries get you—visa problems.'

'You live on a goddamn tree! How do visa regulations affect you?' she squealed.

'They have better trees in Cambodia—Ta Prohm, the tree temple. It is a part of Angkor Wat, one of the Seven Wonders of the World,' explained Arjun.

'And you're suddenly a tree expert? A moment back you didn't know about the Greeks, you buffoon!' she screamed.

That one really hurt, thought Arjun.

'You call me a buffoon, a demigod, some angel of rescue. You don't know anything about me!' he said, suddenly realizing that he was screaming. He continued, 'You talk to me like I'm a moron…'

'You are!' screamed Kelly, louder this time, 'You eat bananas with their peel…'

'That's your cause for judgment? All the nutrients—B6, B12, potassium and magnesium—are in the peels.'

'You grow your nails like some Roadside Romeo…'

'I use them to shave, slice bananas and dig my ears. My nails are as good as a natural Swiss army knife!'

'You play with a jigsaw puzzle that even a kindergarten student could solve!' she exclaimed.

'That's a family heirloom. You would never understand,' screamed Arjun.

'You belch and fart constantly. How the hell do you expect to be taken seriously?'

'If hygiene and manners were so important, you wouldn't have a single politician in your damn country.'

'How is it only my damn country? It's yours too.'

'No, it is not. It's not.'

'You live here; this is your country too. How can you be so blasé about it?'

Arjun pulled his nails out of the seat he had dug into and it sliced through the fabric and metal like butter. He screamed, 'Because, you condescending psychopath, I AM NOT HUMAN!'

One of the seats ahead of him rose and stood up to its full height. Rakesh Bakshi—disguised as a seat—emerged, with a massive grin on his face.

'I knew it,' he said, triumphantly.

Chapter Four

Legend #12

Lord Hanuman was blessed by a rishi that he would never be injured in battle. He was his own bulletproof vest. Or an arrow-proof vest, as the case may have been at that time.

One must assume that this indestructibility rubbed off on some of his relatives and their lineage as well. But genetics is not a gift from a saint but Darwin. Maybe those powers increased with time or even lessened. But one thing is for sure, they passed on to them like a blessing...or a curse.

Arjun should have felt furious at being played yet again. He should have ripped off Bakshi's head and used it as an ashtray. Though he didn't smoke, he was willing to start just so he could use an ashtray. But the food and liquor in his belly calmed him. Bakshi looked like he had just won the Nobel Prize and Kelly appeared as if she had been caught having an affair.

He decided not to kill Bakshi. But he knew one thing; he would not spend another moment allowing humans to tinker with his head. This was the story of his life—to be trapped in a world with a species that constantly sought to play politics. Why couldn't they just leave him alone?

He felt exhausted. He was tired of dealing with bipeds that had evolved for so many centuries only to have their ambitions develop much faster than their brains. Now, dishonesty and blind ambition were their only goals.

'I should have known,' he spoke to Bakshi in a small voice, 'you are a manipulative bastard.'

The man beamed at him, 'Why, thank you so much.'

'*You* would obviously take it as a compliment. Anyway, thanks for the lunch. I'll see you guys,' he said and trudged towards the exit.

'You can't leave,' challenged Bakshi.

'Watch me,' he replied.

'No, you *can't* leave,' said Bakshi and opened one of the window shades. Arjun peered outside and a canvas of clouds greeted him. 'We're 30,000 feet above sea level. Kindly fasten your seat belts,' informed Bakshi and laughed.

'Hmm…' considered Arjun, 'well, as you all know perfectly well, I'm invincible.' He strode across to the emergency exit, and muttered, 'But, you guys aren't.'

'You won't kill us,' said Bakshi and calmly sat down on the seat Arjun had been sitting on. That was the last straw—the little Leprechaun had taken his job, his house, his guardian and now he had taken the seat he loved. It was too much. Arjun charged towards him but Kelly blocked his path, 'Please,' she said, 'please.'

Arjun moved away from Bakshi, back towards the emergency exit.

'Alright, if you won't let me kill him, I'm opening the door.'

'No,' said Kelly, and moved towards the door.

'Oh, stop being such a drama queen,' said Bakshi and leaned back on his chair. Arjun charged again at Bakshi, picked him up with one hand and pulled him towards the emergency exit, 'Maybe I'll just beat the door down with your head, it anyway looks like a hammer's head.'

Just as he was about to smash Bakshi's head on the door, he heard a voice.

'Pawan XXIII, please cease and desist,' said the voice from the screen.

Arjun put down Bakshi and looked across at the video screen. The impressive figure of General Taunque filled the wall. Arjun looked at it in a resigned manner.

'Game over,' said General Taunque.

'It's been a while,' said Arjun.

'Too long,' said Taunque, 'can you put the man down?'

Arjun tossed Bakshi aside like a sack of potatoes. 'The hell do you want?' he asked the image of Taunque.

'The hell do you want, *General*,' corrected Taunque, 'I want the same thing I've wanted for decades from you, Son of the Wind.'

Arjun sat down on his beloved seat and stared at the face of his adversary—a man he had held off for longer than most.

'You two know each other?' inquired Kelly.

General Taunque's aquiline face was striking. His thick beard was gelled down and neatly combed to reveal his sharp features. He was dressed to impress, attired in full military regalia with all the medals and honours pinned on him—the Param Vir Chakra, the highest military award for times of war; the Ashoka Chakra, the highest military award for times of peace; and the Taunque Award, the highest military award for times of being General Taunque. His bushy moustache quivered as if in fear of his own gallantry. But his brown turban remained fixed on his head, just like his principles.

That was him; General Gian Singh Taunque, or as he was known for all his exploits, The Battle Taunque and later in his career, GST, after Goods and Services Tax. After all, he united the country and was feared and respected.

'Across history,' began the General as his moustache quivered, 'the best commanders have tried to push the limits of their arsenal. The Nazis tried to train dogs, dolphins, gas, even balloons. The Russians once tried to train bears to fight for them. Hell, even Hamas claimed they used dolphins to spy on their enemies.'

'So, what is the lesson? Use a zoo to win a war?' said Kelly.

'The lesson is that a good commander tries to maintain secret assets because you never know which asset will win you a war.'

'I'm nobody's asset,' said Arjun, 'I'm not a goddamn dolphin.'

'To answer your question about whether we know each other,' said Taunque, 'I know him, but he does not want to know me.'

'Man, all along, I thought I was the master manipulator, I thought I was Bigg Boss! But it was *you*,' said Bakshi.

'Keep your mouth shut, you fungal infection. Your ridiculous Republic Day shenanigan almost derailed this whole op,' said the General.

'It was full swag, General,' said Bakshi. 'Plus, I got away. I broke the law but they broke a hundred. Allowing a charlatan into their Republic Day parade. What idiots.'

'No, you testicle of a barking deer. You got away because of *me*. While you were running around in diapers, I was making terrorists shit themselves. And some influential people fortunately still remember that,' said Taunque.

'Can we get to the point? I really want to go home,' said Arjun.

'Absolutely, Mr Singh,' said Taunque, 'but before that, introductions!'

He took out a folder from the desk in front of him. Arjun had seen the vellum folder several times before: an ancient parchment made from the skin of a goat that had probably been turned into biryani centuries ago. He could not believe it still existed.

'You still have that? After all this time?'

'Always,' said Taunque.

The General put on his reading glasses. On any other person, it would have looked homely, but Taunque's reading glasses made him look like he was about to rip your eyes out. 'This is an English translation of a language that is too ancient to comprehend—"Arjun Singh", born to: unknown, date of birth: 9 September 1936...'

'Wait, wait, wait,' said Bakshi, '1936? You're…' and he tried to do the math.

'83 years old,' volunteered Kelly.

'No wonder you're such a goddamn grouch. You're not cynical, you're just senile.'

'According to the age graph of my people, I'm still a teenager. We live longer than you humans. In fact, three times longer. Everything about us is three times longer,' he said, sizing up Bakshi.

'…sanctioned to be part of the unofficial assistance to India's defence from 1954,' continued Taunque, 'based on voluntary status. Like every Pawan before him, the Son of the Wind…'

'I am not a Pawan,' said Arjun, 'do not call me that.'

'What is this Son of the Wind business? Is it about his gastric problems?' said Bakshi.

'That, Son,' said Taunque, 'is a secret I am not at liberty to share.'

Arjun looked guiltily at the floor. It was a secret he would never share mainly because he didn't understand it himself.

'…Pawans that have served India's defence unofficially since (disputed date) 2643 BC,' continued Taunque.

'I have no idea what is happening,' said Bakshi, 'are you a vampire or something?'

'Yes,' said Arjun, 'and I'll drink your blood.'

'To explain better, "Arjun" comes from a long line of the vanaras…'

'If they form a boy band, will they be Van Direction?' said Bakshi and roared with laughter.

'What is the joke?' said Arjun.

'One Direction,' replied Bakshi.

'What is that? Is that a movie?' asked Arjun.

'No, it's a boy band. How can you not know One Direction? God, you're so old,' said Bakshi.

'He doesn't know anything about pop culture,' explained Kelly.

'He doesn't know anything about anything,' said Bakshi.

Arjun took a sip of the rum and spat it out on Bakshi.

'You're a goddamn monkey-man!' screamed Bakshi, looking genuinely put off.

'Don't you dare call me that,' said Arjun, his voice edged with old malice. Once again, he attacked Bakshi. Kelly leapt to his rescue. The plane shook with the sudden movement of the giant.

'You're…causing…turbulence,' said Bakshi between hushed breaths as Arjun grabbed his neck.

'You're…the…turbulence,' retorted Arjun.

A sharp sound filled the cabin and Arjun dropped Bakshi to shield his ears. It was a deafening screech.

'Everyone,' said the General, 'maintain some decorum. This is not a boys' school. We are an unofficial army to protect our country.'

'No,' said Bakshi, 'he is not. He's an unevolved primate.'

'Bakshi,' said the General, 'kindly shut your pubescent mouth.'

Arjun sat down with folded arms as Bakshi wheezed in pain.

'The vanaras?' asked Kelly, 'The same army that accompanied Rama to Lanka?'

The General looked at his file, 'Kindly excuse the term but it says here that they are "a monkey people".'

Arjun growled, 'No. We are not "a monkey people", or shape-shifters. We cannot fly. The word "vanaras" means forest dwellers. We have often been mistaken for monkeys, Yetis, Sasquatch, Bigfoot, Daeva in Iran, Hibagon in Japan, and Yowie in Australia. We are neither human, nor superhuman, and we are definitely not Gods. We do not owe allegiance to any country or man. And,' he paused for effect, 'we are not *your* Pawans.'

'You don't look like a Yeti,' said Bakshi, 'Yetis at least take baths.'

'When you bathe, you must use the shampoo as soap, right baldy? Like Anil Kapoor,' he retorted. If they were going to be juvenile, why should he be above them?

Kelly smiled at him, 'I thought you didn't know Anil Kapoor.'

'I learn fast,' replied Arjun. He had finally gotten her to smile.

General Taunque cleared his throat, 'We have five PMs in India. Our government is in disarray.'

'Your government has always been in disarray. When it's not in disarray, *that* is an exception,' said Arjun.

'Since 2012,' continued Taunque, 'Privatization of Indian defence has been on the rise due to improvement of Indian manufacturing. And then, Make in India…'

'Let's do some hash and Bake in India,' said Bakshi.

'... But privatization like everything else turned into an exclusive boys' club. And obviously, an alcohol company could never make it. Despite decades of The Old Baxter assisting the Indian armed forces, it's a pariah. Our official efforts have failed but there's a lot a secret private enterprise can do.'

'Like this,' said Kelly.

'We've met the five PMs. Their priorities are off whack. Nitesh is honest but suddenly obsessed with banning alcohol, Mayawali is a statue, Gandhi is consumed with finding Doraemon on Netflix, Powaar has mentally retired and Momatha thinks the world is conspiring against her. It is terrible. We are out of focus and weak. The economy is tanking, everything is chaotic. But that can still recover. Land, however, will never come back. We are in defence paralysis. And India cannot afford that—we're in the most volatile neighbourhood on the planet. We have brave men protecting our nation with no one to lead them. Those men have asked us. They can't act in the midst of government inaction, but we can. We must do what little we can, for them.'

The room silently digested this thought.

'Why have you not been a part of Indian defence since 1954? He mentioned that date,' asked Kelly, turning to Arjun. Arjun gave it a thought. It was a question he had pontificated for decades. According to him, each government was consequently worse than the last. And the cynicism within him had festered like a magnet attracting more cynicism, till it wasn't merely an emotion but a floating planet of Distrust.

'We don't believe in you anymore,' said Arjun, 'why should we? In 1948, the man who helped get you your independence was killed. Sadly, assassinations happen—it is part of history. But six years after that, depressed and broken at his failure to protect that man, our last Pawan killed himself. None of you cared. No one. So, why should we care about you?'

'Yes, we messed up. We did. But, it's time to move on,' said Taunque gently, 'it's been over six decades. It's time to step up. Our armed forces are exhausted. It's your duty as a Pawan...'

'I am not your Pawan,' snapped Arjun.

'We're being bullied from all sides and our government is busy building statues. We've decided to do something about it. Join us, Mr Singh. Welcome to India's second ever-unofficial armed forces...'

'... The Boses,' said Bakshi, 'dedicated to the man who shaped the Indian National Army, our first unofficial army—Subhas Chandra Bose.'

'The Forgotten Army was great. But didn't it also side with the Nazis?' asked Arjun.

'Almost eighty years ago. Just like the Italians and the Japanese. Bose did whatever he could to rid India of the British. Even if that meant siding with people he morally disagreed with,' replied Taunque. 'Your enemy's enemy is your best friend.'

'Okay. It's a good name, after a great man,' said Arjun.

'We have help from people in all the three forces who

are tired of doing nothing. All we need is a push and you as our doorman,' concluded Taunque.

'This is your army? The only thing this guy can fight,' and he pointed to Bakshi, 'is a comb. And then there's...' he looked at Kelly, 'I'm not even sure what she does.'

'Don't worry about us, Mr Singh,' said Kelly, 'worry about yourself. We have four more soldiers.'

'That's not an army, that's a gang,' said Arjun. 'You may as well become pickpockets.'

'How else do you think we can afford this plane?' said Bakshi, 'I operate at Nazafgarh Railway Station.'

Arjun considered it all. He couldn't understand his emotions. Was he jaded or cowardly? He had been in a state of stagnation since 1948, when he had seen it. That assassination. It had broken him and he had never recovered. He didn't think he could and more importantly, he didn't think he cared enough to.

'So, what's the mission? You're taking down ISIS, the Taliban, murderous Naxalites, what?'

Taunque seemed a bit embarrassed, 'No, fishermen.'

Arjun's brow furrowed, 'Fishermen? And after that, do we defeat an army of mermaids?'

Kelly stepped between the screen and Arjun, 'Four fishermen were illegally detained by China. We're going to rescue them.'

'That seems like big news. Why doesn't anyone know about this?' asked Arjun.

'If we are successful tonight, no one ever will,' said Taunque. 'Technically, China says they haven't arrested the

Arunachalese fishermen. They have just been "detained for questioning". It's been four days. That's a lot of questions.'

'Wait, wait. Why have Indian fishermen been caught by China? Isn't that a Sri Lanka or Pakistan kind of thing?'

'Four Arunachalese fishermen allegedly stumbled into a lake in Cona, Tibet. It is 30 kilometres from Tawang. Makes no sense why they'd go to fish all the way there. Hence, "allegedly". Either way, we have to avoid embarrassment,' said Taunque, 'before it escalates into another Indo-China border fiasco. That is the plan. We go in, rescue them and leave. Nobody will ever know it happened. We don't look like soldiers…'

'That's for sure,' said Arjun.

'…we return them to their homes and we're done. Search and rescue, that's it.'

'I'm not getting involved in murders. Or any wars. Official, or otherwise,' he clarified.

General Taunque smiled, 'You think soldiers like wars? Good soldiers avoid wars. Bad soldiers seek it. What kind of a soldier do you think I am? Our modus operandi is justice without bloodshed. Whatever happens, unless in extreme circumstances, we do not kill.'

'Sounds too good to be true. How the hell can you have a battle without casualties?'

'Oh, I don't know. What if we had someone who could deflect bullets and not get injured?' said Kelly with a smile.

Arjun considered her and the faces around him. All of them looked at him like he was a piece of cheese and they were starving rats. That is when he realized why one of India's most celebrated soldiers and busiest businessmen had spent so much time and effort pursuing him. He was not a part of their plan, he was *the* plan.

'You need me to be your Kevlar vest?' he said, 'Your entire plan rests upon my participation?'

'No,' said Taunque.

'Yes,' said Bakshi.

Arjun stared at both of them and then at Kelly who looked non-committal. It summarized her general attitude towards him.

'All such plans inevitably lead to bloodshed and we, vanaras, are a peaceful race. We will not be dragged into another human charade of peace that will lead to more genocide. Strap up, I'm jumping off,' and he walked over to the exit.

This time, he would not return.

'Did you know why Sikhism was started, Arjun?' asked General Taunque.

'As a branch of Hinduism that would act like the martial arm of the religion and fight to protect the people.'

'Yes. But it evolved. It became a race that protects land, regardless of the religion. Sikhs form the highest majority in the Indian armed forces. And you know why you are a Singh? You are not Sikh, why would you be a Singh?'

'Singh was the name given to the eldest son of any family. A son that would protect the family—the lion of the family.'

'Exactly. Your name is your heritage. You're meant to protect the people of this nation!'

'I know a Parsi called Sodabatliwalla, he doesn't exactly

make soda bottles, General.'

'Think of the lives of the fishermen, you selfish twat,' said Kelly.

'You dishonour all the Pawans before you,' screamed General Taunque, 'you're a Pawan!'

'This is not my problem. I will not be bullied by your manipulation,' he said and reached to open the emergency exit. 'And I am *not* a Pawan. Never will be.'

'You keep trying to die. This will be exactly like that,' said Bakshi.

'I will try to die on my own terms, not yours,' said Arjun.

'You selfish son of a bitch,' screamed Kelly.

'You're a coward, the son of a hen. Poodles are braver than you!' screamed General Taunque.

'You're inhumane. You hate humans because you're an ass.'

'I will piss on your grave, Son. Free of charge.'

'I'll pay you ten lakhs for one mission,' said Bakshi, cutting through the cacophony of insults.

Arjun turned to him, 'Including or excluding Goods & Services Tax?'

Bakshi shook his head, 'Whatever, fine. Excluding GST.'

For the first time in an hour, Arjun smiled. 'Okay,' he said, 'eleven lakhs eighty thousand it is.'

Taunque and Kelly's mouths flapped open like a goldfish's. They all looked at him, especially Bakshi, who seemed surprised that it had worked.

'That's it?' he said, 'We could have all saved two weeks of work, buddy.'

'Don't call me buddy,' said Arjun, 'I only have one condition. If you don't pay me, I get to kill you. When does this mission start anyway?'

Kelly opened the door behind Arjun. He didn't know when it had happened but she was suddenly dressed in all black—with tight pants and a large black sweater. 'The mission just started,' she said and jumped onto the tarmac. Arjun stared at the night sky outside.

'Welcome to China or technically, the Tibet Autonomous Region, whatever that means,' said Taunque. 'Best of luck with your mission.'

Arjun turned to the screen at Taunque, 'Wait a second, aren't you leading this?'

Taunque shook his head, 'No, I'm afraid I cannot. For legal reasons, of course. I've shared a detailed plan with Kelly, she will lead the mission.'

'Sorry, I can't come. I've got a thing to do,' said Bakshi and pulled out his phone to begin a new game of Clash of the Clans. He was fighting a proxy war in reality and in binary.

'Nobody even asked you,' muttered Arjun and watched his new leader impatiently gesture to him from the tarmac. He wished he hadn't been so greedy.

∞

Arjun got off the plane. There was pitch darkness outside and it mirrored the blackout within him. Too many doubts were racing through his mind. If he wouldn't have been so excited by the possibility of knocking on Yamaraja's door, he would have been thoroughly depressed.

'How did we sneak into China so easily?'

'The aircraft,' said Kelly, 'it's a special edition. Only twelve of these exist. Six with the Americans, one with us.'

'And the other five?'

Kelly did not answer.

'Let me guess. China has them. Brilliant.'

Arjun berated himself for impulsively agreeing to the temerarious mission. If it hadn't promised him two years' salary in one night (plus GST), he would have walked back into the aircraft there and then.

'So, what do we do?' he asked Kelly.

'There's a lake prison off this coast of Cona County, Tibet. It's a region China claims to be theirs, as a part of Arunachal.'

'Don't they claim most of the world anyway?'

'There's a lake prison there. We have no details regarding the lake. We do a reconnaissance; rescue the four fishermen and leave. Minimum fuss because…'

'Yeah, yeah. Public embarrassment.'

'Yes and also to prove we can do this. That is the only way we will get the backing of Taunque's connections.'

'So, this is basically an audition?'

'An audition with lives at stake,' she said, 'we're currently unofficial.'

'The Boses,' said Arjun.

'We are the unofficial idiots who can do what India officially can't. With Bakshi's money in tow,' she replied.

'Sigh,' said Arjun, without a real sigh.

She replied with controlled calmness, 'He's not what he

appears to be,' and beneath her loose shirt, Arjun noticed something wriggle.

'Nothing is as it appears. Your lineage used to be a part of this. Before you mock those trying to make history, let's see if you can make some of your own,' continued Kelly.

Arjun stroked the bump on his face and thought about his forefathers. He knew he didn't have Hanuman's blood in him. He didn't feel like an atom of the legacy. Hanuman was a glorious legend who had been pure and pious—an expert on the Upanishads, a faithful follower and a disciplined fighter. Arjun, on the other hand, was an expert in chartered accountancy, a faithful follower of rum and disciplined about hating life. Not the stuff of legends.

Kelly left him to his thoughts and walked away.

The cockpit of the aircraft opened and four men jumped out. They walked towards him. They couldn't see him in the darkness but he was a creature of the dark and could clearly make out The Secular Gang approach him. All four were dressed in black camouflage gears and vests, just like the Black Cat commandos.

Arjun felt joy on seeing them. They had conned him but there had been something genuine in their facade. He felt embarrassed that he was happy to see them.

They approached him with sheepish smiles. The four men ran towards him and before Arjun could stop them, they enveloped him in a group hug.

'Sorry, bro,' said Manoj.

'We had to do it,' said Afzal.

'Job profile and all,' said John.

'Hey, it's that guy from the hospital,' said Darius.

Arjun smiled, despite himself, 'It's okay. I'm err...' and he stroked his hair nervously, 'happy to see you.'

The four of them exchanged glances, 'BFFs, bro. I told you Arjun is the man,' said Manoj. Arjun was happy. In the many decades of living with humans, he had never had friends. He felt some of his gloom dissipate. Maybe it would all work out after all.

'Right, BFF. Whatever that is.'

He then asked the question that had been bothering him, 'So, how many missions have you guys been on?'

Manoj looked at him and then at the three men on his side, 'How many missions? Well, there was...'

'The one with you,' said Afzal.

'And the months of training,' said John. 'That took a while.'

'And of course, there was Paintball. That was a kind of mission,' volunteered Darius.

'Guys,' interrupted Arjun, 'is this your first mission?'

'Yes,' said Manoj and stepped into the light of the airplane cabin. The man's eyes were darting like he was on drugs.

'What's the matter with him?' he asked.

'Chaar Bottle Vodka, Kaam Mera Roz Ka,' sang Manoj loudly with a dreamy glaze in his eyes, 'Na Mujhko Koi Roke, Na Kisi Ne Roka.'

Arjun backed away, 'What the...'

'Endorphins. Happy chemicals!' said John, defending his friend.

'We had to listen to him belt out a Backstreet Boys playlist on the way here. He's on a new experimental potion. Don't worry about it. It makes him annoyingly happy.'

In the middle of a verse, Manoj's eyes closed and he collapsed backwards. 'There's also that one second blackout, but we are managing,' said Afzal, propping up his friend.

'I'm okay. I'm okay,' said Manoj, once he was upright. It occurred to Arjun that the man was considerably more muscular than he remembered. And much more volatile, as if he had snorted some form of happy cocaine.

The severity of the situation began to dawn upon him. He was on a mission with three inexperienced men and a man on drugs, and that too, with no precise plan and equipment. He stood there in his unwashed pants, crushed office shirt and red tie. He felt his dormant gloom resurface; they were utterly screwed. He suddenly felt depressed.

They began climbing a steep hill and barely halfway through, Arjun began panting heavily. Kelly looked at him and rolled her eyes, 'Are you okay?'

'I'm just…not…used to…cardio,' said Arjun.

She sighed. Arjun regretted ignoring his exercises for the last few days, in fact, for the past few decades. They soon reached the lake and he leaned on a pine tree, his heart beating furiously against his chest. Manoj patted him on the back, 'It's okay, man. Don't die because you climbed a hill.'

Arjun smiled. He looked around. The beach had Yunnan pine trees lined across it, as if the trees were sentries of the water body beyond. The area was deserted. It was 4 a.m. and the howl of stray dogs was the only sound one could hear in the distance. Kelly pointed towards the lake, at a white building on a faraway island.

'Gentlemen,' whispered Kelly and gestured for all of them to huddle, 'we have to be stealthy. It's a simple mission but I want no screw-ups. We sneak in, free the fishermen and lead them to our aircraft. They're in cell 38B. I'll be your point man; any instructions will come from me. It's a sparsely guarded prison, so this should be easy. But the worst thing we can do is slack off. Everyone ready?'

'Yes, Ma'am,' whispered the four "soldiers". Arjun simply nodded.

'Everyone ready?' asked Kelly again, looking at Arjun.

'Yeah, yeah,' he said.

Kelly had her game face on. Arjun had underestimated her seriousness.

'Mr Singh, now that you're on board, I'd expect you to at least behave professionally. You're being paid a lot of money. Behave like it.'

'He's being paid?' asked Manoj.

'We haven't gotten our salaries in months,' complained John.

'My health insurance is Combiflam,' said Afzal.

'We get paid?' enquired Darius.

Arjun raised his hand, 'Question; how do we go to the lake?'

Kelly walked to the left and pulled out a plastic sheet that covered a dingy dinghy. It was a rickety wooden boat that looked like it could be responsible for at least twelve drownings. The four men opened their backpacks and quickly assembled plastic oars with the solidity of chopsticks, as the choppy waves danced invitingly to the tune of the full moon.

'We paddle in. One person waits in the boat. The rest run in, rescue our citizens and come right back and out. Simple.'

Arjun gulped, 'What? I… I…err… That's not um… how do we?'

But the tiny army was already on the rocky beach, pulling out the alleged "boat" towards the water. No one in the group had noticed his discomfort.

He had always been fearful of water. He was mortally afraid, like normal people were afraid of death. So much that he had moved from his first base in Kolkata because a part of him thought that Hooghly was a demon which would swallow him. He didn't know why, maybe it was genetics or childhood trauma. He stood there on the beach transfixed as the others quickly loaded the boat. Kelly finally noticed him standing afar as she was about to climb in. She gestured to him and he walked towards her.

'What's the hold-up, Mr Singh?' she asked.

'Oh, nothing. Is there no other way to the prison?' he asked.

'Well, did you expect a free shuttle service to drop us at its doorstep?'

The men behind her giggled. It made Arjun even more uncomfortable. He couldn't admit that a man of his size was afraid of something as ridiculous as water.

Instead, he said, 'I've changed my mind. I'll sit this one out,' and walked away.

He didn't see the fury on Kelly's face or the confusion on the faces of his new friends. He didn't want to. He sat down by the bark of a coconut tree.

'You wheeze climbing a hill, you fear water. You pretend you don't want to help. But the truth is you can't. Because you're a sham, a coward,' said Kelly, the wind blowing her words into his ears. 'You look down upon Bakshi, but his word is stronger than yours,' she said and pulled the swaying boat towards the water.

Manoj leapt out of the boat and ran towards Arjun. He sat on his haunches and looked Arjun in the face, 'Hey man, you can do this. You just need some motivation.' And then, he pulled out something from his backpack.

It was a small bottle of liquid, 'You like rum? Well, this is better. There should be another boat here somewhere. 'Aaj Blue Hai Paani Paani Paani Paani,' sang Manoj as he patted Arjun's knee. With that, he and the boat both disappeared into the darkness. Arjun sat on the coconut tree, gripping the bottle of liquid and his own shame, questioning whether he was a man, mouse or a cowardly simian.

∞

The Boses sat in the boat, observing the lake prison for an hour and calculating the movement of the non-existent guards. Fortunately, the security was inept because waterlogging was a larger threat than a breakout. They climbed up an unguarded wall past an unmanned courtyard and ran into a big locked wrought iron gate. It took them an hour to break it in silence. Finally, they made it to a corridor that was lined on both sides with cells.

The cells were not the worst that Kelly had seen—good lighting, decent flooring and none of the squalor one associates Asian jails with. The four soldiers with her were professionals despite their off-duty awkwardness. They quietly snuck in. After some trial and error, they located the Indian prisoners who also happened to be the only prisoners in the jail. *Did they build a prison only for this*, thought Kelly; *is this Chinese efficiency or just ego?*

They had just broken into the jail cell housing the Indians when things went downhill. One of the Indians howled in their Nyishi language, 'No! Let us be. No more questioning!'

That was all the sound needed to alert the jail staff. Within moments, four Chinese soldiers arrived on either side of them, holding up their unused rifles. Kelly had limited options.

So, she did the logical thing, 'Don't shoot,' she screamed. 'I submit,' she said, raising her hands in the air. This gave the four soldiers a chance to find cover and while the Chinese soldiers considered their options, she removed her jacket shirt and the sight shocked the guards. *It is peculiar*, she thought, *this is Poonam Pandey's life—take off your shirt to get attention.* Two of the guards looked at what lay beneath and were on their knees instantly, screaming, "The Goddess!" in Mandarin. Kelly could not understand a word.

There she stood—with her two extra arms holding two stun guns and her other two hands raised in the air in submission. Four arms on one woman; it was mythology coming to life. She fired and all four guards collapsed, writhing as the electricity coursed through them. What

Kelly didn't account for were the four guards on her left. She turned milliseconds too late as one of them fired at her. Time slowed as the bullet raced towards her torso, but suddenly, it was stopped by a giant flying figure.

Two bullets slapped onto Arjun Singh's torso and ricocheted harmlessly.

'I always wanted to do that,' he said, 'take a bullet for the hero.'

Kelly recovered from his entry and stunned two more soldiers as the giant picked up the remaining two like sacks of wheat and tossed them into the courtyard outside. He leapt on the wall and stood between The Boses and the Indian prisoners.

'Might be a good time to run,' said Arjun, his eyes twinkling. And then, he noticed her arms, 'I guess we all hide something beneath our torso.' Kelly saw his long tail waving behind him—both their secrets were out in the open.

'Only mine is bigger,' said Arjun with a wink. He felt exuberant and more full of life than he had ever felt; positivity had replaced his white blood cells. Kelly tried to pull the Indian fishermen but they refused to move. She had experienced it often; many Indian men could not accept help from a woman—even when there was no other option. Masculinity always seemed to trump logic.

'I'll get them, you run!' howled Arjun, amidst gunshots from two guards that had recovered from the stun gun. Obviously, they were over the mythological aspect of their assailants; divinity had been replaced by duty. Walls cracked and the prisoners shrieked in protest. As the gun smoke cleared, the guards saw a man with a furry chest and a tail waving behind his head, smiling from ear to ear.

'Sorry, guys. The only guns that work on me are these,' Arjun said and kissed his pulpy biceps with more élan than they deserved.

It was a good line, thought Arjun but the guards didn't seem to feel the same. They looked at him and then at each other, saying something in Mandarin. His line was too good to be wasted. Arjun tried again.

He repeated in broken Mandarin, '*Duìbùqǐ dàjiā. Duì wǒ lái shuō wéiyī de qiāng shì zhèxiē*!' Then he kissed his biceps. The guards followed this time and laughed, despite the circumstances. Arjun smiled and said in Mandarin, 'I'm invincible. So, don't waste your bullets.'

The guards held up their hands. Arjun referred to his mental dictionary and translated "bye bitches" in their language. They laughed once again and wagged a finger at him as if he had said something extremely naughty. He raised two fingers at them, gesturing a goodbye, entered the prisoner's cell, and grabbed the panicking fishermen like errant little monkeys. He tucked two protesting men under each arm and began running. A red light with a siren was already screaming around the island cell. Other guards would soon join the pursuit.

'You speak Mandarin?' asked Kelly, racing to his side.

'There's a lot you don't know about me, baby,' said Arjun with buoyancy and added further, 'or, B ob o, as they say.' But "flirting" could wait. He had to be quick. He ran past the courtyard, leapt the wall with consummate ease and almost crushed The Boses who were about to jump into the water to swim back.

'Whoa,' he said, 'what are you doing?'

'Swimming back,' said one of them, 'the boat sunk!'

Arjun looked at them. 'You really don't need to,' he said and walked straight into the water. He took a few steps. It appeared as if he was walking on water. 'Turn on your torches,' commanded a grinning Arjun.

Kelly turned on her torch and the sight that greeted her was surreal—lines and lines of pine trees were tied together, their leaves popping out of the water like seaweed. They were tied horizontally against the water and extended all the way to the beach ahead.

'You made a bridge out of pine tree?' she asked, with disbelief.

'Yunnan pine. Their needles are a bit spindly, so watch your steps.'

'A five hundred meter bridge in two hours?' she asked.

Arjun shrugged, 'My ancestors had a gift for building bridges. They used rocks, I use trees. We better run. This is the fastest way out.' He began running on his bridge with alarming dexterity. The rest of The Boses followed him, but with markedly less pace and conviction. Within four minutes and after having to fetch Darius out of the water only once, they were on the beach. Arjun handed over the confused prisoners to The Boses and instructed, 'Take care of them. I've got something else to do.'

Arjun leaned down and with massive grunts, he began pulling the enormous bridge. The whole unit moved towards him, slowly but surely. It was a tug of war between a man and his own creation.

'What the hell are you doing?' asked an alarmed Kelly. 'We have to run!'

'You…run… I…have to replant the trees,' said Arjun, panting. Kelly noticed that each tree had been removed with care and there were giant holes in the ground to allow them to be planted back.

'Mr Singh, you're not Dogmatix. We will get caught. They are just trees,' she said.

He spun around; sweat dripping down his furry face that had reddened with the effort, 'They are not just trees to me. You won't understand,' he said, as if that explained it all.

'I could marry a tree. I guess that would make me manglik…' said Arjun and then swiftly added, '…baby.'

'Anyway,' he continued and his flushed face burst into a toothy grin, 'I'm invincible. Believe me…' He was about to say "baby" again, but Kelly interrupted, 'Please don't say baby.'

'Nothing can destroy me. Exoskeleton and hairy Anil etc. etc.,' he said, puffing as he pulled a tree and held it up like a fishing pole. As he said these words, light exploded from behind the floating jail cell and with a cantankerous roar of machinery, a large flying object rocketed towards the party. They looked up to see what it was.

'Run!' Arjun screamed at Kelly behind him, 'I'll take care of this.'

'What in the world is that? You can't take it on by yourself,' screamed Kelly over the roar of the engines ahead, 'and how the hell will you find your way back?'

'My lineage will help me find a way. I can't explain it but I have a mental GPS,' he said and grinned with confidence. Nothing could batter him. He knew it from the moment he drank the potion. As he had sat alone after the others had left, the voice of the creature inside him had said he would be safe. He believed him.

Kelly looked unsure, but collected her party and ran towards the waiting plane, over the hill. She kept an eye on Arjun as he picked up a big rock with both his hands. The light from the flying machine silhouetted him as he held up the rock on his right hand, ready for action, his tail waving behind him. In that image, Kelly saw the unquestionable proof of his lineage. She ran towards the plane, reassured that he would take care of them. Arjun, for his part, stood on the beach and roared. His voice echoed across the ocean like the call of a wild animal protecting its territory.

A louder roar erupted as the flying machine exploded past him at a speed that broke the sky in half, heading straight for the plane behind Arjun. He aimed with his rock and flung it towards the flying machine. There was a large clunk as the rock crashed on the machine. It shook in the air above and spiralled out of control towards Arjun, distracted from its mission by the upstart who dared to fling rocks at it.

The blinding light didn't allow Arjun the chance to see much. All he could see was the outline of a missile fired towards him. He braced for impact, delighted he had taken the attention off the plane, as the missile moved towards him.

It slammed into Arjun and exploded with a deafening boom. It knocked him off his feet, towards the lake behind.

He almost crashed into the water but somehow managed to steer away, like a cat from a bath.

'I hate swimming, you floating truck,' he screamed at the flying machine. The machine seemed like it was pondering mid-air why the missile had no impact upon its target.

Arjun grinned and yelled, 'Indestructible, you son of a bitch. That's right!'

The lights of the machine turned off suddenly and the ensuing darkness was even more blinding. Arjun blinked twice to adjust his pupils but before he could, the machine began emitting red coloured lights. It growled angrily and two ducts emerged from its front.

Arjun finally realized what it was—a dragon; and not just any dragon. It was Shenlong, the Chinese dragon God. Arjun did not remember how he knew that but he did. The resemblance was uncanny and unnerving. The two angry ducts paused and then there was sheer cacophony. Hot blazing fire stormed out of the dragon's mouth and Arjun tried to move away. The fire ignited his tail and he felt the fur at the end singe in protest as his tail caught fire.

'My tail is on fire? Am I in Lanka? This is déjà vu! You have an unfair advantage, you flying dragon!' he cursed the machine. The adrenaline in his body submerged any torpid instincts and he felt himself do something he never thought was possible.

It began with an explosion of wind from every orifice in his body. At first, he dismissed it as a terrible case of gas. Had he eaten too many bananas? Thoughts stopped as the wind jettisoned out of him and he exploded like a canon. The sand on the beach parted as Arjun flew in the air towards the dragon.

The dragon seemed stunned and floated mid-air as Arjun flew right into its centre. He felt as if he was the wind. His heart thumped against his chest as he inhaled and exhaled more air. With his tail still on fire, he looped twice and thrice around the machine, setting its outsides on fire as well. He smelled the burning of plastic and metal.

'I'm the Son of the Wind,' he screamed into the wind, 'you son of a bitch!'

Up close to the dragon, he saw a man looking at him—an old man with penetrating, almond eyes—and just as he was about to give the man in the cockpit a final blow that would send him to kingdom come, Arjun felt his heart pop.

He felt the wind stop.

He was devoid of air, in the air.

He clutched his frozen heart in panic and hurtled towards the water below.

In his last moments of blackout, he could not help but read a sign on the undercarriage of the machine.

Zhōngguó zhìzào or "Made in China."

∞

At the head of the dragon, Dr Ling could not believe his eyes as he saw Arjun fall from the sky. It was the Flying Humanoid and it was back after decades.

Dr Ling was lucky to be alive—again.

∞

Tawang Tract (Indo-China Border), 1949

General Mao's People's Liberation Army was established in 1949. It would eventually become one of the strongest armed forces on the planet. But before 1949, the PLA (then, The Chinese Red Army) could not let go of a great opportunity—India's freedom.

In 1949, India was so busy celebrating their victory over the British; they were too distracted to notice any infiltration. It was the perfect time to make a bid for land. As General Mao once said, 'In waking a tiger, use a long stick.' Especially if that tiger was asleep because it was tired of vanquishing some silly Queen.

The following extract is a part of the memoirs of a mysterious "Major General Ling", who allegedly served during a secret '49 battle. The battle was apparently so secretive; it had no official records until now.

I will have to be ambiguous about the specifics in this report. It is a precaution I must take for I still live in the People's Republic of China, the greatest country in the world and also the country where people of the world disappear.

Years later in 1962, we were at war with a country, India and as always, we won. China has never lost a war. We couldn't lose the war since the freest country in the world owns its history. The Indians instigated the war because we would never instigate. After all, we are the most peaceful country in the world.

That war was easy. But years before this win, we suffered a terrible defeat. Fortunately, no one ever knew about it. In 1947, when the Indians beat the British with the landmark tactic of refusing to fight them, while some in China worried about its impact on trade, one man saw an opportunity. Who needed trade when they could get free land?

Getting independence is remarkable—it gives people a false sense of security, especially when the largest army on Earth is at their doorstep. The man who sought to seize this opportunity was General Mao.

His plan was simple—while the Indians bickered over things like constitutions, we would grab some land. Some of us would reach a spot of land and pretend we had always been living there. If not, we'd simply massacre those that did and take over. It was so simple, it had to work! So, we proceeded to a land that was perhaps beyond Tibet and near Tawang town, close to the future "Arunachal Pradesh". Perhaps. I cannot confirm or deny the same.

Maybe we could go around the mountains and take over the whole of India—the mood was jubilant. We walked on, unopposed. We sang as we crossed these beautiful valleys. The sun shone bright overhead and the temperature was cool below. It was that wonderful feeling of being perpetually defrosted. The valley itself was sparse of any vegetation but the grey and brown mountains were carved as if by the hands of God. Men sang, some did a jig —we were the happiest conquerors.

"Happy" because there was no force to stall us, this wasn't a march; it was a long walk in the woods. General Mao, the father, mother, uncle, aunt and the entire family of our nation was in an expansive mood as he moved with his troops, inspiring us with just the weight of his quotes.

'Revolution begins at the barrel of a gun,' said the God amongst men, 'socialism begins at the end of a stick and democracy begins after you take a gun and shoot it with a stick!'

We were confused and inspired by his words. Later, we realized that he was testing quotes for his forthcoming book, *The Little Red Book*, which obviously needed editing. But Mao's words, even in excess, were like manna from heaven and one could not get enough of heaven.

'Men, remember, an army of people is invincible,' he said, his loud voice carrying across our battalion, 'unless, the people are pansies. So, don't be a pansy. Be strong, be brave. Be a sunflower.'

One must sincerely thank Mao's editor for salvaging many of his words. But despite his odd words, we were excited to be in his company. Our souls were soaring and our guns were ready at the helm even when we knew we scarcely needed to use them.

I had the General's attention because I had something no one had actually used in wars. Writers with visions of sci-fi grandeur had written about it but I had actually built it—the world's first fighting robot, me.

I was not technically a robot. I had simply built reinforced armour, crafted from fortified stainless steel and equipped with a gun that blazed from my forearms with more clicks than any gun on our force. Parts of me were so well-armoured, I may have been invincible. For the 40s, it was the greatest manifestation of a war machine and General Mao was impressed.

Thinking back now, I was akin to the 80s Hollywood film, *Robocop*. Chinese military reality was decades ahead of American fiction. I was the most impressive sight on any battlefield. People cowered at my sight. Or at least they did until that fateful day.

I saw it first—a little speck on the horizon. I dismissed it as a really large bird but as it approached, I realized it was larger; a human-shaped aircraft flying overhead. *Did the Indians actually have the gumption to send their air force?* I thought.

The aircraft whooshed past the army and this time, everyone noticed. It then flew back and with a final flourish, stopped right in front of us. We finally discovered what it was—it was a man but not a man, a monkey but not a monkey, a bird but not a bird. For a moment, we were stunned. This was new, even to us, and we had invented the greatest defence weapons of the last century. How was this creature flying?

Without the General's sense of control, we would have broken right there. 'It's nothing,' shouted Mao, 'just a large creature flying. Even Icarus flew, comrades. But he flew close to the sun. And *we* are the sun.'

We all clapped but the creature was unperturbed. It raised its hands and spoke in a deep rumble, all in broken English, 'Maoji, I respect. But you are stop. Now. No more ahead. Stop.'

Few of us spoke English. The ones who did conveyed the message to the others. By the end, the message was convoluted but the intention was clear. It was the worst game of Chinese Whispers in our great history.

'The only thing Indians gained from the British was their language,' said Mao, 'and this creature cannot even speak that!'

Mao was unflappable. We all laughed at the flying creature. We were an army of thousands and this was just one creature. Those odds favoured us, we knew.

The creature's face crumpled in anger at this defiance and he shook his ape-like head. His enormous tail flapped at his bare back as it simply asked, 'No?'

We all replied in unison, 'No!' That much English everyone knew.

His face broke into an evil grin. He burst into the skies and extracted a bottle from a pouch and gulped the content, smashing the bottle on the ground. The shattered bottle smelled of distinctly cheap alcohol. It smiled again. I could see ancient evil in those canines, as if power radiated from its bones. Something told me this was no mortal and I had a feeling of impending doom, but Mao was also no mortal and he urged us to stay firm. The creature floated above us and we stood on the ground as one, a stalemate—one creature versus an army of thousands.

Finally, General Mao screamed in Mandarin, 'Forward, men, come on Ling—robot him!'

I prepared to annihilate the creature with my ammunition and the unit moved forward with my shining spectacle in the centre. And then suddenly, we all collided into each other, for the men in front had been knocked off their places and were now sailing past and over our heads to the back. The creature had punched eight of our best men and had sent them flying over the heads of their own comrades. That was when chaos broke out.

We decided to fire at the creature simultaneously. He hovered over us drunkenly and his laughter boomed across the valley, echoing past the walls of the mountains. It reverberated into our core, disturbing the molecules in our souls. The bullets harmlessly bounced off his body—his face, his hands, his legs, his eyes. It ricocheted all over; some of our men were shot by their own bullets rebounding off the creature.

'Barrel of a gun,' screamed Mao, 'barrel of a gun!'

I fired my incredible ammunition with a meteoric pace at the creature, but it simply looked at me like I was a mite on the bum of a panda. It laughed at us. Uproariously. Drunkenly. His invincibility mocked our mortality. Then it snarled like a monkey and roared like a lion. I felt my body break when I heard that sound. It still haunts me and my nightmares are filled with that creature's shrieks. After our ammunition was exhausted and the smoke cleared, the creature landed on the ground, clicked his heels like a bull and charged. At a speed incomprehensible to science, it flew right through the battalion. Men were knocked to the side and in the air like butter melting through a hot sword. I saw a man lose his hand because of the sheer momentum.

General Mao lay fallen near me. His balding head trickled with sweat and mud, and in that moment I realized, he was a mere mortal. I could see the fear of death in the face of a man who had never feared death.

'How is this happening?' asked Mao. 'I think I've soiled myself.'

It was not going to be one of the quotes that would make it to his final book. Someone picked Mao up—it was the last time the great man would be so humiliated.

Meanwhile, the creature was back at the front of the army and it roared in its broken English once again, 'Stop. No more. I stop. You stop. No more kill. Go!'

There was a stampede of trained men losing their wits. Many were trampled underfoot in their eagerness to break away from the colossus. I was pinned beneath the marauding retreat, men piled on top of me—some dead, some shell-shocked. My body was frozen and the weight of my own robot crushed me. The creature was mesmerizing. He finally looked away from the retreating soldiers and at my shivering frame below. Maybe he recognized how unique my armour was or maybe he saw how young I was. The fierceness in his eyes receded as he flew down and lifted me up from under the collapsed men around me.

'Are you shaving machine?' he asked as he fidgeted with my stainless steel hand.

I scampered back in fear. With him so close to me, I could smell the forests and the trees with a healthy helping of alcohol.

'You're my son's age,' he said as he lifted me. 'My son,' he said and tears fell down his big face, on to my bruised body. 'He is gone. My son is gone,' he cried, 'taken from father.'

I was scared out of my wits but I had to know. 'Who... are you?' I managed to ask. The flying man looked at me with his red eyes, trying to understand my words. He clicked his tongue, 'They call me Pawan...the...the XXII. Father of one.'

He added as an afterthought, 'First they take my Gandhi, then she take my son!'

Overcome with sudden sorrow, the creature roared. It was the howl of an animal injured beyond physical pain. He cried, his fangs and face stretching in anguish. He was invincible but his heart was broken. He was injured from the inside out and that is the worst kind of injury. He howled, trying to cure himself, but couldn't.

I gaped, still frozen and then, I scampered. I looked back and saw him hover mid-air with the verdant mountains behind. Even with his body defeated by his own soul, he flew away like the God of the mountains—floating in his melancholy.

Years later, I would question my sanity as would my entire squadron. Some of us would even be dismissed and our sanity would be doubted for "retreating" without reason.

None of the psychiatrists who analysed me, none of the doctors who tried to help me could ever see what I had seen or smell what I had smelled. I had sniffed an ancient truth and to this day, I question whether our truth had the scent of a lie.

Chapter Five

Legend #89

The Chinese dragon is a symbol of positivity, unlike its Western version—a creature to be conquered with the sword of Gondor, Westeros, Gururgram or other mystical lands. Neither do they look reptilian nor do they breathe fire. After all, the Chinese invented matchsticks and gunpowder; they didn't need a mythical creature's help for the same. Their traditional dragon is a long snake with four legs and a beast's head, making it considerably more fearsome. A flying, slithering beast that can poison, swallow and sneak up on you almost makes you wish that you were reduced to cinders instead by his fire-breathing cousin from Europe! It's a good thing though. At least, they are a sign of optimism and not destruction.

In a country laden with secrecy, Dr Ling worked in a department for the government of The People's Republic of China that was so secretive, it almost did not exist.

Officially, it never had. Dr Ling had never earned money, he had never done any work and he himself was unsure whether he existed at all. The department didn't have a name. Because how can you name something that does not exist?

Initially, it had been hard for Dr Ling to explain to family or friends where he worked. He used to respond with silence and everyone just assumed he was a drug trader. Then, he committed the mistake of mentioning that he worked for the government at a random party and that was the last time he had any friends. Now, everyone who knew the Anguo family regarded them with a mix of fear and reverence. Drug traders were acceptable, but you just couldn't mess with the government.

Everything in Dr Ling's life was ironic. His office didn't exist but it was also the most important office in China's defence, he had a staff of one but the power to take down thousands and then, there was his name. Dr Ling He Anguo, literally translated, meant, "Peace, peace, peaceful country." It was the opposite of what he did and Dr Ling sniggered whenever he read his own nametag.

And now, his dream project was on the verge of completion. It had taken decades of isolation and focus but Dr Ling was pleased with the result. He pulled back the blowtorch, took off his safety goggles and stared at the magnificent creation glinting back at him.

'Is it ready?' asked his assistant/secretary/maid/lab partner/ Sole Renren (Chinese Facebook) friend, Sun, for about the twenty-five thousandth time.

For once, Dr Ling grinned and answered her with

certainty, 'Yes, it is ready.'

Sun scratched her head, 'So, now are you going to tell me what it does?'

Dr Ling cleared his throat; he had kept the secret from his own assistant for almost eighteen years. This was his moment.

'It is,' he began, 'the ultimate fighting machine, undetected by radar, mostly indestructible, with an expected firing range of three hundred kilometres and a special feature with fire. I present to you not a fighting machine, but God in a technological form.'

Sun looked at the big hunk of metal in front of her, unimpressed. She then asked, 'Does it have a charging socket for my iPhone?'

∞

If Dr Ling thought creating the ultimate fighting machine over decades of incessant hard work was the tough part, he had underestimated Chinese bureaucracy. It had been very hard to get an appointment with his Defence Minister because ministers were not usually prone to giving appointments to non-existent secret government departments.

But somehow he had managed to get an appointment with Mr Jin, The Defence Minister. At Mr Jin's office, he stared at the man across the table. The room was built according to the standard bureaucrat template—simply furnished with a table at the centre, bookcase on the side and a seating room on the left. Plastered across the room were scrolls of Mandarin sayings. Mr Jin was reading one of them out loud as Dr Ling sat in front of him.

'There's an old saying from Sichuan province that says "A fish can never mate with a bear and my time is precious so don't waste it." Have you heard of it, Ling?' said Jin, absent-mindedly.

'No, Sir. I have not,' replied Ling, 'especially because you just made that up.'

Jin looked back at him with thunder in his eyes, 'Don't question me, mortal. I'm a bureaucrat. Now, who are you and how did you even get an appointment with me?'

'My assistant hacked into your diary. It's not important,' said Dr Ling, 'I run a secret government department that has been working on a secret project that is now complete.'

'If it's a secret, how come I don't know about it?' asked Jin.

'Well, because it's a secret,' replied Ling.

'How can I believe that you're not some fraud?'

'That would be a secret.'

'I'm the Defence Minister. How can I not have any knowledge about this department of yours?'

'Because it does not exist.'

'How can it not exist?'

'Because,' said Dr Ling, 'it's a secret.'

Jin's eyes squinted at Dr Ling who was sitting in front of him and he slammed the table with his fist, 'Goddamn it. A secret department so secretive even I don't know about it. What is the project, Dr Ling?'

'I can't tell you. It's a secret.'

'Then why the hell would you even come to me?'

'We still need government approvals to move forward.'
'Move forward with what?'
'It's a...'
'...secret. Yes, I understand. But I can't give you approval until I know what the approval is for.'

Now it was Dr Ling's turn to squint at Jin. He said, 'Can you keep a secret, Mr Jin?'

'No,' said Jin, 'they appointed me as Defence Minister because I enjoy leaking our secrets to our enemies. Just recently, I learned that there was a secret department so secretive even I didn't know about it. But hey, don't tell anyone.'

Both men stared at each other, wondering who was winning this battle of nerves. Both leaned on their elbows, looking at the other suspiciously. Both held their breaths as if holding their breath meant holding the other in power.

Finally, Dr Ling pulled away from the grip and simply said, 'India.'

Jin looked at him, 'I'm sorry?'

'India is the focus of my attention,' said Dr Ling.

'Who?' said Jin, genuinely confused.

'India—the country to our west, the second most populous nation after us. You're the Defence Minister, how can you not know India?' said Dr Ling, flapping his hands to indicate his incredulity.

'Oh, right. *Them*. You don't need government approval to mess with them. Oh, they're such grand pansies; sorry, the technical term is "soft state". In 1962, we took land from them—thousands of kilometres—they didn't do anything.

We staple their visas, they talk of negotiations. We claim states that don't even belong to us, they talk of elections. Have you heard the old Mandarin expression, "When a Chinese man is bored, just lean across and fuck with India?" Have you heard it?' asked Jin.

'You just made that up, didn't you?' said Dr Ling.

'You're an old man, Ling,' said Jin, 'how old are you?'

'I was 17 years old in 1949,' replied Ling.

'That is a weird way to answer the question. But if it's India you want, go for it. In fact...' and the Minister began contemplating something.

'In fact, we may be able to work together after all. Leave behind the details of your project.'

'They will be emailed to you. The email will delete itself. If you try to share or print it, a malware will attack your system,' said Ling.

'You trust no one, Dr Ling. It's wonderful,' said Jin, 'I will send you a plan of my own. It will not spread any malware. Now please, get out of my office.'

Dr Ling got up to leave—he had not realized the meeting would be so easy.

'Oh, Doctor. Once you go to Arunachal, please get me one of those prayer wheels. They make them better than China. At least they make something better than us. Oh, also get me Arunachal itself. We "own" it.'

With that, he promptly burst into the Laughing Buddha mode.

Once Dr Ling had left, Defence Minister Jin could not help thinking how fortuitous it was that Ling had come in when he had. Jin had secrets of his own and now he could use Ling to take them forward.

∞

Sun was shocked at Dr Ling's recent dealings. The doctor had moved out twice in fourteen days—once to meet that Defence Guy and now, for some secret liaison. This was two times more than the last time Dr Ling had gone out of his laboratory/home. It was bewildering.

'Where are you going?' asked Sun, defying the Chinese rapport between a mentor and ward by asking questions. The rules didn't apply to her because Dr Ling needed her: to wash his clothes, keep his quarters clean and to hack into banks whenever they fell short of cash. It was primarily for the latter, though sometimes when she smelled Dr Ling's clothes, she wondered if it was for the former.

Dr Ling didn't notice her. He was busy with cranes that were hauling his massive new invention into an even bigger open backed truck. He was so involved he almost knocked Sun down while picking up his creation.

'Dr Ling!' screamed Sun, straining her mentor-ward relationship for the second time, 'What are you doing?'

Dr Ling was in a trance, his sparse grey hair askew and his eyes wild as he stopped to look at his fallen assistant. 'Um… Right, where? Of course,' he managed before swivelling the crane over Sun's head.

Sun was about to raise her voice for the third time when Dr Ling spoke, 'I'm taking this baby for a test drive.'

Sun considered this and screamed, 'Shotgun!'

'There is no shot and there is no gun, Sun. I am the shot and the gun,' Ling said with panache before moving his head around and whacking it on the ornament hanging from the crane's rear-view mirror. It was an ornament of a cartoon minion, holding a metallic saw.

Dr. Ling looked at the ornament with dissatisfaction.

'Who put an ornament on a crane?' he said, ripping it off and flinging it to the ground. 'The world is my crane ornament,' he howled with a manic laugh.

The minion landed on the floor, crumpled into pieces.

'Hey, that's my minion,' yelled Sun.

'No,' said Dr Ling, 'you are my minion, Sun. Go eat a banana.'

Sun raised her eyebrows; her boss had finally lost his mind. She bowed in a Japanese style and said, 'I'm going off to play PS3. Call me when you're back.'

'I am PS3,' screamed Dr Ling to the empty room, 'whatever that is.'

'You're more PSY. I can't understand what you're saying but at least parts of it are entertaining,' said Sun, mocking her boss.

∞

Rakesh Bakshi was at Justin Bieber's second concert in India. The popstar and karaoke expert had shocked his fans in his first show by *not* lip-syncing one song. Hence, the crowd at Chinnaswamy Stadium in Bangalore went ballistic with joy when they heard that the singer would actually sing at his own concert. Bakshi knew only two songs by Bieber, "Baby

Baby" and "It's Too Late Now To Say Sorry", which made good sequential sense. Bakshi had been there. Thrice.

Over the raucous screaming, Bakshi felt his phone vibrate and read the text, 'The Chinese are on board. Your plan better work. We get only one shot. Dhoble—P.A. to the PMs.' Bakshi smiled and deleted the text. His plotting was on cue. His work for the day was done. Now, it was time for fun.

He handed his phone to Kelly, and said, 'JSK, let's rock!'

He ran onstage behind a gyrating Bieber, pulled down his pants and screamed, 'It's too late now to say sorry!' only to be violently tackled by Bieber's security team.

It had been a great day.

⁂

Somehow, Dr Ling had flown his shattered robot back to his laboratory. He was glad he had built it to be amphibious; otherwise he wouldn't have returned from Tibet. It had been two days of torture both in water and through the bumpy roads, but he was finally back.

He reached his workshop, extricated himself from the shattered seats and collapsed next to his greatest creation. As he lay on the cool rubber floor, the image flashed in his head—the flying monkey-man shattering his impenetrable glass with his fist. The creature would have laid him to rest if he hadn't collapsed mid-air. *This one had his weaknesses*, Dr Ling thought. He did not have the fearless brutality of the creature that appeared in his nightmares.

He would not be defeated by it this time; he would not

turn tail like he had. He would bring the creature crawling to his knees and then destroy him. He raised his bruised fist in the air to signal his intent.

'What's up, boss? Where have you been?' said his assistant behind him.

Dr Ling turned to see Sun standing behind him, 'Make me some ginseng tea. We need to get to work.'

Sun scowled, 'But, I have a date. It's a Sunday!'

Dr Ling whipped around at the young woman, 'You have a date. With destiny, Sun.'

'Lame,' said Sun, but proceeded towards the pantry anyway.

Chapter Six

Legend #14

Hanuman was known for his insatiable appetite and once desired to eat food cooked by Sita, who was more than happy to comply. But dish after dish was polished off by the vanara over a period of hours, exhausting even Sita's endless patience. Finally, Krishna intervened and gave Sita a blessed Tulsi leaf, which finally satiated Hanuman's appetite.

One leaf was all it took for his hunger to end. Astronauts have used the same form of food packaging on their missions, which proves that Hanuman was technically NASA's first dietary consultant.

It is a wonder he could fly after loading himself with so many carbs.

Arjun plunged into the water but it was icy cold; which was odd for Sri Lanka. He had been flying and now, he was drowning. He flailed but the panic and the cold consumed him. His left hand was held firm by a strong grip.

His lungs filled up with water as he saw the man next to him. The man looked exactly like him—the same protrusion on his face, but older and more resigned. His eyes were sad, as if they had already accepted their fate.

This is the end, thought Arjun and the water pushed its way down his wind pipe and chill filled his body. His grave would be an icicle, frozen forever. Try as he might, he could not swim. He felt his body quit. The man's eyes were now closed and Arjun closed his too. Suddenly, he was pulled up. He felt an arm drag him up through the water as he blacked out.

The next thing he was aware of was someone leaning over him and pumping air into his lungs. He felt ground beneath his body and the cold fire in his lungs receded. He opened his eyes and could see Kelly's face looking down at him. But it quickly morphed into another person that looked exactly like him but was female.

The woman's eyes were browed with fear as she blew more air into Arjun's lungs. He arose with a spurt of water on a snowy shore. *This is definitely not Tibet*, he thought and finally, found the strength to sit up.

The sad man was sitting by him and he looked confused. He was sad that he had lived, but how could anyone be sad that they had lived? The woman got up and slapped the man across his face. He accepted his punishment and his gloomy eyes made Arjun want to weep.

'How dare you take our son and force him to your own end?' screamed the woman.

The man's face was wet but Arjun could see his eyes fill

with tears, 'It was time. If the water had been cold enough, it could have worked. But it was not,' he said.

'I failed. It was time.'

'Maybe it was time for you but he's a child,' she said.

'They will use him and dump him. They will say he must protect them but no one will protect him. That is our fate and when he loses his way, they will let him be lost. It is better he die than live such a life,' said the man, lifting his face to the manifestation of fury in front of him.

Another slap greeted him, 'You will not make a decision for your son. He will make his own mistakes and his own choices. I will not let you drown him in your depression.'

'I let him die,' said the man and more tears fell down his face, as if misery of decades had finally found release.

The woman kneeled next to him and lifted his face towards hers. In a softer voice, she said, 'You are a Pawan, the bravest Pawan I've ever known. You saved him innumerable times. In Shimla and beyond. He always said so. He died after he got his lifelong dream, his way. Using a method nobody had ever used before.'

'Independence!' said Pawan, 'Pah! It's not worth it if he died. This is all worthless.'

He got up, looking at the valley of snow and the frozen lake in front of him and said, 'Our purpose is worthless.'

'It was three years ago. It's 1951! The man you sought to protect got his wish, he got his independence. For an entire nation. Get your freedom from him. He would have wanted you to. You have to be strong for your son,' she said.

The man sighed and turned away, 'I have no strength

left. All I have to give is torment.'

And he bent down towards Arjun and whispered, 'There's no one worthy left to protect, Son. No one. There will never be. Don't let them tell you otherwise.'

The man walked away into the windy snow, his fur bellowing in the breeze. He was soon swallowed by the white wind like a ghost of the past. The woman looked at Arjun with a sad smile, 'Our choice is simple. You are bound by your duty, Arjun. But not by the sorrow of your blood. I'm going to have to hide you away. Away from this. Into their world.'

Her eyes welled up with tears and Arjun knew then that he would never see his mother or father again. His mother leaned towards him and kissed him on the forehead, as if it was a goodbye.

'Goodbye,' he whispered, 'goodbye, my mother.'

The tendrils of the dream cleared. Arjun's eyes slowly opened and he discovered Kelly's face looking down at him. She saw his eyes open and blushed that she had been caught looking. He couldn't tell how long she had been standing there.

'Okay, you're up, good,' she said and abruptly turned around and walked out of the hospital room.

The epiphany drifted off in smoke as he saw her face. He knew it was an insight but it had dissipated like a fog in the bright sun. He closed his eyes. He didn't know if it was a vivid dream of his past but Arjun's head was about to explode. He'd never had a hangover but right now his brain felt like it had been used for nuclear testing. It was the potion—the thing that had inflamed his instincts and then abandoned him halfway, much like his father. He wanted silence and rubbed his forehead, hoping the nausea would go away.

He reached into his pocket and stroked the pieces of jigsaw that were fortunately still there. He rubbed them for calmness and then opened his eyes.

'Bhai!' screamed Afzal, 'You're alive!'

'We thought we'd never see your ugly face again,' screamed Manoj.

'Boss, you flew like Air India. And then you crashed like a North Korean missile,' howled John.

'Why are we always screaming in hospitals?' asked Darius.

Arjun flapped his hands, 'Quiet, guys. Quiet.'

'Oh My God!' screamed Manoj, 'We can't be quiet, you're alive!'

'Everyone, please leave,' hushed Kelly, who was standing behind the four men. His four friends obeyed her order and left the room without another chime.

Kelly walked to Arjun's bedside with the professional front she carried so effortlessly. She had a few sheets of paper, 'Mr Singh, since you helped with the successful completion of the mission...'

Arjun took the papers. There was a cheque attached to an invoice that said, 'The amount of 10,00,000 rupees to be paid to Mr Arjun Singh as accountancy fees for R&D for The Old Baxter.'

'Please sign here,' said Kelly. 'Also, I need you to fill

out a couple of hundred forms to register you as a vendor, which I'm sure you're familiar with.'

Arjun sat up and looked at her. He had just flown. A human or humanoid or whatever he was had just flown! He remembered the wind coursing from within him. He had never felt more alive. He wanted to do it again, to defy gravity and rub his gas in its face. And yet, here he was with Kelly, who was telling him to sign forms and invoices, not even vaguely amazed. She should have been impressed by him, not this.

'I flew. That was pretty amazing,' he said and put his hands behind his head in a suave pose, 'quite incredible, if I may say so.'

'It was expected,' she said, 'we spent considerable time and effort finding you and expected nothing less.'

'Oh, and did I just save your life back there? Wow, quite amazing, right?'

'You helped save the fishermen and for that, we thank you.'

Arjun's exuberance dissipated. *Helped save? He effectively ran the mission by himself.*

'Helped? I effectively ran the mission by myself! Did no one happen to see that there was a dragon in our midst? Helped the mission. I mean, seriously?'

Kelly gave a mirthless smile, 'Not before almost jeopardizing the mission by flaking out. We didn't know you were afraid of water, we would have accommodated accordingly.'

This was not how this exchange was supposed to go.

Kelly was supposed to find Arjun amazing, fawn over him, kill Bakshi, buy a nice house in a small hill-station with him and then...then what? His pipedream would always be just that. He took the cheque, signed the papers and handed them brusquely back to Kelly.

'Thank you. You'll also be happy to know that we are analysing the footage of your flight. And after conducting some minor tests while you slept, we've concluded...'

'Wait, you conducted tests on me while I was asleep?'

'It was not my choice. But yes, we did. We needed to accommodate for any future surprises.'

'Oh, as long as you had a valid reason to poke my body while I slept. I feel violated.'

Kelly looked at him, unsure. He gave an impish smirk. Kelly scowled and went on.

'We discovered that when you flew, holes...'

'...opened up across my body. On my feet, hands, torso and even my underarms. And of course, my butt!'

'Yes. How did you know?'

'And, the holes resembled the blowholes of a whale. And some kind of light gas exploded outward. I'm assuming, hydrogen?'

'Err...yes. Did you read these tests?'

'No, Kelly,' he said and leaned back on his bed, 'I don't need your tests. I'm a vanara. We know exactly what's happening to every molecule of our body if we concentrate. I felt the churning of gases in my body. I felt the carbon dioxide break down into other gases. I felt my pores open. I felt explosion.'

'Your lungs...'

'Yes, my lungs are triple the size of a normal human being. My chest is fifty-six inches into three.'

'And, your body itself...'

'Is largely impenetrable. I don't have skin; I have something which resembles an exoskeleton. This includes my hair and my nails. And I am assuming you guys tried repeatedly to take blood samples and others and broke a ton of injections and other equipment doing it?

'Um...'

'You could have saved a lot of money if you'd done something you don't seem capable of doing, asked nicely.'

Kelly tapped her pen on the clipboard in front of her, looking embarrassed. But it was too late to back down now.

'You've not exactly been the most cooperative,' she began.

'You know who the first person was to simply ask me to be a part of this operation? You. Before that, it was all lies and scams. You don't know how to simply ask.'

'And you lied about your fear of water. And your fitness. Please don't tell us how to run our operations, Mr Singh.'

'Why are you being such a bitch all of a sudden?' said Arjun, ever the smooth talker. 'You were perfectly nice to me before.'

Kelly sighed, 'Mr Singh, I was nice because I was recruiting you. You are now under my command. We are not friends, you are an employee,' and then, as an afterthought, she said, 'and if you call me a bitch again, I will find a way to harm you, with or without your impenetrability.'

'Okay, but I'm not your employee,' said Arjun.

Kelly's eyes glinted like angry little diamonds, 'Mr Singh, I ran The Boses solo for four years. I have also run successful missions in Naxalite camps, and in Al Qaeda sleeper cells. I thwarted ISIS recruitments and more. To contextualize, you helped rescue fishermen. If you aren't around, it may take us a little longer to get things done but they will get done. So, please get a reality check.'

For a being that had just defied the laws of gravity, physics and biology and flown large above the Earth, Arjun felt very small. With fumes of anger trailing off her body, Kelly turned around to leave the room.

'FYI,' said Arjun as she left, 'your entire operation was a sham. There is absolutely no way you would be able to get into China that easily. And there is no way that dragon would spring into action so quickly, as if it had been waiting just for us.'

'No, the dragon was spotted in Tawang, barely thirty kilometres away. Hardly coincidental,' replied Kelly.

'Why?' he asked, 'Why was the dragon in Tawang in the first place? Hi-tech machinery like that over there? Why?'

'We are asking those same questions, Mr Singh,' she replied, 'anyway, I thought you didn't care.'

Arjun shrugged, 'I guess I don't. But...' he hesitated, 'I got a very strange feeling that the man in the cockpit of the dragon recognized me. Either he's seen me before or he was expecting me.'

Kelly heard him out, agape, 'Are you...are you sure?'

Arjun nodded, 'I know what I saw, Kelly. Just letting

you know.'

Rarely had anyone seen Kelly Matthew look confused but at that moment, she looked as if someone had told her she had been raised by wolves.

The certainty on her face was replaced by a darker look, 'Mr Singh, there's something you need to know about the potion…'

'It shoves adrenaline, ups my heart rate till I feel like my heart is about to explode, driving away all my fears as a consequence. Then, it causes temporary cardiac failure leading to momentary shutdown of bodily functions. Am I right?'

Kelly shook her head, 'Okay, yes. But also, there is something else…'

She seemed to wrestle with a decision. She paced up and down in front of Arjun, deliberating with herself. The door of the room flung open and Rakesh Bakshi rolled inside atop a unicycle, for no particular reason.

'Hello, children. There's my favourite fighter and my favourite employee,' he said, his evil smile beaming, 'and Arjun as well.' He fell off the unicycle that he obviously had no idea how to ride, dusted himself and stood upright.

'How are you, buddy? Champ, you're feeling good. What a display that was day before, friend. Amazing!' said Rakesh, reaching to high-five Arjun's hand and slapping his chest instead.

'Kelly was just telling me something,' interjected Arjun.

'No,' said Kelly nervously and exited the room without further explanation.

Arjun first looked at her depart morosely and then at Bakshi's face which was exuding joy.

'So, are you ready for your next mission?' said Bakshi and laid a vial of the potion on Arjun's bedside.

Arjun thought about it. He didn't want to work for this man. But the potion called out to him. And flying called out to him. And despite Kelly's unfinished declaration, Arjun knew what he was going to say and he knew he would regret it.

'Yes. I'll sign your goddamn vendor forms,' he said, 'how do we get to Tawang?'

'Tawang? No, no. You got bigger fish to fry. Forget hilsa, you'll eat a whale...'

'That's not a fish.'

'I have six missions waiting for you, Son,' said Bakshi, holding up six folders in front of his face. 'Which one would you like to start with, homie?'

Arjun grabbed the folders from Bakshi's hands, 'All of them. Standard rate. Ten lakhs plus GST per mission.'

Bakshi pulled out another vial of the potion and placed it next to the one already on the table, 'Now, come on, champ. That was a one-time thing. Ten lakhs for the six missions. Some international ones. No visas. You know you want to.'

Arjun's teeth clenched against each other, 'One day, I'm going to rip your head clean off your shoulders, Bakshi.'

The bald man smiled, 'Looking forward to it, champ. They say my head's too big for my body anyway,' and he placed a phone, a kit, a lighter and the two vials of potion on the table next to the bed, 'are you ready?'

Arjun concentrated on his body. He lifted up his underarm where a tiny blowhole opened up. He rose from the bed as hydrogen reluctantly popped out of his body. He reached across to his bedside, picked up the lighter and clicked it on. A little fireball lit up in the air and almost burned Bakshi's hand. The man ejaculated in surprise.

Arjun smiled, 'Now, I'm ready. Also, you owe me one lakh eighty thousand. We agreed on GST.'

Chapter Seven

Legend #66

Goddess Kali appears to be the symbol of destruction of all evil forces. Her long tongue, her four hands—one holding a demon's severed head, one a weapon, one caked in blood and one a trishul—all endorse the capacity of women to multitask. She also wears a garland with fifty-one heads of demons and a tiger skin—for a full ensemble.

But all of it is symbolic. The sword of knowledge exists to slay the ego of the demons along with the fearlessness of the trishul and the blessing of blood. Her red tongue represents greed, pressed by her white teeth symbolising conscience. Kali is proof of the thought women put in their accessories.

Additionally, her ebony complexion also embodies her all-embracing nature which hopefully transcends into destroying anyone that endorses fairness creams.

Every political party in India had attempted to woo the venerated General Taunque. But Taunque always declined because of his commitment to neutrality, the country and most importantly, punctuality. Politicians, in Taunque's experience, were raised on a diet of tardiness. It grated his nerves. He swore by two secrets to success: punctuality and backups. He was always on time, and according to plan. And if what he attempted didn't work, he would be on time with four other plans.

But these were surface traits. The big reason behind Taunque's success was extracting the best out of people; his training would break them, rebuild them and turn them into the best versions of themselves. He was a physiotherapist of the soul.

People that had gone through the Taunque programme went through changes that transformed their personalities completely: it resulted in divorces, breakups, physical changes and in one case, a soldier even claimed that Taunque's training had helped him grow taller by three inches—it was as if his body had also risen to the occasion.

Taunque was meticulous, obsessive and inescapable. Currently, he was invested in three people: Kelly Matthew, Manoj Sharma and himself. His ageing body could not cope with handling more. He had attempted to recruit Rakesh Bakshi into his program, but he swiftly realized that it had been a mistake. The only way the Taunque program worked was by utter devotion to Taunque and Bakshi could never do that because of his utter devotion to himself.

Kelly had been his protégé for two decades and his

project with her was his backup plan after his military career, The Boses.

It was time for The Boses' weekly strategy meeting at Bakshi's conference room and Taunque was finding this one more taxing than usual because of Rakesh Bakshi's unusual efficiency. He was not used to Bakshi coming on time, being sober or informed. Today, the man was on the ball and it did not make for easy viewing.

'I've assigned Arjun Singh six missions. Missions we were unable to execute because of border patrols, visa issues, distances and budgetary constraints. Neither is an issue for him. It's costing me less than—what is ten lakhs divided by six?'

'1.67 Lakhs,' volunteered Kelly.

'Exactly. I knew that. He's flying and he only needs bananas, rum and the potion. It's a military goldmine!'

Kelly was not pleased, 'I'm not sure handing him so much responsibility after one mission is such a good idea. He's a free agent with no military experience.'

Bakshi laughed, a little too quickly for Taunque's liking, 'We spent three years chasing him down. Why be precautious now? We'll only know his worth if we test him.'

'We could have at least sent Manoj with him,' she said.

'He flies by himself. Manoj would be extra luggage. No check-in allowed.'

'Or tested him out on another mission.'

'We are testing him out on multiple missions.'

'But…' began Kelly.

'Which missions?' asked Taunque.

'Kony, Saudi, Baghdadi and the other Big Three. Missions we couldn't undertake. The rewards we make on their completion can finance us for a year. This is what we found him for,' said Bakshi.

'This sounds too sudden,' said Kelly.

'I've attached a tracking device on him. He's got a special phone for any issues; and he's got your research files. All we need to do is give him ground support and help out with permissions, which I'm sure General Taunque will take care of.'

'He's still not seasoned. Soldiers take years of training. General Taunque, haven't you told me the story of Sam Maneckshaw and Nehru?' reasoned Kelly.

The General smiled at her, 'Yes.'

'Sam Maneckshaw did not allow Nehru as a passenger on a plane because he had not tested it for flight with two people. It annoyed Nehru for years that the head of a country was denied a joyride but Maneckshaw refused to apologise. Arjun Singh is an untested plane.'

'Yes, Kelly. But this Sam fellow—what did he know?' said Bakshi, 'Yes, the Yeti is not properly trained. But his genetics is all the training he needs. Plus, he's a secret weapon and a secret weapon only works if it is a secret. If word spreads that something like him exists, people can extract weaknesses.'

'But…' began Kelly.

'The shoe fits,' interrupted Taunque, 'we have discussed these factors numerous times. I can't believe I'm saying this, but great job, Bakshi.'

The bald man smiled as if military strategy had always been his forte. Kelly was discontented but Taunque attributed a lot of that to jealousy. It must not have been easy being the go-to person and then finding yourself ousted by the village idiot.

'When does he take off on his missions?' asked Kelly.

'The doctors have given the go ahead. Only our approval remains. I've ensured his missions are international so we can test him in unfamiliar waters. And we can also get rid of our pending commitments abroad. Two birds.'

'Approved,' said Taunque, not waiting for any other opinion, 'that's Agenda 7. Next on the agenda: the dragon.'

Manoj spoke up, 'Permission to speak, Sir.'

'Manoj, this is not the army. I've told you a hundred times. You can speak,' said Taunque.

'Thank you for granting permission, Sir. Intel leads us to believe we may find evidence of the dragon in its last seen location. We may gather more about it by investigating the site.'

'Our intel in this case is us, Manoj,' said Taunque.

Again, Bakshi was the one who spoke up, 'I agree. But our destination is thirty kilometres behind. Tibet is too risky. We got lucky the first time. Everything points to Tawang town. Something is brewing there.'

'Kelly?' said Taunque.

'I agree with Bakshi,' said Kelly, surprised. The General was not the only one confounded by this new efficacy.

'Permission to agree with Mr Bakshi, Sir,' said Manoj.

Taunque sighed, 'Okay, so…'

'I agree with him,' said Kelly, 'but we've still not ascertained why the same dragon keeps showing up in this region. China always plays a deeper game. And nobody has even asked how we snuck past their borders so easily. It's as if they were expecting us.'

Bakshi laughed, uncomfortably, 'How ridiculous. Preposterous. Expecting us? Hah! Hah, I say. In your face! I say hah! I dismiss you.'

Taunque let that sink in, 'I spoke to the Defence Minister of China.'

'You spoke to Jin?'

'How do you know him?' said Taunque.

'Oh, nothing. General Knowledge,' said Bakshi, 'I read a lot.'

Kelly looked across at Bakshi and smirked. Bakshi's general knowledge was restricted to asking her to Google whatever he didn't understand and promptly forgetting it. He had once had a conversation with the Australian PM and kept calling him Shane Warne. Everyone else in the room seemed to share her scepticism and they all gaped at Bakshi.

'Why is everyone so surprised? I'm not stupid,' said Bakshi.

'Well, not stupid,' began Kelly.

'Actually, you are pretty stupid,' said Manoj, 'you once told me to arrange a visa to go to Kerala.'

'That doesn't prove...'

'You once said that Philippines is the capital of Indonesia,' said Manoj.

'Again, that doesn't...'

'You met Sachin Tendulkar and told him you loved his role in *Lord of The Rings*.'

'He does look a bit like a hobbit, come on…' said Bakshi.

'We're off track. The board agrees that Bakshi is usually a moron. Either way, I spoke to Jin and he told me there is no official sanction for any such technology by the Chinese government. A sentiment I reconfirmed with other sources.'

'Maybe it's an unofficial source,' said Kelly.

'Unofficial? I mean, seriously, come on,' mumbled Bakshi, 'how would an unofficial enterprise have access to military? Okay, I realize you're all looking at me and pointing at the irony. But this is China we are talking about—a citizen in China doesn't fart without the government smelling it!'

'You're behaving very weirdly,' said Manoj, 'like you have something to hide.'

'Weird, me?' said Bakshi, and his face turned red, 'Your mom is weird. Your pop is weird. I'm not weird. You're Weird Al.'

'You're blushing?' said Manoj, 'You never blush. Sir, obviously something is going on.'

Taunque held up his hand, 'Rakesh, do you have something to tell us?'

Bakshi stood up abruptly from his chair, 'I've spent my father's entire legacy on trying to finance this dingus of an operation. How dare you all hint that I'd do something to jeopardize this?'

After saying that, he stormed out of his own meeting room. The door smacked with a loud thud and left three people looking very confused. With a mutual mental understanding, everyone decided to ignore what had happened.

'I agree with him though. It's unlikely. China has a pretty firm grip on its people. A little too firm. But the only way to know their endgame is to play the game,' said Taunque.

'Anyway, it's 4:29:30; we have thirty seconds and two agendas. Let's be quick. Final decision on the dragon?'

'He's right. Tawang is the best bet. My team and I will go there for a recon mission,' said Manoj.

'Decided. Additionally, Kelly you need to ensure Singh is on the ball. Brief him and make sure he does what is needed. Motivate him,' said Taunque, and walked out of the conference room.

'Yeah, right,' mumbled Kelly, 'I'm not bloody Shiv Khera.'

Manoj stood up by her side, 'Motivations aside, if this dragon is not an official Chinese op and if it is unofficial, how would anyone finance such an operation? It doesn't add up.'

∞

Dr Ling was a genius, and also a pain in the ass. But Sun did not mind. She could tolerate his temperament because the man had made her very, very rich. And, very, very cool. This meant she got very, very laid. The world was a superficial place and Sun revelled in it. Men were so foolish and so easily impressed by rich women. Her line of boy toys was longer than the assembly line of robots in her factory.

Sun found others' perception of the Chinese way of life

idiotic. Some outsiders still assumed that *all* Chinese people were oppressed. It was only when they visited that they discovered the ground reality. Her social life was vibrant and her work life was incredible—she had no complaints.

To Sun, China's alleged oppression was logical. The government looked at groups of four or more people with suspicion—that made logical sense. They didn't tolerate public expression of religion—that also made logical sense. The people in urban towns were successful, fashionable and smart—what more would they want?

Yes, the rich-poor divide was obscene but that was the case with each of the world's 196 countries (including Taiwan)! She loved being Chinese. She had Earth's best technology and a happening social life. The only oppression her people faced was when they attempted to rise against the Chinese government. But why would anyone want to? She was having fun. What the hell would she be an anarchic for?

She looked at Ling's factory below and marvelled again at his genius. It was a large campus and manufactured sim-card slots for one in two phones manufactured in China. Since China manufactured over 90 per cent of phones on the planet, it meant this factory manufactured a component that was in almost half the phones of the world. And yet, it only had twenty-six employees—Dr Ling, Sun, twenty security guards and six maintenance experts.

They harnessed solar energy and compost waste like the time machine of *Back to the Future,* but without the malfunctions. Over a thousand robots worked full-time in the assembly lines. In the decade she had worked at MIC

INC. LTD ULTD (Made in China Incorporated Limited Unlimited), the total profits had hit 7.4 billion dollars. Sun got a few millions and the rest went to Dr Ling's robotics projects. It seemed wasteful to spend that kind of money on something that never made a profit but as long as she had her updated Google Glass, iPhone, Maserati and a boy to enjoy those gadgets with, she didn't care.

Dr Ling often lectured her on Chinese manufacturing. It was the same lecture every few weeks, 'Sun, people say China doesn't have many global brands that the world buys.'

'That's not true. We have Lenovo, Huawei, Tsingtao and...'

He'd interrupt each time, 'We manufacture most of the world's electronics for cheap. An iPhone manufactured in the U.S. would cost $1400 i.e. the sale price of an iPhone. Same for Samsung, Sony, LG etc. We may not build the most popular brands but we build half the world's everything! We are the turtle holding up the world's entire output. Do you know what would happen if China shut down for a day?

'The world would collapse and all economies would shut down?'

'No,' he would reply, 'the world would collapse and all the economies would shut down.'

His eccentricities didn't matter. His secret project meant a strict "No Visitors" policy. Even deliveries were made a kilometre away by self-driven trucks. The twenty-six employees were committed to work in the factory for the rest of their days, a fate they had embraced because the work was minimal. No visitors, rare maintenance issues and six hours of deliveries to oversee—it was the cushiest job in China.

Today though, they had a visitor and Sun was surprised. It was the Defence Minister. Mr Jin and Dr Ling were having a long animated conversation. Sun had been told to leave the workshop because they wanted privacy, so obviously she had to eavesdrop. She looked at her phone screen. Usually, it showed her the latest PewDiePie video or a World of Warcraft update, but at that moment, it gave her a direct telecast of what was happening down below.

'…you will follow orders, Dr Ling,' screamed Jin.

'I don't answer to anyone, Mr Jin,' screamed Dr Ling, even louder.

'I'm the Defence Minister; I could have you shut down in seconds.'

Dr Ling laughed, loudly. His cackle echoed throughout the workshop.

'You couldn't do shit. If we stopped work, one of China's biggest manufacturing units would come to a grinding halt. Turtle holding the world.'

'What turtle? What the hell are you talking about, you senile old fart?'

'Plus my dragon would probably take a big bite of your stupid army.'

Jin's face puffed like a bullfrog and he stared at the older man. He looked like he would punch Ling and Sun wondered if she should run down and rescue her golden goose. But then, Jin smiled and placed his heavy hand on Dr Ling's shoulder. The doctor recoiled at the touch. Nobody had touched him in decades. He tried to shrug off the bigger man's hand but it stayed put.

'Dr Ling, you're a genius, but also an idiot. What you say is true. But what you forget is who you are. And with a snap of my finger, I could let the whole world know your entire history,' said the Defence Minister.

'Hah,' said Dr Ling, 'the country would celebrate me for creating the world's supreme fighting machine.'

'Like they celebrated your failure in 1949?' said Jin, 'No Chinese would support a man who turned tail despite Mao. Especially the lies you've recorded about General Mao. It is defamation of our moral architect. Yes, I know all about that, Ling. I've read your records.'

Dr Ling's face fell and he looked pale, as if he had seen a ghost.

'You're 87. No one trusts a geriatric on his deathbed to protect their land. How you are even standing is beyond me. We could take your dragon. Take over this place. By any means necessary. It's not hard. Much like your privates at this age, I'm sure!'

Jin placed his other hand on Dr Ling's shoulder, 'I will tell you precisely what you must do next. You failed once, Ling. You failed terribly. You can't fail again.'

With that, the Defence Minister turned, his shoes clicking on the floor as he receded. This was definitely something Sun should not have seen, which is why she enjoyed it even more. Dr Ling turned straight to the camera that Sun had planted and his eyes narrowed, furious, 'Sun. You're grounded. For a month. No allowance for you.' And then, the video went dead.

'Aw, come on, Dad. Come on,' said Sun. She flung her brand new golden iPhone on the floor and stamped all over it. She sometimes forgot their *other* relationship.

∞

Kelly Matthew was crying, or at least a part of her was crying. Doctors had often misdiagnosed her with schizophrenia and bipolarity. She had neither because bipolarity is symbolized by mania and depression that is often out of control. Schizophrenia is characterized by not understanding what is real. Kelly had none of those issues; her moods did not oscillate and she had a vivid understanding of reality.

Her dual personality was caused not by mental issues but because she was supposed to be two people. In her mother's womb, she had consumed her twin and formed one entity. And she could clearly feel the presence of her twin. In the rare moments she lost control of herself, she knew her phantom twin was in charge; like right now.

Kelly's birth could have been a media sensation like Lakshmi Tatma who was born with four legs and four arms. But it wasn't publicised because Kelly's parents were as protective of her identity as they were about the country's defence.

Both her parents were in the armed force—her mother in air force and her father, in no official department. He was simply called by his code—Mr Serene, for his unflappable temperament, or Saran Matthew, spy for a defence branch, unknown.

Kelly's earliest memory was an explosion in her house and her father unaffectedly carrying his handicapped daughter out of the fire to the garden and then plunging back in for his wife who didn't need the help. They had walked away from the house like it had never existed. Kelly was three but that memory didn't get buried. She never knew why they had been attacked; she had just felt her parent's serenity in crisis and inculcated it.

When she was born with eight limbs, her father's assessment had been, 'She's twice the person she would have been. And already a great spy. She infiltrated another human being!'

The Matthews decided to make her extra arms her strength. For her first eleven years, she wore a spinal brace, went through operations worth crores that included separation of the failed twin's lower limbs, ribs and kidneys. Titanium was added to parts of her body where normal people had bones. But none of the pain mattered because her mind was stronger than her vessel. She took her first steps when she was twelve, her first run at thirteen and had never stopped sprinting since.

'You're Forrest Gump with the aggression of Muhammad Ali,' her dad used to say. The man who helped source funds for her recovery and became a foundation for the family's strength was her godfather, the unmistakable General Taunque.

Since Kelly had to be home schooled, her parents were her only tutors with Taunque as a guest lecturer. Before she got out of her wheelchair, Kelly had learned military strategy, military history, psychology, body language, weapons analytics and math—when she had spare time.

When she could walk, she was trained in martial arts, weapons, strength training, and distance running. The Matthew's hill station home in Ooty transformed into a training camp for one little girl. Kelly never questioned her place. She was delighted to be with the three people she loved the most. She became stronger than she had ever imagined and her extra set of limbs meant that while some manoeuvres were hard, others were astonishingly easy. She could scale up sheer rocks, buildings and impenetrable areas; and her firing speed for weapons was rapid. They spent over fifteen years prepping her for an unforeseen mission.

Then, as it happens to most people, her parents passed away. They died of natural causes which surprised them both. Kelly's world would have fallen apart if it hadn't been for Taunque.

At twenty-two, Taunque began sending her on clandestine missions. Naxal hideouts, terrorist sleeper cells and even to religious riots. Kelly was Taunque's army of one, the genesis of The Boses. Then came Rakesh Bakshi and all the discipline she had flew out the window.

Bakshi approached Taunque, offering aid to The Boses. How he knew about them was a mystery. For three years, Bakshi and she recruited men, lost men, recruited more men, spent private money solving military crimes—and also had inordinate amount of sex.

While turning her into a superhuman, her parents had not realized that Kelly was human and had hormones after all. And like most spectacularly fit people, she had an ocean of raging hormones. As Bakshi once teased, 'Jaanu', because she hated that term, 'if your sex drive was harnessed into electricity, you could light up all of Madhya Pradesh. That would be a great NASA satellite image!'

Taunque disapproved of his goddaughter's liaison but as most fathers—honorary or otherwise—discovered with their kids: a battle between a child's lust and a parent's choice is usually a lost cause. Taunque switched to a purely commander-soldier relationship with his mentee/goddaughter.

Kelly cared about only three things: Taunque's missions, Bakshi and her country. And one of those things was slipping out of her control.

She lay on Bakshi's bed, wrapped in a silk blanket, watching him pack a carry-on briefcase.

'You're doing your own packing?' she asked, 'Don't you usually just land up in a country, buy what you need and throw the rest?'

Bakshi's plump torso didn't look appetizing topless until that brash smile lit him up, 'What can I say? I'm maturing.'

'Where are you going?' she asked.

'Clandestine operation. Can't say,' he replied, closing the briefcase.

'You don't do clandestine. And one tiny briefcase is not enough for a trip to China,' she said.

Bakshi was startled. 'How did you…oh,' he said with a surprised smile, 'I forgot you're a spy.'

Kelly recoiled at the accusation, 'No, you idiot. Your

printout is poking out of your bag. Why the hell would I spy on you?'

Bakshi looked embarrassed which was a bad sign. Nothing embarrassed him; he basked in a carnival of embarrassment. His blush meant a terrible secret.

She was attracted to Bakshi for his disregard for conventions and his commitment to her cause. He was a workaholic and she loved him for it because she was one too. But mainly, she was with him for his unpredicted faithfulness which had been drifting further and further away into something unseen.

'We've done it only eleven times in the last four days,' she said, 'that's terrible!'

'Eleven times is a lot for normal people, Kelly,' he replied.

'I'm a woman with six limbs and you're an insane person—we are not normal,' she said, 'if something is bothering you, let me know.'

Bakshi sighed and put on his shirt, 'Kelly, I like you a lot and all, but let's not ruin this with emotions.'

'Agreed. Emotions are terrible things. Especially, emotions like hunger for power. Or greed. I hope you understand,' she said, and with an action that only someone with four hands could have achieved, she got off the bed, put on her clothes, shoes, haversack and was at the door in nine seconds.

'Enjoy China. Don't scale walls that are greater than you can climb,' she said to her paramour or whatever Bakshi and she were to each other. She shut the door and felt pain.

She ran across the corridor, tears streaming down her

face. She tried not to cry, but her phantom twin won. It was too *emotional*. She needed to distract herself with more work. So, she dialled a number on her phone, 'Mr Singh, I'd like to be more involved in your operations.'

Chapter Eight

Legend #35

Many pseudo sciences conjecture that dragons may have been real. Their presence across myriad cultures gives this theory weight. Dragons existed in Celtic, British and most European mythologies. India had the Nagas, snake people, now commonly called house brokers.

The Greeks had Chimera, a fire-breathing, winged creature with the head of a lion and a goat—a mashup of the animal kingdom.

Even The Bible's Satan is a modification of Leviathan, a sea dragon, to which the Loch Ness monster may lay copyright claim.

The closest we have to a real dragon is the Komodo Dragons—giant lizards, all of whom live out their retirement on islands in Indonesia, and barely invoke the legend of a flying, reptilian predator.

The symbolism of a dragon across various cultures is no coincidence. Dragons do represent something very real: human fear.

Bakshi looked at the group seated in front of him and smiled. He loved an audience, especially one that was unsure about him. Taunque and Manoj did not trust him but it was Arjun's hate that really made him happy. It was amusing that the strongest being on the planet was so consumed by him. Bakshi was less than five and a half feet and the only people physically threatened by him were really young children. But here was the big man seething because of his mere presence. Bakshi's ego danced.

'Alright, now that our Yeti has joined us and we're all friends, I have some news,' said Bakshi, 'there is something I got in my email inbox this morning that might interest all of us.'

'*Your* emails? You never check your emails,' interjected Kelly.

'I don't check my work emails but I do have private emails,' said Bakshi.

'No, you don't. You once couriered your laptop and asked me if I got your email! And you broke two phones when you got pissed...'

'We established this three days back, I'm not a moron,' said Bakshi.

Kelly let that one slide but Arjun interjected, 'I believe you are a moron. If there were awards for morons, you'd win a Nobel Prize and then forget to collect it, winning three more of them in the process.'

'Good one, bhai,' said Manoj.

Bakshi's smile vanished but he went on, 'This is a video from the man who attacked us last week.'

'Why would the attacker email you?' asked Arjun.

Everyone looked at Bakshi and though he was usually impervious to hate, he could sense the antagonistic waves flood him. But he was ready, 'Manoj, can you dim the lights? Maybe the video will answer all your questions.'

Manoj dimmed the lights and Bakshi said, 'I present to you, the lead villain of our little story.'

And then, he stood by the table and stared at the screen. Nothing played.

'I think you have to press the "play" button,' said Manoj.

'Of course, I knew that. I was just building up the drama,' said Bakshi and fumbled with the buttons, 'which one is the "play" button?'

Kelly got up and pressed "play".

The screen filled up with the face of a Chinese man. He was clean-shaven and thin, with an aura of a man who knew more than others. He looked like he was seventy, but had the demeanour of a much younger man. In his eyes was the fire of a twenty-year-old conqueror, a young Mandarin Alexander. His hair was thinning at the front and his age had ensured his nose drooped, all of which made him resemble a hawk.

He spoke in the measured tone of someone not used to talking at length; every word in English was precise, despite the slight Chinese twang.

He began without preamble.

'It is a temptation to paint the person opposing us as our enemy. This foolish misnomer makes men lose wars. Calling a man your enemy makes it emotional. And emotions are a terrible way to fight a war. Emotions can drive the cause of a war but rarely the result. A man's ego can drive him to invade a land, but eventually, his ego will derail him. I, your so-called enemy, am not driven by ego; I'm driven by logic. And that logic is simple: India is a failed concept.

'You've been one of the world's leading economies for decades, but right at the point of surge, you always collapse, an erection without direction. You're torn asunder by a horde of leaders each of whom wants precisely the opposite thing. You had four metro cities, now you have twelve—it is not something to boast about, especially for a land that claims to be a contender.

'Worse yet, parts of your land are completely ignored, which is why you have militancy, Naxalites and general chaos. You can't control your own people because you don't care about your own people. You've ignored them in the Northeast, Chhattisgarh, Madhya Pradesh and belts elsewhere. Your own people are in denial about the very concept of "India" that you've tried half-heartedly to shove down their throats. People that make it in India have made it despite your governance, not because of it.

'You are a shameful failure. And here's the best part, if I was an Indian, you may have me arrested for being anti-national and seditious just for criticizing you. Ah, well, in that case, India and China are similar. Just in that case.

'You like to pretend. You have hope in this concept. Yet, you fight over cows, food, faith, class, anthems. I'm sure that helps promote economic security. Everything you do to perpetuate India is superficial surgery. Some of your leaders had vision but you quelled them. All the rest promote is politicized secularity and the only currency they seek is votes. And you think we are the enemy.

'China is not the enemy. You hate us because you know we are winning. We've been winning for centuries. You're about to overtake us in population. We congratulate you. Maybe you can throw all those spare people on us as ammunition and win a war.

'You are a population of one and a half billion, with a billion that are never allowed to be useful. You're inefficient in managing resources. China has very few useless people. Everyone who works in China works for China. Some do it reluctantly and some with joy, but most of the People's Republic works for the People's Republic with the utmost belief that our concept is the most dominant.

'I'm not saying we have no weakness. But our strength conquers it every single day. We are a strong race, stronger than the machines we manufacture. This is why in a few decades; we have conquered the world in manufacturing, production, inventions, engineering and even that tomfoolery called the Olympics. And now, we will dominate the world in one other thing: land.

'You've seen us do it for years now. The Asian and international media questioned our highhandedness in Singapore, Hong Kong, Tibet or even with oil wells in the sea across Southeast Asia. You all whined about our dominance. But nobody listened. Who will listen? China is not a concept like you, we are a movement. We will take over the world not because of ego but because our way of life is more powerful than others. You can complain about us today, but we will own you tomorrow.

'We are not distracted by idiocy like religion, politics and often, even individuals. Some people are disposable. If it is for the higher cause, those people are our—excuse the term—jihadis of progress. We are not the enemy. We are the answer. If you're willing to work for China, China will take care of you. And we will take people into our fold along with their lands, only to fulfil our big aim of a People's Republic of Earth.

'Every bit counts. Even a small province of under a hundred thousand people counts. Even Tawang counts. The people there are our people. They are part of the glory of the Chinese empire. And we will bring them back to where they always belonged. I believe the Indian term for that is "ghar waapsi".

'We will not harm a single person in Arunachal i.e. a single Chinese citizen. They are our own and we do not massacre our own people irrespective of all the lies the international media may spin time and again. We will take over the land by proving to the people the failure of the Indian state and the power of the Chinese republic.

'Word will spread. Tawang may be a tiny speck but it will turn the tide over your so-called claim on the Northeast India. The Arunachalese shall be free from your bumbling and will embrace our superior ways of life. They will be there to see our inevitable dominance of the world.

'Of course, anyone who stands between us and our people will be blown away. A mother does not hesitate to kill predators that claim to be guarding her children by slowly poisoning them. You are the poison and we, the antidote.

We see you have this "creature" fighting for you. He and his ancestors have helped you for eons. Their existence is an aberration, an evolutionary coincidence that happened to work in your favour. Your one advantage is coincidental! How typical.

'I ask him, what is he fighting for? A country that drove his father to madness? Yes, I met him. Your Pawan. This nation you serve turned him into a depressed drunk that wept while he fought. Yes, he beat us once. But at the cost of his own sanity.

'The most potent fighting force on Earth was turned into a sad drunk by a country of imbeciles that didn't even care for him or his family. That's what you're fighting for.

'If this evolutionary marvel happens to make the erroneous mistake of fighting for the side of confusion, then, we will be forced to defeat him. Chinese engineering will conquer Indian randomness. One small man and his brain against a beast of presumed impenetrability.

'Either way, after this little battle, the people of Arunachal shall find themselves in the fold of China. And for once in so many decades, they will be on the right side of the future.'

The man's eyes burnt with possibility and then, the video stopped abruptly. The darkness of the room reflected what the five people sitting inside it felt.

'For a psychopath, his psychosis could not be more methodical, 'said Taunque through the blackness. For once, the Major's words rang hollow. Nobody turned on the light. They were all hypnotized. How could a man reveal his plans and still leave the opposing side flabbergasted?

'So damn intense. That dude really needs to get laid,' Bakshi finally broke the silence.

***

Sun had never seen a man happier with defeat than Dr Ling. The man was glowing despite having had his ass kicked. Sun had been forbidden from accessing the footage of the Tibet attack, which was why she had accessed them. The creature was something out of *Age of Mythology*, a game Sun had won more times than Zeus. Right now, Dr Ling looked like he was Zeus himself.

He was in his favourite contraption—his Tesla conductor—where he smiled as his hair stood up due to magical bursts of electricity coursing across the laboratory. This calmed him. Some people went to massage parlours, a steam or a sauna, but Dr Ling preferred getting electrocuted by his favourite creation.

'How will you defeat it?' screamed Sun over the noise of the bursting lightning bolts.

Dr Ling continued smiling but his words were a rebuke, 'You were ordered not to see that,' he said.

'Yes. I accidentally accessed your files by hacking into them, purposely. How will you defeat it?' she asked again.

The hair on Dr Ling's head was erect as if greeting a passing parade of soldiers as he spoke, 'Him, not it. He's a living being. And I will defeat him mentally and physically.

Through mind games and physical pain. He's my prime goal.'

Sun was puzzled. This was the first she had heard of this new prime goal, 'I thought your prime goal was Arunachal?'

'Ah, yes. It is. A man can have two prime goals…'

'No, in fact, you keep telling me a man should have only one goal and be focused and dedicated and blah blah.'

'I know what I keep telling you,' replied Ling. 'Normal men should have one goal. I can have two. Once I get him, you'll know.'

'Okay,' said Sun, not understanding her boss' sentiment. He was never impulsive. She wondered if she should read the diaries he had written as a soldier in order to understand him more. He had often told her to read them, which was precisely why she hadn't. Why read something someone wants you to? Or maybe, that was reverse psychology. That bastard genius! He knew exactly how he could keep something secretive from her—by not keeping it a secret at all.

'I will look into him. Look inside him. And forget Arunachal. I will conquer the whole of Southeast Asia for China. All I need is what's in him,' said Ling and smiled.

She hated his smile; his happiness was a sign of danger. She went to his desk and opened the drawer with his old diaries; her old man was too consumed by Tesla's electricity to give a damn.

∞

The conference room was silent even after Bakshi's comment; everyone was contemplating what they had seen. Taunque from a military perspective, Bakshi from a financial perspective, Manoj from a soldier's POV, Kelly from all the discussed perspectives and Arjun from a suspicious angle. The words brought out the core of each person's personality.

'This is the problem with being an unofficial unit,' said Taunque, 'we can't even take an aggressive recourse to a direct threat.'

'Can't we send the clip to the Indian Army?' said Kelly.

'I will. But only to the ones who can keep a secret. If this reaches the top echelons of our government, we will be up shit creek without a paddle. Or a boat,' said Taunque.

'Why, Sir?' asked Manoj.

'Any of the five PMs could see this as fodder to further their political future. Blinded by arrogance, they'll assume we can take on the might of the Chinese armed forces. Oh, we could, if the centre could provide basic amenities. The last time Indian soldiers fought in Tawang, a quarter of them froze to death because the Indian government didn't have the sense to send them woollens. We got beaten by thermals!'

'I could get Rupa underwear as a sponsor,' volunteered Bakshi, 'I'm working on a plan for sponsors. Like the IPL, but for war.'

'So, we can't beat them?' said Kelly.

'Maybe. In the right circumstances. But this government can't. It requires an Indian PM to truly understand our armed forces. Leaking this will be a security issue in the borders of the Northeast. The idiots at the centre would completely make a mess out of it.'

'So, what do we do now, Sir?' asked Manoj.

'Well, we know where the enemy will be, so we go there and wait. It's anyway where we were planning to go.'

Kelly looked across at Arjun, 'You seem pretty silent.'

Arjun shuffled and shrugged his shoulders, 'Can't argue with this Ling fellow's logic,' he said, 'I don't understand why we need countries. I mean the tax laws between countries are really titillating. But, barring that...'

Everyone looked at him, puzzled.

'I'm sorry, "why do we need countries?"' said Taunque.

'He believes having countries is pointless. Something about visas,' said Kelly.

'That was a joke. It's about dividing humans into sections on the basis of mountains and rivers...' began Arjun.

'I think we're getting off track here...' interjected Taunque, 'this is not a philosophy debate at Oxford, Mr Tharoor.'

'No, Sir. I think we're on track. We should know precisely how our latest recruit feels about his country before we ask him to defend it,' said Kelly.

'A: I'm not a recruit, I'm a freelancer. B: It's your country because as I said, I don't believe in countries. C: There is no C, it just sounds better when making a point.'

Kelly tapped her pen on the conference room table, 'The reason countries are created is to protect land and ideologies that a large group of people agree with.'

'I know *why* countries are created. It's this instinct you have to constantly form groups because you're inept at protecting yourself alone. Ideologies are thrust down your throat from birth which causes you to continue fighting with each other. It's daft.'

'We have a very long agenda,' said Taunque.

He wasn't used to being ignored, but Kelly was bursting with anger, 'So, soldiers are just a bunch of idiots protecting something that is not worth protecting?'

'You're putting words in my mouth. I admire soldiers. The armed forces are noble people driven by nationalistic pride to protect a bunch of ungrateful idiots who often don't even care that they're doing it! They basically give up their lives just so some idiot in Mumbai can continue going to McDonalds without being shot by religious zealots. While they are quelling a terrorist threat, a random person living in the city goes on Twitterbook or Facetree or whatever to whine about how his life sucks because his new phone doesn't have an app which gives him a personality that makes women want to have sex with him.'

'How did you know I'm on Tinder?' said Bakshi.

'We have a credible threat from a Chinese superman,' said Taunque, raising his voice.

But the tennis match of words between Kelly and Arjun was just heating up.

'So, you don't want to defend your country?'

'Nope. Not interested.'

'It's your country.'

'No. It's your country. Vanaras are neutral. Always have been. I just happen to live here.'

'You have a gift.'

'It's a curse. I never asked for it. I wish I was short, useless, and untalented. I wish I was Bakshi—look at him.

He'd get beaten up by a seven-year-old boy.'

'He's one of the smartest men in this country.'

'Speaks a lot about your country. 1.5 billion people should take some cyanide and end it.'

'You're just a coward that'll use mental masturbation to convince yourself that you're not. Why are you still here?'

Arjun slammed his fist on the table and it cracked in half, surprising everyone including himself with his sudden outburst. His voice rumbled, 'Because, my family was ripped apart by people like you. My father killed himself because he tried to defend your stupid ideologies. How is Dr Ling wrong? My father is like the Northeast. Every few decades, you do something half-assed to help them but do you even care? Really care? Why won't you prove it? Maybe China won't treat them like second citizens just because their vote bank is not populated enough! All you people want to do is destroy each other, over different excuses.'

Kelly sat down with a slump. Nobody wanted to admit it but their newest asset was sounding more like a liability. And the last hour had caused a tear in their convictions.

'Did you and Dr Ling study at JNU?' asked Bakshi.

'Have you even seen your missions? You're going international. Our agenda is for innocents across the world. Not just India,' retorted Kelly.

'Yeah, yeah,' said Arjun.

'You were much nicer over coffee,' said Kelly as an afterthought.

'When did you guys have coffee?' asked Bakshi.

'Oooooh, controversy,' said Manoj.

'It was a work thing,' said Kelly, blushing a little, 'I was following Taunque's orders.'

'Oooooh, coffee, tea or monkey?' said Manoj.

'Please shut up,' said Bakshi, 'my standing is without question.'

Arjun snarled at him, 'And let me ask you questions nobody else is asking. How was a dragon made by China found in Sri Lanka? How did the email show up at Bakshi's doorstep? And more importantly, where the hell does Bakshi go? Where are all his mystery meetings?'

Kelly, Manoj and General Taunque did not look directly at Bakshi because these were questions neither of them wanted to ask, but the man spoke up for himself and for a change, his voice seemed genuine.

'I sacrificed my entire company for the good of my country. I am the CEO of this mission, General Taunque is the COO. Yes, I know those designations. Do not dare to question my allegiance. Everything I do is for the long-term good of this country. Otherwise, I could be sitting on a cool beach in Ibiza sipping tequila off the belly of a supermodel; not helping India fight its unofficial war,' said Bakshi and then, for good measure, he added, 'you monkey man.'

Before Arjun could leap across the table and attempt to rip out Bakshi's throat, Taunque's commanding voice broke through the chaos.

'Enough!' screamed Taunque. 'It's 4:34, there is exactly one minute for this meeting to end and it will end at my call. Understood?'

No one responded.

'Do not make me ask this again. Understood?'
Everyone nodded.

'Operation Tawang shall proceed as planned. Arjun Singh, your missions have been given to you already by Bakshi. Go execute them. I don't care about your feelings for your country, but I do care about your feelings towards people. Are you willing to fight for the people? The people of Northeast India and the rest of *India*?' he asked, putting special emphasis on the word India.

'Yes, as long as it is a just cause. I have no issues fighting for people, but don't expect me to wave flags in the air. I will fight for people that...'

'Mr Singh,' said Taunque, interrupting another one of Arjun's tirades, 'are you willing to fight for the people of India?'

'Yes,' said Arjun, sulkily.

'Meeting dismissed. Everyone knows what to do. Also, Bakshi, I don't question your dedication, but if I find out that you've done anything to jeopardize India's interests, I shall personally pluck out your eyeballs and shove them down your throat—just so you can see where I shall stab you. That goes for everyone else in this mission as well. Including our new recruit,' he said, looking pointedly at Arjun.

'Get on with unofficial work, your stupid opinions and politics be damned. Let's go out there and save the world the best we can. Dismissed! It's time for my daily haircut,' concluded Taunque.

Chapter Nine

Legend #90

Lord Hanuman's faithfulness was his essence. The defining story of this attribute is when Lakshmana was grievously injured in battle with Ravana. Hanuman was sent to get the sanjeevani booti. The greatest booty in history other than a Kardashian, it was an herb that could cure all ailments.
With time running out, Hanuman plucked out an entire mountain that housed the precious herb. That is the true definition of a BFF. Maybe one could ask him for other stuff as well. I need oranges—here's Nagpur. I need plankton—here's the Atlantic Ocean. I need corruption—here's Robert Vadra, enjoy.'

Hafiz Saeed could not believe his luck. One of the world's top ten terrorists, he had always been proud of the US bounty of ten million on his head. He joked with his fellow terrorists, 'Who knew my head is worth so much? Imagine how much they would give for my parts below the belt. Six million minimum, right? One for each inch.'

His comrades always laughed even though they knew Hafiz would only get three million if such a bounty existed. They had seen him urinate and they knew what was what. But they laughed, because when your boss laughs, you must too!

Either way, it was rare for Hafiz to meet anyone who had a bounty similar to his. But today, he was in elite company. He sat opposite ISIS supreme, Abu Bakr al-Baghdadi, a man that also had a US bounty of ten million (two million for parts down below). Baghdadi was said to be dead but death is sometimes just a rumour.

Hafiz had landed in the city of Fallujah, Iraq, and was pleased to see that after all these years, the city was still reduced to rubble. The only structures that stood were ISIS camps and mosques and that's all that really mattered. The swirling dust, sand and men with guns who pillaged and raped whoever they pleased gave Hafiz a warm glow. The fallen city was so wonderful.

He picked up his silver cup of tea and munched on a date as Abu settled down on the carpet in front of him. The room was simply decorated—carpets adorned the floor, the walls and the bed. There was a large hookah under the bed and behind that, Hafiz noticed a stockpile of weapons. Both men looked at each other and smiled.

'Would you please get your boss for me?' said Hafiz to the man in front of him, as he took another bite of the date.

A man appeared from behind "Abu", and the difference between the two was minimal. The real Abu now spoke to

Hafiz, 'You could tell my body double from me, Hafiz?'

'I am not CIA, Abu. I know which one is living or dead,' said Hafiz smiling, 'and how can I not? When I've admired that face for so long? His beard has a few sparse spots, whereas yours has none.'

The two men embraced and sat down on the carpet, 'These bloody Americans have ruined this city,' said Hafiz.

'Yes,' agreed the ISIS chief, 'Laid it to rubble. Interfering spawns of Shaitan. Harams. Ruined this city.'

'Maybe with all the Saudi money you get, you should build schools, hospitals and generate employment. You could rebuild the city,' suggested Hafiz.

Both men looked at each other and guffawed, 'You are a hilarious man, Hafiz. Hilarious. Everyone knows that the will of the Almighty is for us to plunder and destroy all humanity. Progress, bah!' said Abu, sipping on his tea.

'How shall we ruin the name of the Almighty if we start thinking about progress?'

Hafiz sat up, alert, 'I was so impressed by your use of women jihadis in Europe. Those white supremacists didn't see it coming. So many women and children killed—I was so delighted.'

'Well,' said Abu, 'I've always said. Women are good for two things—cooking and blowing things, if you know what I'm saying.'

Both men laughed at the classy joke, 'I'm thinking. We've killed young brainwashed men, women, and children. But Abu, there is a whole segment we haven't even thought of. A segment that can get past X-Rays and blow up more people.'

'Babies,' ejaculated Abu.

'How the hell did you know?' said Hafiz, holding up a suicide jacket that could fit a nine months old baby, 'I got this made for precisely that. Baby jihadis. No one will suspect it.'

'I agree,' said Abu and held up his own suicide jacket for a six-months-old child, 'Mine comes with a diaper holder.'

The two men admired their weapons of destruction, 'We are two bodies with one heart. So, it shall be!' exclaimed Hafiz, 'Babies are angels and who is a better angel than the one who meets his maker after killing innocents?'

'I agree,' said Abu, 'babies are the future. You're so smart, Hafiz,' and in a burst of passion, Abu moved away the table that divided them and kissed Hafiz on the mouth.

'Oh, Abu,' said Hafiz, 'what we do is against the will of God,' and kissed him again.

'Come back to Pakistan with me. The hospitality for people like me is just wonderful!'

Just as the two men were on the verge of discovering each other's bounties, the window near them exploded. Explosions were the norm in the region but both Hafiz and Abu were not used to actual combat, preferring—like most men in charge—younger men to sacrifice lives in their name.

Both men gasped and from the fragments of shattered glass, brick and mortar, a gigantic man spoke to them in a rumbling voice, 'Well, isn't this a happy coincidence? Hafiz Saeed and Abu Baghdadi. Two for the price of fun.'

Abu's body double and Hafiz's bodyguard responded, simultaneously firing bullets at the figure that merely stood there, allowing the bullets to rebound from his body like squash balls. The body double's bullet bounced off and killed Hafiz's bodyguard and Hafiz's bodyguard's bullet bounced off and killed Abu's body double in a perfectly synchronized equilateral triangle—surely a delight for all mathematics fans.

Hafiz and Abu took a step back, but the man in front of them bowed, 'Don't worry, friends. I just want to take you for a little ride on my magic carpet.'

He removed his backpack and quickly filled air into a blue tarpaulin, 'Now, get inside. Treat it like your honeymoon suite. You are about to get deducted,' he said as he shoved both men in, 'I'm also a Chartered Accountant. Excuse me while I try out new Accountant/ Superhero catch phrases. Hope you like it. Now, watch out, there will be some turbulence.'

∽

For once, The Secular Gang was quiet. No insults, no racism and no testosterone infused faux fights. All four sat on their chairs, silently looking at the scenery in front of them. They were quieter than a church mouse in outer space.

Perhaps it was the view. Tawang Province in Arunachal Pradesh had the view of most of the Northeast of India which was nothing less than dazzling. The valley below was docked with little homes enveloped by green trees and a hint of snow in the mountain peaks beyond. A cricket ground that doubled as a football ground, skating rink and wedding hall dotted the landscape along with the edges of a lake hidden beyond the trees.

The view was like a painting, untouched by pollution and vagabond progress. The sliver of the lake itself was worth the arduous travel to the town. Nestled between two mountains, the Shonga-tser Lake—or Sungester Lake for easy pronunciation for foreign tourists—came into existence because of an earthquake in 1971, one of the few times an earthquake had caused something beautiful. Tour guides later bastardized the name of the lake to Madhuri Lake, after a song shot by Madhuri Dixit at this location. Like most things in India, places changed their names only for Bollywood celebrities and dead politicians.

Perhaps it was the weather that caused their silence. The sun politely warmed them as the coldness tried to bite into them, leaving a perpetual state of goosebumps. It demanded silence. Or maybe, it was just the man seated next to The Secular Gang who spoke at the speed of a bullet train.

Druk Lepcha, the owner of the Lucky restaurant/gym/ cyber café/ parking lot/ hotel/ medical store/ wine shop/ but, no cigarettes, was explaining the origin of his name.

'My father from Bhutan. My mother from Arunachal. So, I'm Druk—like dragon. Though, you should have met my wife, she was more dragon than woman,' he said and laughed at his own joke.

Manoj, as he heard this man roar with laughter, finally had empathy for those that had been faced in this situation before. Mr Lepcha was a wonderful old man but Manoj sincerely wanted to gag and toss him into the lake. But unfortunately, according to the locals, Mr Lepcha was the most lucid about the "dragon" that had appeared in Tawang. Manoj raised his hand in front of Mr Lepcha and clapped it twice—it was the only way to distract the man from his own words.

'Please tell me what happened with the dragon?'

'You heard the joke about the man from Arunachal?'

Manoj shook his head, 'Mr Lepcha, please focus...'

'First hear my joke, young man.'

'Fine. Tell me your stupid joke, uncle.'

'There was man from Arunachal. A man from across the border came to his coffee shop and ordered coffee. He spoke Hindi, so he tried it and said, "Friend, do you want some cheeni?' So, the coffee shop owner said, 'No, I don't want Cheeni, I'm part of India.'

Once again, Mr Lepcha roared with laughter.

Manoj sighed, 'Hilarious.'

'You are not laughing.'

'Hahaha. Hilarious. Now, please tell me about the dragon.'

'Okay. It came twice. Like my wife on our honeymoon,' said Mr Lepcha and smiled mischievously. 'First sign of it was loud screeching from beyond the valley. As soon as the screech came, everything shut down. TV, phones, electricity. The first time, we thought, well, there goes the light, as usual. Our municipality is really not very good. We get electricity through wires from main Arunachal. I'm thinking I should run for elections in the municipality, shape things up...'

'The dragon...'

'All lights were off. I came out to this balcony. Best view in all Tawang, you can see the valley below and the stars above. It is beautiful. I looked at the valley and I saw a red shape in the darkness below. Then, I was blinded by an explosion of lights. I thought, this municipality was real stupid and that's why it was happening. First, they cut lights and then, they waste them. But, when my vision cleared, I saw it,' and Lepcha's voice dropped. 'It was the most magnificent and fearsome thing I had ever seen. A dragon as alive as my name. It flew across the valley. Then, it screeched again, hurled fire into the air, and flew over our village—impressive display. I soiled my pants. I'm not ashamed to admit it. I'm an old man; I'd never seen anything like it. And then, I saw panic in the streets below—people screaming, running about. It even threw fire at an isolated tree. Burnt it down and flew away. That's it.'

Manoj considered this. The story would have sounded ludicrous if he hadn't seen the dragon himself. He could understand why nobody believed the little town. A dragon that had threatened an entire village had only burnt down a tree and had disappeared? It indicated more the result of mass hysteria and the abuse of narcotics than reality.

Mr Lepcha's wrinkled face was morose and he could tell the man quivered at the thought of this presumably supernatural being. Lepcha had lived his entire life in a happy cocoon in the hills and to see something that shook the entire foundation of his being in the autumn of his life seemed unfair.

'The second time?' asked John.

Mr Lepcha shook his head, 'Same thing. Screech. Lights went off. No phones, nothing working. This time it set fire to another tree, and then, it disappeared. If that thing wanted to, it could have burnt down this entire town. But of course, nobody believed us. Even the army left before. Some Naxal mission in M.P., they said. They were following orders from the Central Government apparently. The soldiers were disappointed but obviously, we don't matter. Only the border is patrolled and there is little fourteen soldiers can do in front of a dragon. There's little fourteen hundred soldiers can do. Period.'

'Afzal, please put all of this in the report,' said Manoj.

'Already sending, Boss. I've even made some Excel sheets for fun. Even though the network up here is terrible.'

'Mr Lepcha, we're here to help,' said Manoj.

The old man smiled, 'Four of you? That's not a battalion, that's one side in a volleyball match!'

Manoj smiled, 'You haven't seen the fifth...'

'Or the sixth,' said Afzal, 'she made us this.'

Lepcha gave him a sidelong glance, 'Made you what exactly? You look like you got rejected by the military.'

Darius guffawed. The truth was so close to the joke he could not resist.

Manoj picked up the binoculars and pointed them at the valley towards China, 'Mr Lepcha. Can I have some tea, please? We have a long night ahead of us.'

The old man got off his chair, affronted that his question wasn't answered, 'Yeah, yeah. I'll get you more butter tea.'

The Secular Gang was relieved to get silence. They stared across at the gorgeous valley and waited for the mythological figure, secretly wishing it would never come.

South Sudan—the world's youngest country gained independence in 2011 and broke into a civil war in 2013. The country was born out of war and thrown back into war. Its neighbours repeatedly found some excuse to invade it—Islamism, extremist Christianity, depraved dictatorship, bored warlords and in one case, an army of children; presumably competing for the U-14 War Championships.

It was inevitable since the country was bordered by Congo, Sudan, Uganda and Ethiopia—four powers so volatile, they gave Plutonium a complex. The country was not prepared for the violence that perpetuated its existence. Seven armed groups planned attacks in 90 per cent of the country, and all of them accused the other of having plans to install a dictatorship.

Now, the leading group involved Joseph Kony, a man who created an army of over a lakh child soldiers and deemed it the will of the thirteen "Gods" that spoke to him. Real Gods had abandoned South Sudan, leaving behind only the psychos.

The UNHRC had refugee camps at the border that housed thousands of the homeless. The refugees were kept "safe", or as safe as living in hell would allow them. Their dingy bunkers had poor sanitation and were strewn with blue plastic sheets, mattresses with holes and steel utensils. The camp smelled of a deathbed. The UNHRC volunteers suddenly found their hopelessness rise, as they saw a tanker approaching them from beyond the hill.

They had been expecting the tanker after Joseph Kony in his weekly address, *My Little Kony*, had declared, 'The

God of War has spoken to me and told me that people who seek shelter from foreign forces like the UNHRC are foreigners themselves. And not African or Sudanese. Death will come to them. Amen.'

As the tanker approached, UNHRC volunteers screamed at people to find shelter but there was no shelter. The tanker fired and as the camp braced for impact, something whirred through the skies, flying parallel to the ground. It blocked the fire from the tanker inches before it reached the camp— just like David de Gea saving a penalty kick from dictatorship.

Arjun Singh slammed backwards and slid across the ground with the impact of the tanker's firing. He was glad he had consumed the potion before diving in front of the tanker or he would have felt pain as the missile had smacked right on his head. But the adrenaline ensured he didn't feel a thing.

He got up from the wiring and dusted himself off. A child was looking at him from behind the mesh of the camp with her mouth open, 'Don't worry, kid,' he told her, 'fortunately, the missile hit my head.'

The tanker geared for another attack, and Arjun ran straight towards it, covering the ground astronomically fast. He turned the tanker's gun skyward, and the missile fired harmlessly into a few trees.

'You son of a bitch,' screamed Arjun at the tanker, 'you killed my friends,' pointing at the trees.

And with all his strength, he ripped out the gun from the tanker and tore off the top of the armed vehicle like a can of beans. When the top half of the tank was ripped off, Arjun saw the people in the tanker—two African men and behind them, one Joseph Kony.

'Joseph Kony,' said Arjun, 'you stupid son of a bitch. How arrogant are you to come to a war with three soldiers?'

'Who are you?' asked Joseph Kony, 'We…we weren't expecting resistance. It is Poker Night at our camp. I…I just thought I'll take a drive.'

'Normal people don't take a drive to massacre innocents,' said Arjun and smashed the gun he was holding on one of the drivers, trapping him underneath. He told the other driver, 'Go back to your camp and tell them what you saw. Or who you saw. Tell them I'll be back. As for you Kony,' he said, crushing the tanker's gun, 'you and I are going for a short drive. Or a short flight.'

He pulled out the blue tarpaulin from his haversack, 'Get in the bag since you are a doubtful receipt and I'm your suspense account. That's my new catch phrase—hope you like it.'

∞

Before being a soldier, Manoj Sharma used to be a gunda—though the technical term was "regional party worker". He enjoyed thrashing anyone that stood in his way without repercussions. The law always looked away if you flashed your political credentials. It was a fantastic job. Unfortunately, Manoj had *some* decency and when he protested to his colleagues beating up a Nigerian woman for "looking like she sold drugs" and then an old man because "his house should be ours", he was unceremoniously fired.

He joined the Short Service Commission. But his unorthodox thinking meant he was fired yet again, only to find out that he had been delisted because his unconventional ways had caught Taunque's eye. He hadn't been fired since. Taunque had saved him from himself and he tried to be to his little group what Taunque had been to him. He was strict when it came to discipline and it was this discipline that was causing The Secular Gang to lose their mind in Tawang.

It had been two weeks of anxious waiting. He had barred his team from consuming narcotics, which was all Lepcha spent his evenings doing—travelling in his mind with the consumption of every leaf-based intoxicant known to man. The man was a botanist. Manoj was sure he could turn a cauliflower into a mind-altering substance. But he couldn't allow his men to lose focus.

'Got some rose plant bhang, if any of you is interested,' said Mr Lepcha and offered them a cane basket full of stuff, 'it's on the house.'

'That's what you call "little"?' asked Manoj.

'Yeah. If you're living your life right!'

Afzal looked at the pipe in Lepcha's mouth with temptation, John looked at Afzal's temptation and felt tempted, while Darius sat by Lepcha, passively smoking.

'Can we have a little...' began Afzal.

'Yeah, come on. Just a bit,' said John.

'No!' cried Manoj, 'We're on duty. We're not here on vacation.'

'It's been fourteen days, Manoj. That dragon is never

going to come. I'm tired of sitting on this stupid chair all day.'

'We can play Antakshari,' said Manoj.

'No! Come on. You're not Annu Kapoor. I'm sick of it. We've played Monopoly, Jenga, we've finished Cluedo thirty times. We can't even play cards…'

'It's gambling,' said Manoj.

'Come on, man. Just one puff.'

'No, Afzal!' cried Manoj, 'We're soldiers. Six more Indian soldiers were killed mysteriously. That's twenty-five deaths in three months. We don't know who the hell did it. If you wanted to do drugs, you should have stuck to engineering. Go for a long run if you want.'

Nobody went for a long run. If they were committed to anything, it was to insult each other and follow their leader. The deaths of the Indian soldiers rankled them. Six soldiers were found dead, all due to heart attacks at the border. It was too coincidental for six men to get a heart attack and meet the fate of almost thirty men before them. Once again, the Indian PMs were more concerned with squabbling with each other to bother about deaths of their toy soldiers.

It aggravated all four of them and they were determined to wait and wreak vengeance on the dead men's behalf, even if their own government failed them. This was what limbo must have felt like—an eternal wait for something that may never arrive. And even if it did, it would probably not leave one happy.

∽

Seven faces of the world's most evil men peered from the

bottom of the deep pit at Arjun, who floated at the mouth of the pit. His laugh bounced off the walls of the pit, making it worse than it actually was.

The stench of the massive pit was palpable. Weeks ago, it had smelled of damp mud and Mother Earth and now it smelled of wet faeces and Father Fart. Arjun waved his hand in front of his face as the stench rose to meet his nose.

'Gentlemen, I hope my hospitality hasn't left anything to chance? Bananas and rum for everyone! I would have arranged for a proper toilet. But since all of you are pieces of shit, we should be okay. Now, you can't see where you are. But has anyone here heard of Olduvai Gorge?'

'Which agency do you work for and who the hell are you?' screamed Al-Baghdadi, 'I've been in this pit for weeks!'

'Olduvai Gorge,' continued the floating giant, 'is in the continent where humanity originated—Africa.'

'I know Africa. I am Africa. What are you?' screamed Joseph Kony.

'Palaeontologists love this place,' continued Arjun, ignoring him, 'I can see why; it's gorgeous', and he took a peek at the landscape. Spurts of green shrubbery and rock met with gentle brown mountains and a sky bluer than the ocean. The sun kissed the land; even the ball of fire that warmed the Earth held a special spot for this land of glory.

'How dare you shove us in a pit?' howled Hafiz Saeed.

'We're in Tanzania, East Africa. Since the 1930s, this gorge has yielded the most beautiful bounty for palaeontologists. Stone tools, skulls, bones, fossils and everything that helps us understand the origin and evolution of humanity.'

'I will put nuclear bomb in your ass, motherfucka…' screamed Kim Jong-Un.

'Somewhere in our evolutionary path, we took a wrong turn. And all of you are proof of the same. You guys are disgusting. Worse than people that wait till 25 March to file their returns. So, it's only fitting that you find yourself in a pit—a pit that palaeontologists in the future may dig to discover the devolution of humanity.'

'Come, you want to be rich? Come! I'll give you fifty billion Zimbabwean dollars. You can buy three eggs with it. Come,' yelled Robert Mugabe.

'But, I won't kill you—that would be wrong, and unjust. I'll just let you do that to yourself,' he said, and opened his haversack into the pit. 'Knives, guns, nunchaku. Kill yourselves. It only makes sense; after all, you're the ones with the problem.'

The weapons clattered against each other on the soft mud below. The terrorists and despots gave each other a cursory glance and leapt on to the knives under their feet. The ninety-five-year-old Mugabe twisted his back with just the effort of bending, and that made Arjun feel a little bad. But just then, a phone ring disturbed his thought process.

He picked up the phone, 'I'm in the middle of something.'

Kelly's voice broke through the line. The reception was sketchy at best, 'We've had some…news. The dragon it…err…returned. We tried to fight back. But we need you back here ASAP.'

'Is everyone fine?'

'Manoj. He, he... We tried our best but...but...bu... he's been taken...'

The phone disconnected abruptly. Arjun tried calling back but the phone crashed.

'Goddamn charging,' he said and in anger, he slammed the phone into the pit. It landed in the middle of the knife fight and shattered.

Some switch went on inside Arjun. Chemicals flew rapidly through his body and straight to his head. He had never felt so much rage. He didn't know if it was the potion or genuine emotion, but right then, he wanted to rip the world to shreds with his bare hands.

All over the world, evil men were killing innocents whose only sin was being at the wrong place. The balance of the world was completely askew. There was no such thing as karma—it was weighted in favour of the rich, malicious and selfish.

With a growl, he flew down and with no mind of what he was doing, grabbed one man by the neck—ripping his head clean off. He held another and flung his body head first into the wall of the pit. He snatched one and twisted his neck off. With two remaining, he punched and pummelled them to death till their insides were like gooey ketchup that splattered against the wall and his face.

He growled again in his pit of death and at the injustice of life. Coated in the blood and bone of some of the world's most despicable men, he blasted off in an explosion towards the sky—to smite anything that stood in his path, with the potion driving his body to aggressive vengeance.

'You came here to be audited, but you got raided,' he swore into the wind. 'Bloody delinquents made me miss my favourite catch phrase.'

~

Manoj had lost his virginity when he was seventeen. He had been very impressed with himself because he had seduced Sudha over months. She was older, out of his league and also, considerably married. He had taken her for movies, dress circle tickets, dinners—Chinese only—and even drinks to a 3-star hotel. He had to indulge in all sorts of thievery to finance the operation, but she had finally consented and it had been quick, embarrassing and wonderful. It had taught him a valuable lesson—if he stayed determined about something, he would usually succeed at it. It also taught him to learn Kegel exercises, but that's neither here nor there.

Manoj was a patient man but it had been a month and a half since their arrival. After a few days, even the most bountiful view can drive the most imaginative man crazy. Fortunately, the locals did not lose patience with them and their exceptional hospitality was still keeping the show running.

The soldiers' prime source of entertainment—Lepcha's daughter, Harithi—was warming up to her favourite theme. Every day as the sun set she would enthral the group with her gossip—from news of the town to someone called Kanye West breaking internet records to why Katrina was a bitch for dating Harithi's future husband, Ranbir. Her company calmed them, especially because Harithi was gorgeous.

This evening, however, her daily grouse was closer to home, 'We were on Indian TV this morning, again. "Locals in tiny village see killer dragons: is drug use rampant? Is it Udta Tawang?" Even Indian TV finds our story incredulous. They believe women marrying snakes, snakes being aliens and women being ichadhari naagins, but our story is where they draw the line. And we've suddenly been downgraded from a town to a village. What nonsense!'

Her father nodded patiently, smoking what Manoj was sure was an apple, 'I admit. It's bad.'

'Bad! It's terrible, Papa. Kailash, my FB friend from Delhi was LOLing at me. It's so embarrassing. That dragon was real. Why doesn't anyone believe us?'

Her father blew smoke towards the setting sun across the mountain valley, 'Would you believe us? Where's the proof? No photos, no videos. There is no proof.'

'Whatever, Dad. And to protect us, we get these four guys. Are you guys even an army? Where is the real army?'

Manoj shook his head, 'Not their fault. They follow orders. Plus, an entire battalion of men has been wiped out mysteriously. The government doesn't care. Even the backup soldiers at the border were withdrawn. It didn't even make the news. Something is shockingly wrong with this whole deal.'

'What do you mean they follow orders? Aren't you one of them?' she asked.

'Not exactly, no,' said Manoj.

'We're unofficially a part of them,' said Afzal.

'It's complicated,' said John.

'Like a relationship status, but real,' finished Darius.

Harithi snorted, 'Sigh, guys. Sigh. At what stage are we supposed to be part of India? We're a border town; we're supposed to be protected.'

'The dragon hasn't done anything yet,' volunteered Afzal.

'This is why it doesn't make any sense. Why have a dragon with the potential to destroy a town and not use it?' said Manoj.

Lepcha took a deep drag and blew it out, 'Do you gentlemen know about Tibet?'

'Of course, we know about Tibet. We're not stupid. It's Dalai Lama's hometown,' volunteered Darius, looking at the apple cigarette in Lepcha's mouth with extreme jealousy.

'A simple no would have sufficed,' said Lepcha, 'let me tell you about Tibet.'

Harithi snorted and got off her chair, 'This is going to be another one of your stories. I got things to do.'

'Sit down!' said Lepcha, raising his voice, 'You need to know this.'

She was surprised. Her father was placid, he never screamed at her. He always said that daughters were like slingshots; the more tightly you pulled them back, the further they'd fly away from you. The quote had never made any sense to Harithi, but she respected her father nonetheless and sat down.

'Do you know why Tibet is not a country?' asked Lepcha.

'Because of China?' volunteered Darius, moving his chair closer to Lepcha to inhale the intoxicants that emanated from the older man.

'No, Earl Grey tea and silk shirts.'

'Was it a shopping mall?' whispered Darius in between the rings of smoke that came in his direction.

'Tibet was a peaceful and arid land with no interest in war. If you were living there, you really wouldn't want anything else. The people were spiritual and peaceful. But Tibet had a problem: it lay between China and India, and was then ruled by the British. And the British love tea and spices, especially because their own food is so terrible. A businessman told me he once tried blood pudding, and got diarrhoea for ten years. Anyway, they wanted a direct trade route with the Chinese and Tibet had the misfortune of being in the way.'

'So, the British turned Tibet into a trading post in the eighteenth century; a supermarket for East India Comedy—sorry, I meant, Company—and Chinese trade. They eventually also interfered in the politics of the region and helped ensure that four Dalai Lamas mysteriously died before they reached puberty.'

'Sounds like *Game of Thrones,*' said Harithi, 'only with less boobs.'

'Ah, but, it was The Great Game between Russia and Britain that led to the current state. A Dalai Lama finally lived to his adulthood with the help of his Russian teacher, making Lord Curzon more insecure than a man whose wife has an Italian tutor. The British believed the Russians would use their influence with the Lama to wrest control on Tibet.'

'This really sounds like GoT, right?' added Harithi to Darius, 'The North is Tibet, but it needs the help of

Danaerys, who happens to have a dragon as well.'

'And Tyrion is Lord Curzon?'

'I have no idea what you're talking about,' said Lepcha.

'You tell us your history, we'll tell you ours,' said Harithi.

Lepcha puffed at his cigarette, 'So, under Curzon's orders, the British attacked Tibet and basically massacred a bunch of people whose only weapons were sticks. Oh, and they also allowed the Chinese Army to take unofficial control of Tibet because what's a few massacres here and there to get silk shirts and Earl Grey?'

'What about the Russians?' asked Manoj.

'They had no intention of coming to Tibet. They were defeated by internal conflicts, Japan and possibly, liver failure. The Russian bear had no intention of hibernating in an arid land that was under such conflict.'

'What a KLPD,' said Darius.

'Is that a military term?' said Lepcha.

'It is—for certain types of artillery,' said Darius and smiled at the giggling Harithi.

Lepcha stared coldly at the obvious flirtation.

'Didn't the Chinese army beat the Tibetans in the 1950s?' asked Afzal.

'How the hell do you know?' said John.

'Wikipedia, bro. We've been sitting here for days with nothing to do!'

'Yes, yes, they did. The Mongols did too. But their control over the region was reiterated because of the British. And, once China rules any land, they believe they own it forever.'

'Dad, that's a great story!' said Harithi, 'But what the hell does that have to do with anything?'

Lepcha puffed again, 'Tawang District has been claimed as a part of South Tibet by the Chinese for decades. We used to be Tibet. Now, we're India. But the Chinese have been figuring a way into us for a long time. Except they can't have another blood bath. Hence, the peaceful threats of the dragons.'

'I still don't get it. Why have a military tool that you don't even use for attack?' said Manoj.

Lepcha smiled at him, 'Technically, what is a country? What does it mean to be part of a country? It means the people are part of a country. But what if the people felt neglected by a country that is supposed to help them prosper? This is not a military manoeuver; this is a manoeuver for public opinion. China is saying India is not taking care of you, why not believe in us?'

'Why us? We are barely half a lakh people. Eden Gardens gets double that many people for a cricket match. We're half of an IPL match!' cried Harithi.

'You know when civil unrest truly took off in Kashmir?' asked Lepcha.

'1990, the year of V.P. Singh,' replied Afzal, 'he got so busy trying to appease the minority vote bank; he removed troops from J&K. Rumours say he claimed that defending our country from Pakistan would aggravate the Muslims. My father was livid with the argument because it meant that some people in power thought we didn't belong to this country.'

'When the centre is at its weakest, that is when it's the best time for the neighbours to jump in.'

Manoj contemplated this. This was not a battle, this was a PR campaign and the product the Chinese were trying to sell to Tawang Province was China. They were saying, *'Humare toothpaste mein namak hai aur India waale namak haram hai.'* And seeing how most of India had generally dealt with the Northeast, it didn't seem that tough a sales pitch.

'How do you know so much about all this?' asked Manoj.

Lepcha took out a locket tied around his neck and handed it to Manoj. It was a silver chain with a metal insignia hanging from the middle.

'What is this?' said Manoj and turned over the memento in his hand. It had a goat with its horns showing proudly and a name underneath, "Ladakh Scouts."

'Wait,' cried John, staring at the insignia, 'Lepcha uncle, you were in the Ladakh Scouts? Wow.'

'The who?' asked Darius.

'Infantry. To protect Ladakh and J&K borders. They've featured in every major Indian conflict since like forever. Siachen, Bangladesh, Kargil, whatever. They're like mountain experts. Goats,' said John, 'I got into this because of guys like him.'

Lepcha beamed at them proudly, 'They mainly took Ladakhi and Tibetan people. It was a cinch.'

'He doesn't stop talking about how things were in the army,' said Harithi, 'even when I make tea for him. He's like, tea was better in the Scouts. Anything.'

Lepcha smiled at her affectionately, 'I'm protective, my

dear. Of all I hold close. The army does that.'

He took another puff and released it lazily towards the setting sun bathed in an orange hue. Suddenly, he got up with a jolt.

'It's here,' said Lepcha, looking towards the valley, 'it's here.'

Manoj and his three companions got up from their chairs, 'Where? All I see below is a fog.'

'That is not fog. It's artificial, look at how it rises like industrial smoke in a cold climate. Now, I suggest you all cover your ears,' said Lepcha and covered his ears.

A moment later, a loud piercing screech filled the valley and the twilight turned into complete darkness. Manoj's eardrums almost shattered.

'It's the cry of the beast,' said Lepcha.

'No,' said Kelly, stepping out from behind them, 'that's a non-nuclear electromagnetic pulse. It stops all electrical devices,' and she took out the earplugs from her ear.

'Who the hell are you?' said Harithi.

'The girl who is going to stop the most advanced LAWS I've ever seen,' said Kelly and removed her poncho. Her four arms popped out from within.

'What are LAWS?' asked Afzal as Harithi and Lepcha gaped at Kelly's hands.

'Lethal autonomous weapons system—a military term for technologically advanced robots or drones. It's also very illegal, by international convention. And very soon, it's going to be an illusion. Everyone in your positions,' she screamed and ran forward towards the source of the screams.

Manoj saw her race downhill through the town, towards the source of the fog from which the red glint of the dragon could already be seen, 'You heard her! Men, in positions! It's time to protect the 8th smallest province in all of India, and the concept of India itself.'

Chapter Ten

Legend #55

The Naga Fireballs or Mekong lights are a peculiar phenomenon reported near the Mekong River that runs through Myanmar and eventually, China. Urban legends suggest that glowing balls mysteriously rise from the water high into the air before disappearing. While no scientific evidence has been found, mythology suggests this to be the work of fire dragons beneath the surface of the water.
Locals must be glad it is merely the dragon's burp and not something excavating from further south of the dragon's anatomy.
What this legend does perpetuate though is a dragon's love for water.

As he smacked into a hot air pocket in the sky, Arjun almost lost control and plunged towards the Earth. Even a one-man flying machine can face turbulence. In his brief foray into flying, an air pocket had almost led him to crash into an aircraft. It was a United Airlines flight though, so

Arjun wasn't sure if he was harming or doing the people on board a favour.

Keeping his eyes open was another challenge. He had tried goggles but they had cracked because of the altitude and speed. The wind buffering into his face made it almost impossible. Bird collision was another problem. Fortunately, he didn't have engines or he would've been in trouble.

But, the toughest thing about flying was maintaining his breath. He had to consciously keep swallowing enough air to power forward. A second of distraction could mean losing control. He was largely indestructible, but he was sure that even he would not have survived a fall from thirty thousand feet in the air.

For most of his flights, the potion powered so much adrenaline into him that he didn't fear death or failure. But as he seared through the clouds at lightning speed, he was also powered by rage. They had his friend, possibly his best friend. They would have hell to pay. He would take their innards, make a necklace out of it and make them wear it.

The face of that old Chinese man kept popping into his vision. He didn't know if he had the gumption to tear that tiny little man into shreds, but he would have to. His rage made him fly faster than ever. He would have flown well above the clouds as he didn't want to smash into an airplane and it allowed him more speed, but he needed air to power himself onwards. So, he flew well below the clouds. It was dangerous and any civilian or more importantly, any air force could spot him. But with a mixture of luck and perhaps Taunque's influence, he had snuck past all radars.

He usually loved to fly because the scenery changed so rapidly over India. One minute, he'd be over languid brown hills in Maharashtra, the next over a tiny city in Madhya Pradesh, then over the gorgeous ports outside Chennai and suddenly, over hillocks of orange clouds above. He was his very own Google Maps and he flew across the country, taking in all its wonders and impossible insanity. But today, he barely looked down.

His rage was too strong to allow any contemplation.

Twice, he lost his way towards Tawang and had to crash in the middle of nowhere to check his orientation. But finally, in the clearing, he saw the little town show up on his natural GPS. From a distance, he could see smoke coming from the valley in the darkness and he flew faster, hurtling towards the town. He slowed at the last minute, and then crash landed, as always.

He left a pit in his wake and even with his strength; he felt an ache in his heart, close to the pain he had suffered when he had fallen from the skies while facing his Chinese nemesis. His head felt light and he lay on the ground, recovering his senses. But then, the rage built up again and he lifted himself abruptly to wreak vengeance on the entity that had Manoj. Kelly's face was wrought with worry. He shook his head and tried to get his bearings. He had flown longer and faster than he had ever flown but now it was time for war.

As he climbed out of the pit, Kelly began talking, 'Same sounds as last time. Our source, Lepcha, confirmed it. All the phones shut down. Smoke and fire. This thing came roaring out of the smoke. As per plan, we took our stations to fire surface-to-air missiles at him. I took my position closer to the ground in a foolhardy mission to pull out the robot's battery, and then...'

Arjun's head was exploding with exertion, 'What happened to Manoj?'

'The robot came,' said Kelly, 'and disappeared instantly. It grabbed Manoj before I could do anything.'

The remaining members of The Secular Gang stood at the edge of town, looking forlorn underneath a street light. They were at the beginning of the valley and behind them were the homes, the cricket stadium and the haphazard construction of an Indian hill station. Everything was lit with weak street lamps. The red rooftops seemed like they were precariously balanced from the edge of cliffs, daring gravity to take them. In the darkness, the town looked like it was preparing for its end, with even the light abandoning it.

'We've ensured that all the people stay indoors,' said Afzal and pointed to the nearest three-story apartment building, 'Lepcha, our local contact lives there.'

Arjun saw a wizened man's face peek out from behind one of the windows and yell, 'Is your friend back?'

'No, Lepchaji. For the hundredth time, no,' shouted back Afzal.

The screaming was ringing in Arjun's head. He reached into his jacket and looked for the potion. He pulled out two bottles but both were empty. He growled in anger and smashed the bottles on the side of Lepcha's house.

'You drank the entire potion?' said Kelly, 'That was a beta test. It's supposed to last you for six months, not two!'

Arjun steadied himself on the bark of a tree, 'I just dispensed with seven of the most dangerous men on Earth. Missions you couldn't do in a lifetime. Please do not lecture me. You let your own man get taken.'

The Secular Gang—or whatever remained of it—stepped forward to defend their leader. But Kelly held her hand at them and moved towards Arjun, 'You're jetlagged. And your potion is dying out. Your body is going through withdrawal and exhaustion at the same time.' She handed him a flask, 'It's tea. It'll rehydrate you. Drink it.'

Arjun took the flask from her and smashed it against the house. 'I don't need your stupid sympathy!' he heard his voice say, but he felt himself a distance away. He knew he sounded like a different person but he couldn't relent.

'We've been talking regularly, Arjun. We had discussed this,' said Kelly.

'Bah, talk, talk. All you people do is talk.'

'If I had your powers, Arjun Singh,' began Kelly.

'But you don't, do you? You have your stupid arms and your disciplined life. Enjoy it,' he said and leaned back on the tree.

He could see her control her temper and deliberate over what words to use to debilitate his mind, so, he stopped her in her tracks.

'Anyway, that bucket of metal will be back,' he said, 'He wants *me*.'

'Your arrogance is...'

'It's not arrogance. It's vengeance. My dad kicked Ling's ass. It took me a while to figure out. Now, it's my turn.'

'Dr Ling. Who the hell is he anyway?' said Kelly.

A loud electronic screech rang through the valley and a fresh bout of smoke exploded out of the dusk air, as if in response to the question.

⁂

The sound of the electromagnetic rays was deafening but the robot that caused the sounds was quiet as a mole's whisper. In the dark, it was impossible to see the source but Arjun could make out the red shapes.

'He's in the north west direction from where we are standing, about 28°,' he screamed to his little battalion.

'Men, ready to fire,' screamed Kelly.

'Ready to rescue,' screamed Arjun, and he took off to fly straight into the robot. He flew just three feet and collapsed back on the ground. Every muscle in his body ached. He tried again, but failed.

The robot hovered over the trees—emanating light that was brutal red—and mocked them. They couldn't fire because from a rod dangling in front of it was Manoj. He looked unharmed and even waved at them though Arjun could see the fear in his eyes.

Headlights went on in front of the robot as it hoisted Manoj thirty feet above them. Holding him up like ragdoll, it began to buzz. A beam shot out from it—a beam of laser. Arjun watched helplessly as the beam made its way to Manoj and with the precision of a surgeon, it chopped his right hand right off.

The man screamed in pain as his limb fell to the ground

at the exact same time the world was submerged in darkness. Manoj's screams echoed through the valley. And then, before there was a moment to react, the laser sliced through Manoj's neck and lopped his head right off. His frozen look of fear fell from the sky in a rainfall of blood.

'Fire at will,' screamed Kelly.

A volley of angry ammunition from The Secular Gang tore at the robot but all they got were harmless pings. Arjun tried to concentrate but try as he might, he could not fly.

Darkness. The kind of darkness that lulled the hill station into peaceful sleep now readied itself for the dance of death. The robot moved—though they heard it more than they saw it.

'Hold fire,' screamed Kelly.

The robot was nowhere to be seen.

Just as they got ready to attack the belly of the beast, they were all blinded. An explosion of bright lights burst through Arjun's cornea. It was like looking at the sun during an eclipse; the humans felt their eyes burn in anguish at the assault of light. Arjun heard groans from Afzal and Kelly and even his eyes were in discomfort. The blinding light lasted for barely ten seconds but it was enough.

It disoriented their little group. Arjun saw the outline of Kelly bent over holding her head and John screaming into his walkie-talkie, 'Don't look directly. Enemy is in. Enemy is in.'

The darkness filled their space, as blinding as the light—the ghosts of furious circles of light haunting their cornea.

'He's using light as a weapon!' screamed Darius, 'Who the hell does that?'

'The Falklands War of 1982,' said Kelly, 'the British used it to blind Argentinean attacks. And it was also used by the Americans in the Iraq War—it was proved useless, much like the Iraq War.'

'It was a rhetorical question.'

'They used it to disable the enemy,' screamed Kelly, 'to sneak up behind them.' She turned 180° and ducked at just the right time. The robot's buzzing laser power and lights turned on again.

Arjun turned less quickly and The Secular Gang ahead of him was a further second slower. There was an electric buzz. And in the light of the robot, Arjun saw the remaining people of The Secular Gang fall to the floor. Without their heads.

The heads of his friends hit the floor before their bodies did. Afzal, John and Darius' brain got the message last—the message that they were dead. And their lips moved in horror at their beheading.

Arjun screamed once again as the robot moved towards them, almost languidly, as if it had all the time in the world and nothing to fear. A hapless Arjun charged at it, attempting to fly again, but it swooped towards him at a much higher pace.

Before he knew what was happening, the robot had plucked him off the ground. Kelly took position near Lepcha's building but her gunfire was impotent to the dragon's engineering. Arjun was picked up in the air, and swung round and round, like a child in a merry-go-round. The robot whirred in the air with great strength and high velocity. Giddy and tired, Arjun was flung and crashed into Lepcha's house.

It could not have chosen a better canon to fling at a building than a large, invincible man with a hard exoskeleton. Arjun crashed on the mid-floor beam and it collapsed with his weight—the whole building fell, floor upon floor of cheap cement and brick collapsing in a grumble of destruction.

Arjun heard screams but he was too out of it to do anything about it. He lay on the ground and he could hear men and women screaming around him, but the clearest screams were Kelly's.

Her scream woke him up and he saw things clearly—the robot's chassis with scratches from the bullet marks, looking over Kelly lying with her eyes closed under the rubble. He saw the bodies of the dead near him and finally, the rage boiled over. These were braver than a man who flew about in a flying robot.

With a burst of air, Arjun soared and launched himself towards the robot. But as soon as he did that, he was once again stopped mid-air. He found himself trapped inside a net. He roared but the net was too strong. Or, he was too weak. The net reeled him in towards the robot, like he was not a giant fighter but a rather large catfish.

In a few moments, Dr Ling had killed everyone Arjun liked. He flailed, he squirmed, he punched and he roared in anguish. Though the net that held him gave way, he could not set himself free. The robot flew in the air, away from the wreckage of The Boses and Arjun howled in anguish again—a feral scream. A smoke was released from within and Arjun felt himself drifting to sleep. And against his wish, he slept inside the net.

In his robot, Dr Ling heard the feral scream and recognized it as something from decades ago. But he smiled with the knowledge that this time the scream meant victory.

❦

Many minutes—it may have been hours—later, a drowsy Arjun awoke. He felt the robot surge towards the ground and before he could gain any perspective, he was plunged into cold water. The Shonga-tser Lake was considered holy but in the slowly turning morning light, it was a temple of damnation. Arjun struggled beneath the water and his panic made him choke. The images of the past came rushing back and all Arjun could see was the chaos of his own limbs uselessly flapping about, against his death.

But then, he was pulled out of the water. He coughed and puked out the water from his lungs. Through his watering eyes, he could see a sliver of the sun. There was enough light for him to finally recognize the quagmire he was in.

Dr Ling's dragon held him in a net six feet from itself. The net was suspended via a long pole attached to the mouth of the dragon. Instead of a Jaguar or a Mercedes logo, he was a dangling living logo of the dragon. The net straightened itself and Arjun out, till his hands and limbs were pulled apart and he stayed pinned to the torn but still steady net like a messiah on a cross. In the cockpit, Dr Ling's unmoving face glinted in the mild sunlight.

That face now twisted into a smile and Arjun knew it

could only be bad news. He saw the laser move and point at where he was held, trapped.

'That's it,' he managed, 'that's all you got, you psychotic son of a bitch? You took my friends—but I'm not human!'

Another contraption that looked like a toilet plunger emerged from the barrel, covering the laser.

'That's it? You think I'm a broken toilet? Hah,' said Arjun, spitting out more water and struggling with the energy left in him.

While they hovered over the water, the dragon whirred with purpose, preparing itself for some colossal task. As Arjun stared into the barrel, still writhing, the suction cup sucked on Arjun's skin, sealing it inside—a vacuum. The laser singed through the airlessness and as he looked down, he felt pain on the bottom of his leg. The pointed, incisive and vacuumed burst of energy pierced through his clothes and his skin. His pants burned and he smelled his exoskeleton crumble in the face of such power.

He had never understood his own invincibility but Dr Ling obviously had. The man knew him better than he knew himself. The vacuum was helping his body erode. It felt as if someone had taken a scalpel and was dissecting his leg slowly. Arjun let out a roar of pain. It echoed through the lake and the mountains and right back at him, causing him to roar even louder. The ray cut through his skin and muscle, working its way diagonally and upward—intending to slice Arjun in half, like a butcher fillets a sheep. With a spasm, he went into shock but the pain did not lessen.

The laser had now made its way to the centre of his

navel. The front of his leg was sliced open and bleeding a river of angry vermillion into the blue lake below. Arjun tried to scream but he was spent. He had no fight left. He had bitten his tongue in the middle of his screams, and spittle and blood came out of his mouth.

The laser veered millimetres from his heart, made its way past his booming chest and stopped at his collarbone. He looked down at himself, sliced and torn and wondered what kind of monster would enjoy doing something so horrible to his enemy. The ray changed direction towards his neck and his face. Arjun groaned and prepared for his gruesome and slow death.

From the right of his vision, Arjun saw a meteor blaze through the dim orange sky and smash into the dragon in front of him. The dragon shook in protest as the meteor crushed the cockpit. The blazing ball changed direction and smashed once again into the dragon. Arjun through his sweaty dying eyes could see the dragon crunch in protest and so surprised was it by the vicious attack; it didn't have time to turn for a third blow.

This one was more furious than the last and it broke the dragon in half. Arjun, still trapped on the cross, plunged towards the water below, his net breaking clear of him. As he fell, the cockpit disengaged itself in an ejection seat. Arjun fell towards the water, his body a bloody carcass and he knew he would still die from drowning.

He splashed into the chilled water and its cold salt burned his wounds. His limbs couldn't move and he didn't even attempt to struggle. Ling's robot sank too but it didn't matter—Arjun was ready to die, death would be better than this pain. As the water filled his lungs and his eyes were about to close, a figure swam rapidly towards him. It released his arms and legs from the trap and grabbed him by his left shoulder, pulling him up.

Just like in his dream, he was dragged towards the bank. His bleeding had subsided because of the chilled water, but his lungs were still filled with water and he felt himself head towards a white light.

Air was pumped into his lungs and he sat up in protest as water and blood poured out of his mouth. Looking down at him was the same figure that had looked down at him decades ago—the face of his mother, but more matted and broken than before.

The face looked at him and let out a concerned clicking sound, just like a female monkey would when she found her new-born child in anguish. Before he knew it, his mother slung him on her back and was flying into the air with a collapsed and bleeding Arjun.

॰

After what seemed like hours or maybe even days, Arjun woke up. He was in snow, with more white snow whirling around him. His entire body was plunged in thick, white snow—only his head popped out, like a man buried by his friends in the sand. All the wounds still hurt. He groaned, wishing he was dead. In his dazed state, he saw a wad of leaves and a brown paste by his face, rolled up below a rock to hold them down. With some effort, he pulled out his right hand and pushed the leaves and paste into his mouth, greedily chewing and swallowing. They immediately brought relief to his torn body.

What didn't bring any relief was the realization that Arjun was in a grave of snow, slowly wasting away. He had been rescued and then, left alone by his mother.

To die.

The Himalayas (Location Unknown)

The following extract is an adaptation of folklore, a series of miniature paintings with words written in a lost language that passed on when humanity was young. The source is disputed but many believe it dates back to 100 BC.
Some believe it was found hidden in a jacket on the dead body of Everest climber George Mallory, but that's mere conjecture. Like Yetis, or flying humanoid creatures.

The prophet descended upon the people after a decade in wilderness. There was serenity around him as he wafted down upon his seat beneath the Banyan tree at the town centre. The clouds parted and the early morning mist cleared as he landed and even the red mud swirled in anticipation—as if the elements were making way for the messiah's entry.

Bathed in the orange tinge of the sun, he landed on the platform beneath the tree. His eyes remained closed as he settled which allowed us, the audience, to absorb his physical appearance. He looked ancient, older than the tree he sat beneath, more aged than the rock the platform was made of and maybe even older than the skies he had emerged from.

His face seemed as if it was carved in brown rock and despite his age, his arms and thighs still held sinews of muscle. His beloved gadda was tied in a cloth belt around his waist and his chest still boomed with purpose. His tail was thick and long and stood upright behind him like a flag. His hair was long and grey; he looked like a warrior and a rishi—precisely what he was.

The entire town of two hundred felt the emanation of his tranquillity and fearlessness. But the spell broke as the prophet opened his eyes. He did so slowly and took a few moments to adjust his pupils to the world outside since he had been so consumed by the world inside.

His eyes were deep and brown and as he saw the congregation around him, he smiled. It was a tired smile, a smile of someone who had pushed his mental and physical boundaries beyond reality. He cleared his throat and was offered a glass of rose water, which he gladly accepted with another wane smile.

'I am not a prophet or a messiah,' he began, 'I am just like you—a soldier and a student.'

His voice sounded like two mountains gently crushing against each other, like the voice of the Earth itself.

'You have heard stories of all I may or may not have done, but it was all mere coincidence. It could have happened to any vanara here,' and he looked at the youngest vanara right in the eye, which happened to be a baby hugging his mother's shoulder.

'It is the work of any student to pass on all we know to whoever may seek answers. So, ask away,' he said, looking at our faces. 'Ask me anything.'

Of course, nobody could. We were mesmerized. None of us could fathom this reality—we would shatter the dream if we spoke.

'I've maintained silence for fourteen years and you're the ones with no words,' he said and smiled. A few people laughed and it somewhat broke the tension. So, he went on,

'Let me ask you a question then? Who are we?'

He looked around for an answer and then at the eager face of Aryabhatta, a boy who knew all the answers and was regarded a prodigy—he was *so* annoying.

'You, Son?' he asked.

'Guruji, we are vanaras—a humanoid species numbering a couple of hundred that remain largely hidden from the world for the safety of all. Some of us can change shape, disguise ourselves, survive in most environments and the very lucky few of us can also…fly,' said Aryabhatta nervously.

'Good,' said the man, 'good. It is what we are. But who we are is slightly different. We are souls. It just so happens that the vessel we command is stronger than the vessel most command. Humans have the same souls as us and in different circumstances, we could have easily been one of them—which wouldn't have been all bad. Now…' he said, and took another sip of the rose water.

'…I have meditated for fourteen long years and it is to answer one simple question: what is our purpose? Does anyone know?'

Aryabhatta's hand went up. It was strange—a group of learned elders were silent while a young boy with nothing to prove took the lead.

'To be the best we can be. To train, to soldier, to learn every martial arts and read every book the land can provide. We are soldiers and scholars and we aim to achieve both physical excellence and mental utopia,' he said, reading out the manifesto of our school.

The man smiled at him, 'You seem like a scholar, that

means you could grow up to be a genius or a coward,' he said, and everyone laughed. He continued, 'But in your case, I would ascertain genius.'

Aryabhatta blushed with bliss at the elders who smiled graciously. Older people loved him, he really was aggravating.

'But our real purpose is the service of the human race, especially, the race of this land. Some of you will wonder why? And to answer that, I ask you one simple question: who needs you?'

He let the question linger. It seemed to make sense; it seemed logical, too logical. I couldn't hold it in any longer—my hand raised itself despite my own reservations.

He looked at me and so did the rest of the crowd. I never sought attention, attention always made me ridiculously nervous. My palms were sweating and my heart was blasting with blood, I really wished I hadn't raised my hand.

'Yes,' said the man, 'young man?'

'Sir...Guruji...Sir,' I began, 'why didn't you kill the ten-headed king when you had the chance? You flew all the way there and you could have killed him.'

Everyone gasped. I could sense my father's eyes burn holes into my forehead. Even my mother shook her head in disbelief at her beloved son's naiveté. But all their tension disappeared when they heard a loud laughter—the echoing, booming, uninhibited laughter of the man on the platform. He rocked back and forth. Tears trickled down his face. Everyone joined in, though no one knew what was so funny. I blushed and wondered what I had done and how I would ever live it down.

He said, 'You look at this boy like he's stolen your goats or set your thatched roof on fire. He's merely asked a question. It is no crime.'

It was now everyone's turn to blush. I smiled uncertainly, relieved that the joke was not on me.

'Questions are good,' said the man, 'they lead to answers. And answers lead to solutions. You've read why I didn't kill him?'

Aryabhatta's hand went up but he was ignored. I nodded my head furiously.

'And?' he asked.

'I don't believe everything I read,' I replied.

More gasps were heard, but some of those were mixed with laughter. This time, he almost choked on his rose water as he roared with laughter, once again.

'Fair enough. There is no better book than life itself.

But this time the books are right. The thing that is most essential about a vanara is faithfulness. And my faith was with my king. It was him who had to conquer. His victory meant more to the future of the kingdom than mine. His victory meant prosperity and that meant peace. My victory would never have guaranteed that. I was a mere soldier. And a soldier ensures victory for his leader—not himself. Plus, I was there as an envoy. Yes, they attacked me but me attacking them back would have been a sign of my weakness, not strength. It would have led to turmoil in both kingdoms. There was of course one other reason,' he said and contemplated for a second, 'their king did not deserve death at my hand.'

The entire crowd went silent.

'We admired him. He was a scholar and a good king, except his dalliance with demons. You can't falsely paint your enemy as a villain when he may be just like you but with different motivations. Any other questions?'

My hand shot up again, 'Guruji, we live longer, are harder to kill, stronger than the humans—why can't we just conquer the world?'

The man smiled again. He was amused by the same questions that had annoyed my teachers.

'Why would you want to conquer the world?' he asked.

'Because, we can,' I replied.

'I can also fly, does that mean I should build a nest?' he said. A few people laughed at this. 'I asked myself this when I was young, all those centuries back. Conquering the world would not benefit anyone, not even us. We are a handful, there are millions of humans. We would need work done, what would we do then?'

'Make the humans work for us.'

'Slaves. Eventually, they'd rebel and figure out a way to kill us. It would just make the humans and us miserable for a couple of centuries.'

'I've seen some humans ride around in grand chariots and live in opulent palaces...' I said.

'Why would you need a chariot when you can fly? Who needs a palace when you have a palace of skies? Superficial joys are only for the stupid.'

'But, Guruji, we could be the most powerful race in history.'

'Ah, power,' said the man and he smiled again, 'the aim of the unenlightened, the fabrication of a soul that equates happiness with greed.'

'I thought…' I replied, '…that it could be something. It could be a way to replace the corruption of humanity with a higher and more idealistic motif.'

The man bore his eyes into mine, glimpsing into my soul to see if there was something faulty there, 'You sound like every mad ruler. Everyone believes their ideals are better than the others. But it is a fool who believes that someone of another faith or moral standing is inferior. Everyone is different and that is good. Are you an idealist?'

I didn't know when a sermon to a group turned into a private conversation with my hero. I just knew he was the only one who could answer the puzzles that had kept me up at nights.

'Yes, you could say that. I don't like wrong things happening to people,' I replied.

'Then listen clearly to what I have to say,' and he raised his voice. 'This is why I have contemplated deeply—to find our true purpose—and this is what I propose. We are blessed. For some reason, the higher beings gave us the ability to not only be incredible fighters, but to also tell wrong from right.

'Not all humans have been blessed with this gift. And because of them, the rest suffer. It is not only our duty but also our purpose to be the guiding force that holds together the entire species and the fate of Earth—to guide them when ego misguides some of them.'

'We are a population of one hundred and eighty seven. Because of our gestation period, our population grows ever so slowly. It is futile for us to dominate this planet but we can ensure that it takes the right path. I propose that every generation of humans shall have one of our best to guide them and since we are of this land, let us guide the land of the Indus, Banares and Kailasha.'

The crowd shuffled uneasily. They were not sure what to make of this pronouncement.

'We will align that vanara to the leader of this land. Let me reiterate, it does not have to be the king or when kings do not rule, the leader of the land. It is merely he or she who is the spiritual compass. We align ourselves on the side of good, the silent messiahs who protect the truly wilful.

'Do we not want to use our blessings to further the cause of righteousness? To protect the land that we belong to? To use our superiority for the benefit of a larger cause?'

His passion was transferred to us and our hesitation was replaced by applause. A few did not partake but I immediately recognized them as the most cowardly in our little town.

'I leave the rules and norms for the same to you, but in times of doubt, ask yourself simply: who needs you?' he said. His eyes were weary with the effort of talking so much.

'And, if that is unclear, know one thing. I need this from you. Will you rise with me for the protection of our land?'

This time, our acquiescence was unanimous. I was delighted—our species had a meaning and we were all jolted with explosions of excitement. Our existential conundrum had gotten a glorious solution. Then, he raised a tired hand at us and for the first time, his age showed on his face.

'Discuss this and arrive at a democratic decision. I'm afraid I...' and he hesitated for a moment, '...my soul has other places to be.'

Hushed silence greeted this proclamation. It was written in our teachings that what he said was impossible—his end could never be.

'Guruji, how is this possible?' said one of the teachers, 'We cannot exist without your blessings! You are immortal,'

He smiled for the last time, 'Ah, I am. My memory, my soul and my very being are immortal if you follow my steps and live the way I lived. You all will be bearers of my immortality.'

'But Guruji, it is said that there is no way for you to be taken from this living world. It is biologically impossible, unless...unless...' said a teacher, with tears streaming down her eyes.

'It is impossible unless I want to. This is my mahasamadhi—my chosen exit from this mortal coil. Do not worry,' he said.

'I volunteer!' I screamed from the back, 'Guruji, I volunteer my life to the quest of being the first one. I will do whatever it takes.'

He looked at me as I bent down my knees. The crowd parted to let him see me. My eyes were red with tears but I'd never felt so sure of anything in my life.

He looked at me and sensed my determination and will, 'What is your name?'

I told him what they called me.

'Ah,' he said, 'much like me. The Son of the Wind, the offspring of atmosphere, the kin of the air. So it shall be.'

Then, he closed his eyes and concentrated deeply. His body rose as he took his last flight and soared towards the clouds and we could sense him feel every pore of his being. He rose hundreds of feet above, just a man with a long tail wafting in the orange clouds.

We all stared up and then, there was a loud explosion, as if a thunderbolt had crashed into a tall mountain and decimated it under its power.

Glittering atoms of his mortal coil descended on us—glowing embers of light. And I wished I was made of the atoms that had created him. And sometimes when one wishes for something hard enough, it becomes reality.

My mother gave me a bittersweet smile and asked in a tearful whisper, 'Who needs you, Pawan?'

Chapter Eleven

Legend #20

The worship of Kali has always been associated with macabre. Thuggee or thugs—the infamous organization of criminals from the 1400s— worshipped the Goddess and even believed that they were made out of her sweat which meant their mortal enemy was deodorant.
Tantric temples are also her domain—some for true worshippers, others for goat sacrifices and some rumoured to house the possessed, the mad and sepulchral creatures from beyond this dimension.
Voluntary and gruesome involuntary human sacrifices have also been closely associated with the Divine Mother.
Her terrifying designation as CEO of The Devourer of Time can make the world stand still. But maybe when you get too close to her, you do so at your own risk.

Birds circled above the spot of the crash. They had been scared by the violence and not even the bravest rook bore the courage to descend to the spot by the forest. They waited to feast on the cocktail of brick and human remains.

One rook bravely descended to the area that normally would have been teeming with curious humans. But over the last few months, the fear in the town led to no one venturing out until well after the robot had left.

The rook looked around at the heads, the torn arms and the buffet of plasma that lay splayed on the ground. To a human, the feast would seem barbaric but a rook can't tell apart barbarism from lunch. And if humans did not think anything of consuming his fellow birds without any guilt, why would he feel remorse when returning the favour? Of course, the rook did not think any of this for he was programmed for one thing—to feed.

He was pecking away when he was suddenly jolted by one of the bricks thrust aside by a tired hand. A figure emerged slowly from the wreckage and while rooks do not have names, humans do, and this one was called Kelly. The rook took to flight with his colleagues; they'd have to return later for their protein.

Kelly's ears rung, not with the building collapse but with what she had witnessed. She kneeled over and as her vision cleared, she saw the carnage that greeted her survival. The world was tattered. Building parts lay collapsed and the stench of the incineration of her former colleagues could not be eluded.

It was the worst possible scenario—dead civilians; the first non-soldier casualty of the battle. From a distance, she saw the bone of an arm stick out from under the collapsed building and she knew they had no chance.

She cursed herself. They should have kept Arjun closer. He was their plan and they had left him alone. Everything in the last month had gone on so well. With Arjun by their side, there had been a feeling of invincibility around The Boses and now the entire team was wiped out. It was all because of *her*.

Kelly's twin wept for the death of the bravest men she had ever met. She wept because they had believed in her. Between her tears, she felt a metal shard poking from her shoulder. She plucked it out and blood gushed out. She quickly wrapped the injury with a torn piece of her inner shirt, and grabbed all the guns near her. She looked up at the sky and tried to remember which direction the dragon had flown in.

Under the slowly rising sun, she plunged into the forest to chase after a dragon she knew she could not defeat; who had captured a man she did not know could be defeated. It was a doomed exercise but she had to explore her limited options. She stumbled through the forest as Darius' face separating from his body haunted her every step. She would die in pursuit of Ling but she could not have one more death on her hands.

Lepcha saw her leave but stayed quiet. He was an old man. He was bruised by the fall but he was too busy rummaging desperately through the rubble—trying to find his heart. He would try finding his daughter all morning and when he finally would, his world would collapse.

Life was leaving him slowly, his organs were freezing and his breath was slackening at the pace of a glacier melting. Arjun lay in his white grave, burning to death in the freezing temperature. He could feel his knee bone scraping against the snow, with no skin to protect it. His chest, hip, thigh, stomach and every sliced part of his body burned despite the numbness.

He felt no anger towards Dr Ling. He barely thought about him. The man's entire life's work lay in the bottom of a lake as did the lives of Arjun's best friends. Everything was over. He chewed the abundant leaves and paste and it helped calm his pain and also induced delirium. He knew what it was—the paste was opium latex and the leaves were Khat. One, a source of natural morphine and the other, a Yemeni source of energy. He didn't know how he had either in the midst of snow-capped mountains, but he chewed away, even though the deliriums were vivid and obscene.

He had seen the sun rise and set from his half-closed eyes at least a dozen times, so that meant, he had been lying there for a fortnight. In his visions, he saw Kelly drown, Manoj running around laughing without any limbs, Dr Ling dicing him into little test tubes and morphing into Bakshi, Major Taunque commanding an army of ghosts and his father killing his own son.

This morning, he felt the sun vividly rise from the mountains, brighter than before. The snowfall receded into a trickle and as the bright sun burned his face, he had his most lucid vision yet—a purple langur crouched by his head.

He opened his eyes wide and wondered if it was an opiate fallacy or his first visit to reality in a while.

The white face of the langur looked down at him. 'You've been busy,' she said.

His heart felt lighter. 'Yeah, I'm broken. I'm so broken,' he said. He felt so tired he wanted to weep.

'I finally figured it out,' she said.

'What?'

'How you can heal so quickly. You thought it was because of your exoskeleton and your thick skin. But it's not that.'

'It doesn't matter now.'

'There's a theory that every atom that has ever existed on Earth exists now in some form. Every atom. So, you could have the atom of Julius Caesar or Genghis Khan or even R.D. Burman inside you. After all, we're all atoms.'

'I don't understand. I'm tired and I want…'

'If we're all atoms,' continued the langur gently, 'theoretically, any atom can repair us. Atoms to atoms, dust to dust. It sounds impossible that a dust atom could repair skin or blood. But what if through some miraculous stroke of evolution, a living being managed to defy everything we knew about biology and science?'

'Science can't defeat human cruelty,' said Arjun.

'You are that miracle. We are that miracle. Your body heals with the air. That's why the vacuum hurt you. You are not impenetrable. Your regeneration is so swift that nanoseconds after any injury, the atmosphere's atoms become yours. You are made of the wind and the air. You can't be destroyed in this atmosphere because you are this atmosphere!'

'All the atmospheres on Earth couldn't repair me now.'

The little langur hugged his head, and Arjun cried. He was a grown man but this little langur knew that deep down, he was just a child who had been left in the wild.

'You'll be whole again. The potion ruined you. But your history is inside you. Movement is our healing,' she said, stroking his unkempt hair, and then she got up and scampered off.

Through his blurry vision, he saw the monkey run into the snow and as she did, her body morphed into the body of his mother and disappeared into the whiteness beyond. *His* mother. She had risen from the recesses of forgotten memory to rescue him from death and had single-handedly destroyed Ling's ode to destruction. But then, why had she left him to rot in this cold, cold grave?

Movement. He understood the truth—she hadn't left him to die; she had left him to find a way to live. She left the leaves and buried him in the snow to allow him to live, but the next step depended on Arjun. His right hand lunged through the snow to his breast pocket and parts that had lain asleep awoke with thunderous pain. But he didn't care. He plucked out the jigsaw piece from his pocket.

A trident shaped rock in front of tall mountains. He saw the tall mountains beyond. With an effort, the broken carcass of Arjun Singh struggled out of his former grave. He tried to stand but his body was frozen. So, he crawled, like a baby learning how to move. *Move!*

He would return from death. The snow he had emerged from was caked with brown congealed blood. He shoved the remaining leaves into his soaked pockets and with another groan of anguish, he crawled away from his death.

The path he had chosen was hopeless but some hope lay beyond the trident rock.

∞

Kelly's efforts to trace Arjun or the dragon had been futile. Her hours of recce had just shown her a chunk of red metal by the lake and blood at the bank, which could only mean that a bloodied Arjun had taken flight. It was pointless. A person could not outrun the flight of a Boeing 747. All she had found was a piece of the wooden jigsaw puzzle. But it was all she needed. So, she trudged back to the town.

The residents were now awake and rescue work was under way in the collapsed building, but the bodies of The Secular Gang were nowhere to be found—she didn't question it because she did not care anymore.

Taking a back route to avoid the crowd, she reached the guest house and snuck into her room, undetected. Beyond the door, the baldpate of Bakshi was sitting on her bed. For once, he was not smiling. Kelly did the logical thing—she put a silencer on her personal weapon and shot Bakshi on his thigh. A flesh wound aimed to stun and lead to bleeding.

Bakshi gasped in pain, 'Ow! Ow! What the fuck, Kelly… what the fuck? I'm the one who shoots.'

She held him up by the collar, the gun still in her hand, 'What the hell did you do, Bakshi? What did you do?'

Bakshi looked at the blood leaking from his thigh. 'This is the worst breakup ever,' he said.

Kelly pointed the gun at his head. This was it. This man had caused all of this, he was the eye of the storm, the epicentre of an earthquake of deception and she would end it now.

She put her finger on the trigger and spoke calmly, 'Bakshi, I'm going to shoot you now. I should have done it days ago. Whatever bullshit you've been up to ends now.'

Her new ex-boyfriend looked up at her with confusion and pain, staring first at her bleeding thigh and then at her face, 'I...I...' he muttered.

Kelly felt the barrel of a gun poke into the back of her head and heard the authoritative voice of General Taunque, 'Put the gun down, Kelly.'

'Thanks, Taunque, you good old fart,' said Bakshi and promptly fainted on the bed.

※

It may have been hours or days or lifetimes, Arjun did not know. Time had become an endless expanse of snow, and he trudged through it with the speed of an old clock. His body was disconnected and he had become pure instinct, a primal impulse that carried him towards the trident rock.

The leaves had kept him going and he could not stop. His body was freezing fire and he knew that if he stopped, he would be frozen in time forever. So, through every painful step, he limped towards the direction his subconscious mind had charted for him. His brain was his GPS and he was hoping it wasn't as muddled as the rest of him.

After an indefinable length of time, he finally stopped. His body broken in half, his mind shattered to little grains of sand. He stopped. Something told him to. Through the mist of cold snow in the distance ahead, he saw the outline of a rock. With laboured breaths, he moved to the rock, every moment agonizing, and every step as heavy as a tectonic plate.

At last, he was in front of the trident rock—there was no mistaking it, even in the snowstorm. It was as tall as a small monument but he wasn't here to appreciate its beauty. He didn't know why he was here. He touched its base and as he did, he collapsed in a heap under it. He was done.

He was at the end of time. His clock could run no more and he lay, his neck leaning on the rock. And then, he howled—a final howl to his Maker, to the guardian at the doors of death—to cease his living. It was his last howl.

∞

'Drop the gun, Kelly,' repeated Taunque, 'think logically.'

Kelly did some mental mathematics. She explored the option of unleashing her extra hands, but the more experienced man would expect it. Then, she relaxed and dropped the gun.

It was the "think logically" part that had got to her and she smiled despite herself, 'Too much of a clean-up job to do it in here?' she asked Taunque.

The older man put the safety catch and placed his gun back in the holster. He then nodded, 'Far easier ways with far less chance of incriminating evidence,' he said.

She sat down on the bed next to Bakshi. And then, she immediately got off it—she'd slept in a bed with him far too often.

'But we are going to kill him?' she asked.

'That depends,' said Taunque and pulled off his shoe and shoved it under Bakshi's nose. When that smell didn't wake him, he smacked the man across his face with the shoe. Bakshi woke up, looked at Taunque and squealed.

'His death depends on his use for us,' said Taunque and smacked Bakshi in the face again.

'One second,' said Bakshi, his voice filled with pain, 'you're going to kill me?'

Taunque hit him hard on his head this time, 'I want you to talk. You will talk now. You will tell us what *actually* happened.'

Bakshi wailed but Taunque cut him short by shoving his sock into the man's mouth, 'Stop behaving like a wussy, you excrement from the anus of Bilbo Baggins,' said the General, 'for once, man up and speak.'

'I…dunn…annfing,' bumbled Bakshi as Taunque pulled the sock out of his mouth.

'Yes, yes. You're in pain,' said Taunque and pulled out an injection from a bag nearby and stabbed Bakshi's thigh with it, 'local anaesthesia. Now talk.'

Bakshi howled but the drug helped soothe his shot leg.

'You've been talking to the Chinese from day one. You sabotaged us. However, they gave you false reassurances that there won't be any casualties. In exchange, they gave you what? Not money. What? It's not brain surgery, you goddamn erectile dysfunction,' said Taunque through gritted teeth.

Bakshi looked at his bleeding thigh and wept. After a few moments of sobbing, he looked up, 'Why do Indians pretend to hate booze so much?'

Kelly looked at Taunque and then back at Bakshi, 'What are you dithering on about, you flaccid condom burst demon baby?'

But Bakshi was no longer listening. His blood loss had made him light-headed, 'It's a scam. We do moral posturing over booze, so we can tax it more. It's a global thing. I get it. But only in India do we find not only a tax on morals but also a judgment. Oh, you drink, well, we're going to charge you more money because basically alcoholism is murder of morals.'

Taunque sat on a chair, Kelly remained standing. This monologue from Bakshi would obviously take its own path. Different people had different ways of confessing. Bakshi's method was to sudden eloquence.

'My father suffered because of it. No matter how much he did for the country, it was never enough—because he sold booze. What an asshole. He built hospitals, schools, donated to charity and probably nobody knows this. But do you remember telling me one of the big reasons India got our asses kicked in 1963?'

'Sweaters,' said Taunque, 'but, I was just making a point. We were outnumbered, outmanoeuvred and out of depth.'

'Sweaters,' said Bakshi, 'in sub-zero terrain, our soldiers didn't have sweaters. Imagine the arrogance of some leaders sitting in Delhi who did not have the basic humanity to assume that a man could freeze to death? It pissed off my dad. After the war, he spent lakhs every year sending thermal wear for our soldiers. You know what someone in the government did? They sold the sweaters for profit, illegally. Then, they dragged my father into a scam. He said he created the sweater scam for black money. It never went public because my dad had to bribe people when he tried to help our country. One neta told him, "Your reputation is anyway kharab, tum daaru bechte ho." You're an alcohol merchant, you have no reputation.'

'So, what?' said Kelly, 'You were sad about dad, so you decided to betray our country?'

'General,' said Bakshi, 'do you remember when we met the PMs? Do you remember how humiliating that meeting was?'

General Taunque was jolted. *How could he forget? In the many decades of his service to the nation, he had never felt more impotent—and more frustrated.*

'What meeting? What happened?' Kelly asked.

'We offered our services to protect the borders to our five PMs, at a cost, of course. First, staple insults about me selling booze. Taunque backed us and had support from top military minds. So, the PMs asked how much we'd give them for offering our services for free. Then, they kicked us out because they decided it was better for our defence to build a statue at the border instead. Apparently, it would scare the enemy away to see their faces,' said Bakshi, 'and they almost got Taunque arrested.'

'They should have. They deserved all my threats for the way they behaved, those regurgitated ass peanuts,' said the General.

'That is messed up,' said Kelly.

'I like my country,' said Bakshi, 'but I will not be fucked over like my dad. I want us to have the best defence mechanism possible, with privatization. Eliminate the babus. A private fighting force that actually helped the Indian army would be the best publicity. I didn't think the Chinese would attack us. I also didn't think they'd have better equipment than a demigod! He turned out to be a disappointment.'

'He tried as best as he could,' said Kelly.

'Please. He's a shadow of what we expected, that monkey man,' said Bakshi.

'He's more of a man than you. At least, he didn't betray us.'

'Oh, you'd take up for him. You have a soft corner…'

Taunque slapped Bakshi in the wounded thigh. The man growled in pain.

'So, let me get this straight, you sold our plans and put us in peril,' said the General, 'so you could defeat the Chinese and then use it as publicity to help get official sanctions for The Boses? That is the most juvenile plan I've ever heard. You caused the deaths of so many, you walking talking abortion!'

'How was I to know that they could defeat a demigod? I thought once we found him, victory was inevitable. I thought I could be George Bush Jr.'

Kelly could not help but smile. Only Bakshi could think

that aspiring to be America's most mocked President was a good thing.

'Don't look so shocked,' said Bakshi, 'GWB had the lowest ratings and then, 9/11 happened. He rose and responded to the tragedy with aplomb. Suddenly, everyone loved him. It was like watching a dog learn how to fly a plane. Though, a plane is a bad example here. I thought I could do that. We're at the worst point of leadership. We need a leader who serves the country. We need me. Worse people could be in charge. I'd make bad decisions but at least, they would be for the benefit of my people. As an Indian's future PM, I'd put...'

Just then, the door smacked open. A man stood at the door and before Taunque and Kelly could react, Indian PM's head exploded.

'You killed my daughter, Mr Prime Minister,' said Lepcha. He threw a metal insignia with the figure of a proud goat towards Bakshi, lowered his desi katta gun and then, he walked off.

Chapter Twelve

Legend #6

Hanuman was a chiranjivi i.e. an immortal, not the South Indian actor, who by some, is also deemed eternal. However, according to Hindu scriptures, immortality doesn't mean a transcendence of physical infinity, since all physical bodies are foretold to end.

It is an allegory, like so much of mythology. Though, some take it as literally as a stick to your head, which is a metaphor for misguided anger.

Believers still say Hanuman lives in Gandhamardhan Hills, the same hills he lifted to get herbs to Lakshman when he lay dying. It would be ironic for the God to continue living in a mountain that he once lifted; surely Atlas would be very jealous.

His dreams were hallucinations and his hallucinations were nightmares. His spirit screeched in anguish inside his head, as his body was dragged through vivid red snow—a photograph of Nehru beamed down at him, a typewriter typed his death letter, water coloured black poured down his face and all along, there was that thought that he was a vampire, drinking blood. He could smell and taste blood; its iron tinge caked him, some his own, but some from another source.

In the midst of all this was her face. It looked at him with worry, anger and care. Those eyes would carry him to the depths of the sun. Time drifted and melted like an Edvard Munch painting. It oozed into his reality. The only change he could sense was in his own physicality. His body was self-immolating, as if he had jumped into the pit of a volcano and he felt the lava in his body gurgle in anger as it moulded into an image of him in blood. He knew the volcano would explode and if it did, the destruction would be his own. He lay there with his dreams, hallucinations and nightmares—waiting for the subsidence of his own ticking time bomb.

※

It was a rare moment of weakness for Dr Ling to ask Sun for help. This time, he was embarrassed and injured. Sun had zeroed in on his distress signal and picked him up from near Tawang Town. She was surprised it was still part of India because it meant that Dr Ling had failed, again. It was a lesson that lightning could strike the same place twice, especially if that lightning was a feral demigod. And if Dr Ling couldn't conquer him—no one could.

She carefully landed the two-seater helicopter; it was an

aircraft of Ling's design—fast, silent and undetectable. She landed it precisely where Ling's GPS chip had told her to and saw her boss lying on a grass knoll beside a riverbank. He had been lying there for almost seventeen hours but had given her specific instructions to come only at night.

For once, she realized his age. His thinning hair clumped to one side, the other side caked with dried blood. His eyes were red and his face bruised, like he was on his deathbed. Sun felt sympathy. She would help but not before taking a selfie—#LingVase, #DyingFather, #FatherDaughterLove. Even though her contract barred her from posting anything in public, it would be irrelevant if he died. She patted her hair into place, wore a big smile and as the flash went off, her boss woke up.

She leaned forward to stroke his hair in a rare moment of affection, when he said in autocratic voice, 'Nutrients, please. Nutrients.'

'Most people call it food,' she said but held the packet to her boss. He took it and sucked the glop inside with palpable relief. It was his own concoction—a paste of tuna, broccoli and ginseng, a precise dietary requirement for a healthy male. Dr Ling did not need more than the packet's 200 grams four times a day. As he told her repeatedly, 'Taste is a human weakness and leads to desire and gluttony.'

'She almost found me,' said Ling, 'almost. They have another freak, a four-handed freak.'

Sun ignored his abstruse statement and looked at what he was holding.

'What have you got there?' she asked, pointing to a

case that Dr Ling was hugging with his left hand. It was the size of a large suitcase though its metal/plastic sheeting ensured that it was internally cooled. This meant it was something biological.

'The future,' said Dr Ling, and got up from his place on the ground.

'Where will we carry it? The copter is a two-seater,' said Sun.

Dr Ling carefully placed the container on the passenger seat and strapped it in. Without a glance at Sun, he clambered on to the pilot's seat.

'What the hell am I supposed to do here?' she asked.

'Take some more of your beloved selfies. It's a beautiful area. I'll arrange your pick up in twenty-four hours,' and with that, he started the engine and was off.

Sun watched him fly off into the wind, and looked down at her phone—11 per cent battery left.

'I had told you to put a charging socket in the goddamn copter, you old ass,' she said to herself. What was she supposed to do for a day without her phone? Food and water never even struck her. She had an App for that.

⁂

He awoke suddenly. His senses had no time to acclimatize to his surroundings. He was hurtled into existence, reborn in the midst of a hurricane and felt himself falling. As his eyes opened against the gust of wind, he realized it was no figment of imagination. He was plummeting at a meteoric speed towards the ground far below.

His vocal capacities rose to the fore and he screamed against the wind, but the words were lost in the velocity. The ground zoomed in on him and just as he was about to crash land to his probable death, something kicked in and he felt rusty old wind rise up from beneath him. It came with hesitation, like a junked car that hadn't been started for long. But it came!

Just as he was about to be turned into a giant pancake on the white valley below, he arose, naturally, without aid. He was the wind, he was the atmosphere, he was the air and he was the Earth. He flew upwards in his ecstasy and immediately wished that he hadn't because his just awoken body protested and he rose ten feet before crashing on the hard ground below, missing the soft landing of the snow.

He lay groaning on his stomach and wondered what the hell had happened. He had been asleep for weeks. And then, he was awoken to flailing down a mountain.

To the left, a happy cackling greeted him. His mother was dancing, swinging her limbs and tail, pointing at him and laughing her head off. It was uninhibited, as if she had held her pleasure inside her for decades. This creature that was his creator—who had rescued him from his death, nurtured him, cured him and healed him, only to fling him off the top of a mountain—was his only hope in the world. This insane broken being was his mother.

He smiled at her and got up from his place on the ground.

He immediately collapsed right back because his limbs were still not used to maintaining his weight. He felt his healing wounds open up again. Once again, his mother howled in glee at his misery. This time, he didn't smile.

∽

Mr Jin—China's Minister of Defence and Land Acquisition—was buoyant, exuberant, ecstatic, delighted and two hundred other synonyms of "happy". As the Defence Minister, his job entailed defending the border—but it also involved claiming lands that other countries did not yet know belonged to China. Disputes were on for land with India, Japan, Bhutan, Indonesia, Taiwan, Vietnam, Philippines and other parts of the People's Republic of the World. No country (barring the U.S. for now) even attempted to seriously question China's border or its land claims since all of them were overawed by PRC's military might.

As Mr Jin said, 'The phallus of our forces is adequate protection. Even looking at its size would impregnate them with destruction.' It had been a bold line to use in a meeting with the PM but his audacity had worked. The PM had laughed which basically meant that Mr Jin might as well be handed the job of PM once this one was done. And by God, he deserved it.

The meeting was held in the PM's conference room in Beijing with dragons in every nook. The wooden table was embossed with a water dragon, the coffee mugs had wind dragons, the red carpet had yellow dragons, and even the view of Beijing outside had two fire-breathing dragons watching for threats.

Mr Jin loved it; he felt he was breathing fire himself. He peacocked around the meeting with the PM's closest allies on the unofficially known matter the policymakers called, "Dragon Fire: The Expansion of the People's Republic."

All the top Chinese officials sat in the meeting and Mr Jin was the star.

'Mr Chang, your efforts at claiming Hong Kong have been embarrassing. Again, there was a protest. Control your people, Chang,' he said, pointing at the External Affairs Minister whose efforts at seamlessly bringing Hong Kong's people into China's fold, much like Hong Kong itself, had been fraught with minor mortifications for years.

'We used to claim lands using swords and guns and now we are quelled by rich idiots in suits demanding packaged bottle water. Maybe you, Sir, should use Evian to defeat them!'

The room snickered in laughter despite themselves. It was not the norm to be so disrespectful and driven by machismo. But, Jin was far from finished.

'We've claimed parts of the seas for oil all across Vietnam and Japan and no one could stop us. How would they? It's like that old saying by Hsing Tao, "Defeating China with their weapons would be like a grasshopper trying to satisfy a blue whale". However, we have to be aware of perception. Inside China, we are deservedly the champions of the people. But public perception on a global scale is the way of the future. We don't want to be another...' and he paused for effect, '...U.S.S.R.'

All the twelve men and the one lady in the room gasped at the mention of that name, as if it was the worst fate any nation could face.

'A vast kingdom on the precipice of conquering every land and becoming the most powerful nation on Earth stumbled over its own ambition and overconfidence. The Russians are our kindred brothers…'

'…with larger livers,' interjected the PM, 'you know—vodka!'

Everyone roared with laughter at this display of joie de vivre from the leader of China. Each laugh was an effort to please their temporary monarch. *Does he really have to spell out a joke like that*, thought Jin.

'America's biggest export is culture. And they used it against USSR through films, news propaganda and manipulation of the truth. Now, social media is culture. We cannot fall into the same trap. We need someone to voluntarily declare the superiority of the Chinese way. No guns, no war—a democratic conquering. Is such a thing possible, you ask? Yes it is,' said Mr Jin, 'and that's where I bring you Tawang…'

'Sounds like Taiwan,' said the PM, 'because, this too is ours?'

More laughter. When Jin became PM, he didn't want to be *that* guy. He wanted to earn the laughter, for real witticisms. It was the Chinese way: your hard work, not your reputation earned rewards.

'Yes, Sir,' he said, shortly, 'we can do this. With little help from anyone…okay, maybe some help from the Indians. But can ineptitude really be a source of our victory?'

A few laughs. It disappointed Jin. His joke was wittier than the PM's ridiculous Taiwan joke, but he motored on,

'I've managed to help Tawang reach a point where our citizens there are on the verge of accepting PRC as their own. Soldiers from the People's Army are already stationed there, helping Tawang rebuild itself after a sabotage attack by the Indian forces. Those people have been ill-treated by that shadow government for too long. This year, we will bring them back home. The land they come with shall just be a happy bonus. It shall mark a precedent for other "disputed lands" and a landmark step in modern warfare, where you win the people before you win the land. Surely, when people of a land want to be with us, the government that claims to own them stakes claim only by force. And as we know, the Chinese government never uses force—just intelligence. The transition to China will happen on 28 June.'

The rest in the room looked at each other with scepticism—the sheer accuracy of that date was preposterous.

The PM spoke, 'Even women cannot predict the date of their cycle with such precision, Mr Jin.'

Again, guffaws. Mr Jin clicked his tongue. *Using a woman's period as a punch line? Really, Mr PM?* But he thought better of it and instead said, 'Yes, Sir. I'm precise. Much like my country. Those people need us, they just don't know it yet. And we will help them find out—on 28 June. As Hi Huan said before committing suicide, "That's it from me."'

He sat down. Everyone on the table looked impressed by his confidence. The PM, however, was bemused, or dubious.

It was the first time Mr Jin began to doubt the success of his plan. But he was sure another meeting with Dr Ling would inspire confidence.

∽

It is tough to argue with an insane person, impossible to argue with an insane person who doesn't speak your language and downright inconceivable if the person is also your mother. Arjun had not won a single argument with his mother. She responded to any protest by slapping him and screaming louder than him. The angry untamed creature used the same strategy as panellists on news debates.

His mother had grown up in icy mountains and had found shelter in a cave, since apartment buildings were hard to come by in this snowy void. She had survived in the cave for decades which had led her to regress to being a primate. And vocal communication was off the table.

His unspoken schedule in the day was to meditate for hours, be repeatedly flung off a mountain to help him fly, then be shoved into a vat of ice-cold water and then rest his broken body. Any inclination to gripe against his mother was quickly removed when he saw the cuts on her body.

'You cut yourself,' he asked her, 'why would you cut yourself? And how?'

She clicked her tongue and dismissed him like he was a fly. As to the "how" part, he could only ascertain that she had conquered her body to an extent where she could control her invincibility. Or, she was old.

It wasn't hard to figure out—she had healed him by using her own blood, an ancient blood transfusion. There was an old steel bucket full of the stuff. He could not bear to look at it but his mother induced fresh cuts on her arms and thighs to heal him. His remonstrations were met with more swatting of his face and ancient primate curses.

Seeing his old mother weaken as he grew stronger broke Arjun's heart but there is only so much you can do when someone who created you insists on giving you their love, even if it gives them pain.

So, he didn't protest. He listened to her and held back his tears as she insisted on applying the tincture of her life force and turmeric all over his wounded body. He still limped because the cuts ran deeper than mere flesh. Arjun did not think about what had conspired before. He did not want to think. He got into the habit of talking to his mother, even though she didn't understand.

'They all must be dead. It is so futile —what are they fighting for? I never had a best friend in my life. Hell, I've never had a friend. Because of what you did...' he said, pausing with guilt, 'or, he did. I owe you my life. Thrice. But I would have been happier dying here than living in that...that corruption. I'm sure that idiot Bakshi is behind this. Some half-baked idea about power,' he took a pause and then said, 'I hope she's okay.'

His mother did not comprehend but he went on. As he did, he realized he was talking to himself and had been for days. And once again, he wondered who the insane one was. The little cave his mother called home was like stepping back into a faulty time machine. It looked like an average Indian living room from the 1950s. Photos of Nehru looked back from the cover of old magazines, stacks of newspapers rotted in a corner, a sewing machine was thrown in one corner and an old typewriter lay untouched. In the midst of it, lay a giant fading photo of Mahatma Gandhi with his John Lennon glasses and of course, bottles of old cold drinks. Not Coca-Cola, not Campa-Cola, but Cow Cola which Arjun assumed was some pre-Baba Ramdev inspired drink.

The warmth of the cave made it seem homely but outside in the freezing cold, instead of a doormat, there was the body of a frozen mountain climber, a white male. The face stuck in a grimace and Arjun could not tell how long he had been there. He tried to move the carcass away but his mother smacked his hand.

'Did you try to save this person?' asked Arjun, but his mother had already moved on to removing lice from his head. It was probably true. Imagine being frozen on a mountain and being dragged through the snow by a mystical Yeti creature—the climber must have died of a heart attack before hypothermia.

All these things in his mother's home were not material goods, but memories, used by his mother to keep her past alive. This wasn't a cave, this was her mind. She wasn't insane, she was holding on. He was the one talking to himself about nothing. In this house, he was the one unworthy of saving.

∞

It had been a peculiar sight: fifty Chinese soldiers working in cooperation with four voluntary firemen of Tawang, three cops, a few locals and one Indian army man at the centre of it all. All of them were clearing debris, using ropes and pulleys to lift up fallen roofs and walls. They searched for dead bodies, four of which already lay on the side with their wailing relatives.

The scene made Kelly's blood boil and she wanted to run and smack the Chinese on the side of their heads. What held her back was the one Indian army man. He was running the show, speaking Mandarin to the Chinese and Hindi to the locals and ensuring things moved smoothly. General Taunque's uniform was caked with soot and dust but he motored on.

'At least someone from our side is there,' she heard a man in the crowd whisper to his friend, 'one Indian soldier and about a hundred Chinese ones. Kind of ridiculous, no?'

His friend nodded.

Kelly seethed further and reached into her kit, looking for her gun. But then, General Taunque moved towards her. He pulled her to the side.

'You know the truth, so you feel the rage. But for those who do not, the Chinese are coming off wonderfully. Rumours are flying that the robot was part of an Indian air force drill gone wrong. And it's gaining traction because there's no one here to deny it. Acting against them would only give them more brownie points,' he whispered to her.

'How has this gotten derailed so much?'

'It's a surprisingly good tactic. Sabotage a land you want to claim at a point when you know the opposition won't thwart you. Remember the dozens of dead Indian soldiers?'

'Of course. Killed mysteriously at night.'

'Drones, I'm sure of it,' said Taunque, 'specialized

drones. Illegal, yes, but, when has that stopped anyone? A weak government would not want to risk more casualties in the region. The Chinese are using subterfuge and sabotage to gain traction and support from the Tawang side. It's a tried and tested tactic.'

'Kashmir,' said Kelly.

'Exactly. Inspired by Pakistan, perhaps. Though, the Pakistanis were inspired by the Chinese, so maybe, the Chinese are just inspired by themselves except this is even worse from a support POV for India. No Indian soldiers. Zero!'

'There's you.'

'I'm a retired General. I'm an old man. Perhaps my presence is giving some positivity to the Indian side or maybe it is reminding people that I'm the only one there.'

'So, what's the solution?'

'The solution will arrive in eight hours and seventeen minutes. When Bakshi and I had met the PMs, they had threatened us with a court martial if we interfered with Indian borders.'

'Sounds about right,' said Kelly, 'you're risking court martial?'

'Over a hundred Indian soldiers and I are. I'd rather be court-martialled for doing my job than let Indian people accede to the opposing side because of the ineptitude of our politicians.'

'What's the point though?' said Kelly.

'Franz Ferdinand,' replied the General, 'and not the singer, I've heard that joke before.'

'That's the kind of joke Bakshi would make,' said Kelly with a sulky smile.

'People say the assassination of Austria's Archduke Franz Ferdinand's death led to World War I. They also say Helen of Troy caused the Trojan War. It's bollocks. Serbia and Austria had terrible relations before the World War, as did the Spartans and the Greeks. Franz and Helen were just the minor catalyst required to throw men into war. Two countries with bad relations don't need much of a reason to start a war. They just need the people in power in both countries to be foolish enough to think that war is the solution. Tawang Town is India-China's Franz Ferdinand or Helen of Troy.'

'Not only are we fighting for the rights of the people here, we're fighting for a future war. If we don't find a peaceful solution, this is the tinderbox that could cause India's ego to far overreach its force. It's happened before, and it can and will happen again.'

'What is the point?' she asked.

The General gave her a sidelong glance, as she carried on, 'If the tinderbox is to be lit, it will be lit anyway. Either way, the Chinese are obviously more efficient, they're more driven, and they're more organized. Arjun was right. Dr Ling was right. Why are we trying to stop a superior force from steamrolling an obviously more inferior us?'

The General stared at her with disbelief. For years, he was used to Kelly following orders, without question. If he said something, she listened. She argued, but she always listened. She had never completely dismissed the General's core philosophy on life i.e. the belief in his country.

'Look,' said the General, 'I know you've suffered tremendously. You've lost someone special...'

'Please, Bakshi was an idiot,' she interjected.

'I'm not talking about Bakshi,' said Taunque.

He let the statement linger and then heard commotion near the building and without a further word, ran off to do what he had been doing since the day he was born—find solutions. Kelly gazed at him and wondered if during birth too, the General had helped the gynaecologist cut his umbilical cord.

She looked at the search and rescue mission and then, she looked at her left, towards the trees in the forest. Why were two Chinese soldiers surreptitiously scouring through the trees? There was nothing to rescue under a tree. What the hell were they trying to find?

'Made in India,' she gasped and ran towards the site where signs of India's sabotage were being hunted for. Even if she questioned the mission, she still had to save it.

~

It hadn't been a good start to General Taunque's day. He'd awoken at 6:43 a.m. and the sun had already ridden out beyond the valley. He hated when the sun beat him. He loved to rise before it, with his chest proudly daring the sun to rise on the Earth that was owned by General Taunque. Today, its orange light shone upon everything below—every tree, every rock, and the distant blankets of snow. Now, it was just showing off.

The last time the sun beat him; Taunque had been diagnosed with a severe case of malaria after a surreptitious battle on the Rajasthan border decades ago. The battle had been successful, measured by the fact that nobody had known it had happened.

Today, he had been beaten by his age. Despite his physical condition, spending thirty-six hours pulling out debris and breaking news to relatives while coordinating the arrival of his soldiers had taken its toll. He had missed his mental alarm and also the knock on his door.

He now saw the gift waiting for him at his table. Someone had entered his room without his knowledge. He really was getting old to allow such liberties. On his study table were four pieces of metal—two flat, one oblong and one obviously extracted from a motor of some sort. All of the metal had "Made in India" embossed on them. The attempted subterfuge was overkill, insurance that there would be no confusion about who had created the robot. It reeked of desperation.

Despite her remonstrations, Kelly had once again pulled through. He put on his robe and stepped out to the corridor, which was lined with red carpets and archaic gas lamps fitted with modern CFL bulbs. He stepped across to Kelly's room and saw the door was ajar. Within, the blankets were folded, the bed was made, and the curtains were drawn—Kelly's yearning for order, even when she knew the job was someone else's.

Taunque smiled but his smile quickly disappeared as he realized that the metal on his table was a goodbye gift.

He leaned against the frame of the door and imagined her leaving.

'Yours has left too, huh?' said a voice behind him.

He turned to see Lepcha. The man had an atrocious habit of sneaking up on Taunque. But his annoyance was soon replaced by sympathy—Lepcha's face was haggard, his eyes burned red as if he had been crying for hours and his sparse hair stood on his head like prairie dogs popping out of their nests.

Lepcha said, 'I have not had a cup of tea in three days.'

It was a peculiar thing to cause such misery for oneself. Taunque had always endorsed the habit of tea—an Earl Grey with a dollop of milk, without sugar—but for a lack of tea to cause such misery was highly unconventional.

'Okay,' said Taunque.

'No matter how late my daughter slept, she'd make me tea,' said Lepcha, 'her face in the morning looked like she needed something stronger herself, but she always did it. It was horrendous, honestly. Awful tea. She always put too much sugar. There was one time she put salt, which was good. I told her that's how we drank our tea in Tibet—with salt and butter. So, she started putting salt every day. Too much of it. It was even worse. Anyway, I've not had tea for three mornings.'

General Taunque felt a twang of sadness as he comprehended that his daughter had also left him. In different circumstances, but she had. He walked towards the man, 'You Ladakh Scouts really love your tea, I know. Take me to the kitchen. I make some horrendous tea myself.

Not as bad as her I'm sure, but I'll try.'

Lepcha almost smiled but then held out a newspaper for the General. The General opened it and saw the front-page headline, "Liquor Baron killed in car crash," accompanied by the wreckage of a burning car.

'Rakesh Bakshi was incinerated in a gas explosion inside his car,' quoted Lepcha, 'his head was burned to ash. Some people are questioning whether there was foul play.'

'Okay,' said Taunque.

'Why?' asked Lepcha, 'Why am I not a murderer? Also, why are the goddamn Chinese here in my town?'

Many had attempted to understand what made General Taunque a good leader. Only those close to him knew that it was his instinct and his instinct told him that Lepcha—despite being a recently minted murderer—was his ally.

'I'm going to make you that horrendous cup of tea,' said Taunque, putting a hand on Lepcha's shoulder and leading him into his room, 'you're going to wash yourself up. And then, we're going to talk about your town and our country. Consider yourself out of retirement.'

Chapter Thirteen

Legend #61

Dragons form an important part of Chinese astrology. People born in the year of the dragon are extremely lucky. Yes, the year of birth can change the luck you represent. It's a Sorting Hat, with the reptiles.

There is the creative Wood Dragon, the extroverted Fire Dragon, the reflective Earth Dragon and the optimistic Water Dragon. And standing arrogantly to the side is The Metal Dragon—the most ruthless. People born as Metal Dragons are inflexible, combative and typified by their unwillingness to accept the undoable. There is an English word for such a dragon—"dictator".

Of course, it is typical that a dragon of metal would be impossible to mould. For how can you mould with words a living being that is smelted from fire?

General Taunque had been involved in wars across India's history—Kargil, Siachen and even a mission against ISIS in Kerala that almost had him assassinated. But he adapted to the violence because that was how wars were fought.

The General understood wars but he did not understand what was happening in Tawang. He had never fought a war for perception and that is what this war was—a battle for the opinion of the people of Tawang. And because of the internet, a battle for opinion of India as well.

When the footage of the Chinese soldiers helping India leaked, #ShameOnIndia trended across India, when Taunque's small battalion was seen in Tawang, #ProudOfIndia trended and when the Chinese and Indians cooperated, it was #IndoChiniBhaiBhai. Immediately after the footage of a Chinese soldier screaming at a local, it was #IndoChiniWhyWhy, and finally, when the Chinese army put up a photo of a reconstructed house smiling with Tawang locals, it was #ChinaKiMaKiAnkh.

And all this happened in seven days. How could public perception swing so drastically in a week? Was the country schizophrenic? Was this a modern ailment where ADHD permeated even into politics? Did people on social media suffer from bipolar disorder?

It didn't help that Taunque didn't understand what a hashtag was. When someone explained that it was merely a key on his keyboard, he wondered how one random symbol could cause such chaos. Then he realized that was what most religious wars were about.

Taunque was from an old world where any perception that reached the brain survived for decades, which might have explained why one family ruled unopposed in India for so long. Had the Gandhis become 'monarchs' only because of shortage of information? Public perception could change the flow of a war or a campaign. He had seen it happen with the manipulation of vox populi in Kashmir and every naxalbari village. But ninety eight per cent of the time, it was because of the impassivity of the government.

Demands for the resignation of India's PMs rose in the morning and died by the evening. Taunque never understood why Indians asked for a politician's resignation if something went wrong. If anything, they should be made to work harder, not stop work altogether.

It didn't take long for the five PMs of India to bypass Taunque and accept praises for sending a battalion to Tawang—as Arnab Goswami screamed —'The most decisive decision-making from any Indian leader I have seen since Kohli picked up the 28th T20 IPL World Cup last month.'

While this chest thumping idiocy took place, the ground situation worsened. Over two months, it became clear that the Chinese were winning on-ground support. They would have already won all of public support in Tawang if it hadn't been for Lepcha.

Lepcha had become Taunque's only friend in the friendly town. The rest of the town was respectful but wary of the man who represented a country that had severely let them down. But Lepcha represented something more to them—a wise, persistent voice of a wrecked local. The two men bonded over their respective losses. Lepcha had lost his daughter; Taunque had lost his entire battalion.

Now, they sat in Lepcha's TV room that was the only room that did not overlook the valley. Instead, it overlooked gutters and storerooms at the back of the hotel.

As Lepcha said, 'If you're in my beautiful town and want to watch TV, I'm not wasting the view on you.'

The TV was switched on but was ignored as the two men played chess. Lepcha was an atrocious player. The challenge for Taunque was to sabotage his own game to ensure that it lasted longer than three minutes. It was a great strategy by Lepcha—to frustrate the opponent with your inferiority so severely that he begins to impair himself.

In his daily dealings too, Lepcha remained the same—impulsive, mercurial, but fortunately, on Taunque's side. He had told everyone who had bothered to listen in town, 'Don't be fools. The Chinese are more efficient and organized than us, but they are also more ruthless and controlling. Choose. Do you want development at the violation of your personal freedoms? Because that is exactly what happened in my Tibet.'

Because of him, the townsfolk harboured some doubts because in everything else, the Chinese soldiers had been miles ahead. Not only had they reconstructed the fallen building, they had built two more. They had even constructed a public toilet with a direct link to water from the lake nearby—a facility that Indian authorities had been unable to provide in years. It did not help that the Indian army had been pulled out from their posts within two weeks.

Taunque's sources informed him, 'They fear a Chinese reprisal and a 1962 type situation. We can't risk it.'

Tawang was left with just ten soldiers who were put strictly on border duty, a strategy that was flawed since the enemy was already inside the border. Sometimes, even Taunque questioned whether fighting for the rights of people to stay in India was worth it after such shoddy decision-making, but Lepcha was insistent. He'd been the reminder of reason for the General throughout the severely declining situation.

'Lepcha, I appreciate your help, but I'm afraid we're on the losing side. It's reached a situation where if an election was held, the people would choose to accede to China.'

Lepcha had clicked his tongue, 'Not while I'm alive.'

He had then moved his Queen right in line of Taunque's King—unless she was a jihadi Queen, it was a suicidal move.

'The legalities are complicated and accession would take decades, but the seeds are already sown. And we've not given ourselves a chance,' continued the General.

'Not while I'm alive,' repeated Lepcha, as Taunque's King killed his Queen.

The TV blared as one of the news anchors—a nouveau prototype of Indian news anchors, dressed in a suit but with the attitude of a village natakbaaz—screamed, 'Breaking News…'

Taunque picked up the remote to turn off his hollering, but then stopped after listening to the anchor's words, 'A Chinese Minister gives us an exclusive insight into the Tawang situation…'

Taunque scowled on hearing that the threat of losing over a lakh Indians to China was being described merely as a "situation". Over the explosion of tickers—stock updates, three thousand breaking news, Twitter updates, Facebook updates and advertisements to sell cement—a face popped up.

'China is a very charitable nation. And we have given Tawang all our resources and assistance because they are *citizens*."

He let the word "citizens" hang in the air as Taunque read his name—Mr Ban Jin, China's Defence Minister.

'And in lieu of our love for the citizens, we come bearing bad news. On 26 June 2019, at precisely 6:47 p.m., there will be an earthquake in Tawang. It will measure 8.1 on the Richter scale with the town centre as the epicentre. Reverberations will be felt in all surrounding parts, but Tawang will be sunk to the ground.'

He paused as he read his notes on the podium, 'If you doubt the veracity of this pronouncement, remember, in 1975, China was the first and only country to correctly predict an earthquake at Haicheng. We saved thousands of lives and today, we aim to do the same for you. It is an old saying by Sun Tzu, "If you need a mink coat during winters, why not skin the neighbour's cat?" China is your mink coat—*our* people of Tawang need not worry. They can evacuate the province and retreat to India or they can skin our cat and come with us to China. On 28 June, at 6 p.m., Chinese trucks will be waiting at your border. You cross over and we will take you to safety. There will be enough for everyone, much like China.'

The footage ended and the coverage swung back to the anchor screaming about patriotism, earthquakes and for some odd reason, animal rights. Taunque turned off the TV.

'Well, 28 June. I guess they have announced the elections. They've bypassed the electoral process,' he said to Lepcha who seemed to have not heard a word. Lepcha concentrated on the board in front of him and quietly said, 'Checkmate.'

Two of Lepcha's pawns had Taunque's King surrounded. He stared at the board in disbelief. Two pawns and the worst chess player that had ever lived had beaten him. He looked up at his friend who smiled at him as if he had unlocked the secret code to all the world's banks.

'Not while I'm alive,' repeated Lepcha, and got up from his chair. He walked towards the door and said, 'Now loser, make me some disgusting tea. The way they used to in Ladakh.'

Chapter Fourteen

Legend #2

Many Kali temples have a monkey guarding the doorway. This custom originated in the Ramayana, when Lakshmana was captured by a sorcerer and was about to be sacrificed to Kali. Hanuman stepped in and tricked the sorcerer to sacrifice him instead. The switch earned him the respect of Kali who deemed him a worthy protector of the Goddess from whom most need protection.

It was inevitable, of course.

For Kali is an avatar of Shiva's wife, Parvati.
And Hanuman is an avatar of Parvati's husband, Shiva.
Shiva and Parvati: the God of Destruction and the Goddess of Love.

Even a smidgen of the combination of those two powers could shatter the world into two.
Buyers, beware.

It had taken weeks for Arjun to understand meditation. He figured out five steps—close your eyes, shut your stupid thoughts, focus on one part of your body, hold and release your breath, become amazing. The stalactites, stalagmites, the sound of the quiet cave and the smell of moss and green helped his quest for calmness. If you couldn't gain calmness here, you were probably ISIS.

He took a deep breath and released it slowly, focusing on the centre of his temple. He felt a tingle throughout his body. He gained control over every pore, including his own powers of the wind. He was Zen, he was Buddha, he was Valmiki, he was a Speaking tree, and he was the manifestation of all types of meditation. He had never felt this good in his life. Suddenly, something smacked him hard in the face and his façade of tranquillity collapsed in a heap of confusion.

'You son of a bitch,' screamed Kelly and hit him hard with a large aluminium flask.

'Ow!' yelled Arjun, more out of mental anguish than pain, 'What the…'

'You colossal piece of crap,' she screamed again and smacked him twice. The bottle had a dent now and resembled less a flask and more a work of modern art, possibly titled "The Slap of Wrath."

'You might want to stop hitting me,' said Arjun.

'Why the hell should I stop hitting you, you regurgitated mass of bullshit?' said Kelly, getting ready to create three more works of modern art.

'Because,' said Arjun, 'my mother might tear you limb from limb.'

Kelly put the bottle down and looked at the snarling gurgling mass of his mother's fury behind her. Arjun's mother was on the edge, her teeth were bared and she was doing everything to hold herself back.

'She tore apart a giant robot; you may be a sand castle in comparison. Down, mother, down,' said Arjun. 'That's a good mother. Who's a good mother? Come on. Down.'

His mother backed off, but didn't stop staring at Kelly. Arjun got up and stood between them.

His mother muttered something in protest at Kelly.

'She is my friend, Ma. You know her. My *friend*,' said Arjun and slowly approached his mother and placed a calming hand on her shoulder. His mother growled but let go.

'Why don't you go hunt yourself a mountain lion or something? Some light recreation,' he said and snarled like a wounded lion.

His mother perked up at the possibility and gave her version of a smile which was more terrifying than her threatening pose. She walked out of the cave and onto the cold mountain.

'That was a lucky guess,' said Arjun, 'I didn't think she actually hunted mountain lions. I didn't even know they were mountain lions. It's…'

He paused his commentary on the extinct species and looked at Kelly who for a human being resembled a predator. He didn't know what he preferred—facing the physical density of his mother or this maniacal look of a woman.

'I thought you were dead,' said Arjun, suddenly realizing that Kelly was not a hallucination, 'how...did you find me?'

'You are the worst kind of living being,' she said, ignoring him, 'whatever series of evolutionary mutation caused you to exist should be wiped out from biological memory.' And with an angry charge and a quick jump, she lunged for Arjun and kissed him hard on the mouth.

He looked down at her with surprise, 'What's happening now?'

'Oh, shut up,' she said, and kissed him again.

'Are you sure, you...' he managed between her thrusting her tongue down his throat. He couldn't tell if this was passion or anger, but he still interjected, 'I mean you must be tired from the journey. And you're supposed to be dead. And...'

He didn't have the opportunity to speak again as he was distracted by the awakening of parts that had remained stagnant for way too long. Every nerve in his body tingled as he meditated on one part of his body. Feeling her warmth flung into his, he felt no calmness—just sheer eruption of passion.

Many minutes later, he felt the kind of serenity he didn't know he had ever been capable of. Despite the pain of his slowly healing body and the cuts that had ripped him in half, he felt elation—the best balm for his pain.

He found it odd that he didn't even question where or how she had found him, he was just delighted that she had. She had a part of his jigsaw and now that she was here, he was complete.

Defence Minister Jin would never admit it but a part of him dreaded Dr Ling. Ling was a psychopath, which was good—individuals with diminished empathy made great leaders. Some of Jin's best friends were psychopaths. In politics, you were either an egomaniac or a piece of meat, to be chewed up and spat by predators.

His dread was mixed with pleasure that he controlled inarguably the greatest scientific mind of the generation. The mind who had laid the plans for the next level of Chinese conquering—made for a modern world where people's emotions were a weapon—was under his thumb. Without Jin's support, Dr Ling was nothing.

But there was *something* unnerving about Ling, something deeper. The doctor's assistant led Jin towards Dr Ling's laboratory. *How did his assistant work with him?* Jin wondered. Maybe she was his paramour, relative, or all of the above. Jin did not judge.

She led Jin through acres of automated robots working on sim-card chips. Or maybe it was ball bearings or circuit boards for automated weapons or chips for vibrators. Jin did not judge.

The assistant kept her head in her phone at all times, not once looking up to respectfully ask Jin if he needed anything. This, he did judge. He understood the young generation's proclivity to shove their lives into their phones; Jin himself had been similarly obsessed with Mahjong as a youth, but not at the cost of disrespecting his superiors. It was too western.

'He's a little off today,' said the assistant as she used her key card to beep them through a metal door, 'if I were you, I'd be really nice.'

'I'm the Defence Minister,' said Jin, in a bristling tone, 'he's the one who has to be nice to me.'

'Whatevs,' said the assistant and closed the door behind him.

Jin wished this meeting hadn't been so surreptitious; one interaction with his assistants would have intimidated this young upstart of a woman.

He adjusted his eyes and discovered he was not in a laboratory, but a gymnasium. Grunts greeted him from within and after the bright foyer outside, the dim lighting here was disconcerting. Jin moved with trepidation as the rubber floor squeaked under his feet. No one came forward to welcome him. It was not a welcome one of China's most powerful men was used to. Obviously, Dr Ling was trying to disorient him.

He straightened his back and reclaimed his authority, 'Ling! Where the hell are you?'

A grunt and a clank of weights crashing was the response and then, an annoyed voice followed, 'What do you want?'

This is too much, thought Jin, *what do I want? I want you to respect my authority, you arrogant little silkworm.*

'Get out here, Ling,' he screamed into the shadows, 'now!'

His order was met with another clank, another grunt and then the shuffle of sneakers on a padded floor. The room smelled peculiar—the smell of sweat and freshly unwrapped plastic, with a tinge of something rotting.

From the dimness, he felt Dr Ling approach him, but he

could barely make out the man. He could, however, sense a savage aura, something askew. A subconscious instinct for survival induced sweat to trickle down his back. It had been years since he had been in a physical fight and Jin wasn't sure if today was the day to start.

'I've emailed you the proposal, Jin. Email. It's 2019—why do people still need to meet?' said Dr Ling, curtly. There was threat in his tone that Jin did not care for but a fact echoed in his mind—he was in an underground lair on a secret mission and no one knew his whereabouts.

Dr Ling's voice sounded heavier, oozing with more testosterone than he remembered. Jin struggled to impose his authority, and tried again.

'There was once a fox that dressed as a sheep to mix with a flock of sheep, so he could eat them. You know how the sheep found out his reality?'

'By running a DNA test? Dolly the sheep cloned them? I don't care, Jin,' rumbled Dr Ling.

'By talking to him. They didn't send emails. There was no Firefox at the time, Dr Ling,' said Jin, proud of his joke—that would have made even the PM's sycophants chuckle.

'Face to face meetings ensure clarity. And I need to weed out the foxes to protect our citizen sheep.'

Dr Ling's silhouette moved with disdain, a black and white portrait of condescension, 'You didn't just come here to make stupid puns, did you, Jin?'

'Is Phase 3 ready to roll, Ling?' said the Defence Minister.

'As my assistant's email should have clearly helped you understand, yes, it is. We're prepared for the worst.'

'Yes, I read that part. What do you mean prepared for the worst? We execute Phase 3 and if that doesn't work, we exit. This is the order of the Chinese government. It is our mission, not yours. It's like that old saying by Navjot Singh Sid…'

'Save it, Jin. This is no longer your government's mission, it is mine. You told me I could do whatever I wanted with India. I asked you for clearance merely out of courtesy.'

Jin blinked in the dimness and reached for the walls for a switch that would turn on the lights—both in reality and metaphorically. But, there were no switches.

'Now, if you're done, I'd like to resume my experiments.'

'You were working out.'

'It's an experiment.'

'Whatevs, Ling,' said Jin, using the term he had learned moments back, 'you will go ahead only with Phase 3, Ling. That is all. Anything beyond that is not sanctioned by…'

He felt Ling loom closer to him—a figure that appeared larger and more intimidating than he remembered, 'Do not dare to tell me about what's best for China, Jin. I was fighting wars with Mao before your mother had pulled in your little penis into a cloth diaper.'

'Why would my mother pull my penis into a diaper, that doesn't even make sense…' interjected Jin.

'It was so tiny; she had to pull it specially.'

'Yes, but all babies have tiny penises. You aren't exactly born with a full-grown phallus. Or delivery would be far more complicated.'

'Yours never grew.'

'Look, Ling, you're terrible at insults. You should have said, "Jin, your peepee is so small only a microbiologist could see it because it's a DNA strand". Bringing diapers in...'

'This is not about your goddamn penis!'

'Everything is about that, Ling. For example, maybe you are overcompensating.'

'Shut the hell up about genitalia! I've been fighting wars since before you were in your diapers.'

'Wow, good one. Original,' said Jin, letting his sarcasm hide his fear.

'...I will do what needs to be done. Phase 3 will be successful and we will triumph and bring back our citizens to our fold.'

Jin considered this. He was glad he had at least aggravated the scientist enough to understand Dr Ling's mental state and the news was not good. The good doctor had gone bad.

'I expect you to follow orders, Ling.'

'And I...' said the doctor, moving towards the minister, 'expect you to leave the conquering to the real soldiers.'

A ray of light fell on Ling's face and just a glimpse was enough to disturb Jin. His face was bloated and his jaw swollen as if it had been broken. Pulsing blue veins popped from the man's cheeks. It was as if he was evolving or devolving into something new and something very wicked.

'I'm becoming more than you can imagine. I have the DNA of invincibility and my plan will go as we've discussed,' said Dr Ling, retreating back into the shadows, 'now leave, unless you'd like to be a part of my experiment.

I need someone.'

For once, Jin did not push his authority. He retreated with a sigh of relief. The grunts and clanking of metal resumed and Jin wished he hadn't seen this human-wolf cannibalize the body of a sheep.

∞

'Your chest is a couch,' said Kelly as her head lay on Arjun's chest, avoiding the deep scars. His body was a mixture of pain and satisfaction.

With her eyes closed, she said, 'And why are your nipples so red?'

Arjun smiled, 'Why are yours so puffy? They're like Chocos.'

He felt her lips curve into a smile. If he had known that meditation could feel so wonderful, he would have tried it before. But it was not the lust that calmed him, it was her. She lay where he felt she belonged.

'Bakshi wanted to become Prime Minister,' she said, out of the blue.

'Uhuh,' he said. He didn't feel anything when he heard the name, which was odd. 'Thought as much.'

'He was in cahoots with the Chinese to gain political traction. He wanted to be the man who saved India from a Chinese invasion.'

'That could've worked,' said Arjun.

'Sadly, yes,' she said, 'but he's dead now.'

'Sounds about right,' said Arjun, not asking why.

'He didn't kill or help kill all those soldiers, though.'

'The mystery of the sixteen dead Indian soldiers?'

'That was Dr Ling. He used drones in the dark. The drones would read heat signatures and approach a soldier when he was alone. Then, they would pierce the soldier's heart with the spine.'

'Horrible way to die,' said Arjun, picturing a soldier braving the cold in a tiny bunker, all his thoughts on a magazine or the radio or nursing a cup of chai that was rapidly turning lukewarm, looking out at the blackness of the night. The soldier might have been thinking of a movie, a moment in his life that mattered, or even something as arbitrary as a cricket match when he must have felt a piercing needle in his heart and a moment later, he would have been choked to his sudden death.

'Is there a good way to die?' she asked.

'Maybe,' said Arjun, contemplating the stories he had heard as a child, 'how many drones?'

'Eight maximum. A man who can invent one of the most horrific weapons of destruction by himself is capable of whipping up a small team of killer drones.'

Arjun's thoughts wafted slowly to his dead friends, 'What about The Secular Gang? What did you do?'

He could feel her tears wet his chest, 'I miss them. They were…we had to stage a car crash. Their families received notifications of their death in an unfortunate car crash in the Northeast. And a compensation of twenty lakhs from The Old Baxter, as if money can buy back life.'

Arjun felt his own eyes well up, 'He comes in my dreams sometimes—Manoj. Smiling like a goofy idiot. Says they chopped off his right arm and that's okay because he uses his left one for *important* work. Then, he says he had chosen this life, and was thankful that at least he had once banged a married woman and broken up a marriage. What a completely reprehensible thing to be proud of.'

'He had much more to be proud of,' she said, 'why are you suicidal?'

The brusque question took Arjun by surprise. He looked at her and then smirked. He tried to think of that dream.

He began, 'You made me forget once, with your face. I realized why in a dream after the Tibet incident. My father tried to commit suicide when I was young. He tried to take me along with him. He was my hero. When he hugged me, he enveloped me. It was like being back in the womb, protected from all sides. I felt so safe. I felt like he'd defeat God and tear the universe apart to save me. I worshipped him. And, *he* tried to kill me. Life had beaten him. Humans had broken him. What could destroy my God? How could their violence break my hero? He was so broken. Shattered. Life is futile. It's meaningless. We're all pawns in someone else's chess match, drifting out of control, deluding ourselves that we have free will. Why am I suicidal? It's because you're never in control of your life. Never. The only thing you can control is your own death. Like my father did. I'm suicidal because that's the only time in my life I'm not playing by someone else's rules. Committing suicide is the one way I can be me.'

He could feel Kelly's tears against his chest, but he felt

like he had no reason to cry. He could not weep over his own meaning. He could not lament his truth.

'Are you still suicidal?' she asked between sniffles.

He thought about it and gave her an honest answer, 'Not right now. Not with you. No.'

His words lingered in the air and in the silence of the cave, he felt the vague tendrils of joy.

'Ling used DEW,' said Kelly.

'Daman and Diu?' asked Arjun.

'Directed-energy weapons. The U.S., China and Russia have been trying to develop them for years. India too. They emit highly focused energy, way more than conventional weapons. Ling beat all the nations to it. Those lasers are some hard-core Star Wars shit.'

'Some who?'

Kelly smirked at Arjun's pop culture debacles and looked around the cave, 'So, your mother rescued you. Did you know she was alive?'

Arjun considered this, 'I think some part of me knew. She's spectacular—protective and insane.'

'Going with the little I knew about my mother, that's the definition of every good parent,' said Kelly.

Arjun smiled, 'I'd read news stories about a convicted terrorist, murderer or rapist. And when they'd interview the mother, she would always defend her child with no proof. It always aggravated me. I always thought they were not defending their children, they were defending themselves. I never understood why they would defend their love so much till I was reunited with my mother.'

'So, you think she will defend you if you were convicted of a crime?'

'Oh, no. She'd probably kill me before the state has a chance. If she knew I did it. I'm just saying, I now understand why *those* mothers would defend their kids. The love part.'

They descended into silence in each other's arms, not talking about what lay ahead, if anything at all. From the corner of the cave's mouth, Arjun's mother looked at them and cried. She missed her husband, she missed his warmth, and she missed the soul that had been entwined to her even after he tore himself apart. She felt a tinge of joy to see her son finally experiencing peace. She had done all she could. She had brought him back and given him a second life.

Her son was as good a man as he would ever be and that is the best a mother can hope for. She was happy that he was happy at last. And it was time for her to say her final goodbye.

Every part of his body was aching and he was happily tired. Kelly and he had spent the entire night awake. The last time they had counted, it had been seven times. When Kelly was about to give up, he had joked, 'That's what you get for hooking up with a seventy-three-year-old virgin. I have a lot of catching up to do. This is the Narmada Dam exploding!'

'I don't think you know what the dam contains,' she had said and then with a laugh, had plunged headlong into it.

Afterwards, she had asked him, 'Why were you a virgin before tonight?'

'Well,' he said, 'do you see a lot of my kind running around in Lucknow?'

'But, I'm not your kind either. I'm human,' she said.

'Yeah, keep telling yourself that,' he said and received six playful slaps on his face, with a punch for good luck.

They had finally slept and Arjun was glad that at nights, he had the cave to himself. His mother never seemed to sleep and rarely stayed in the cave except to treat him. The moments she slept, he saw her lolling on the frozen rock trident outside, like it was a tree. She never truly rested because her mind was attuned to being alert all the time.

At some inordinate time the next day, Arjun woke up feeling satiated. In all his years, he had never attempted to do to himself what most men do ordinarily. It was a combination of lack of interest and self-control that came from sources he didn't know. The wait had been worth it. He had cashed in all his chips on one hand and had won a Royal Flush.

He woke up and looked towards the mouth of the cave, with Kelly curled up against his chest—thick blankets coated her. In the constantly raging snow, he could never tell what time it was. And that's when he knew something was strange.

The light that came in from outside was not one he had ever seen before. He lightly moved his hand from under Kelly and got up from the old bed. He walked to the mouth of the cave. A newspaper cutout was hanging from the cave's entrance, stuck crudely with a sharpened rock.

It was a photo he had not seen before—his father with Gandhi. In the photo, the giant vanara protectively towered over a smiling Mahatma, who seemed bemused by his protector. Arjun stared at the photo—the weird lights made it appear like it was from some other dimension. Gandhi's face had been circled with a red pencil and next to that, in almost child-like handwriting, were written in an ancient language, the words, 'Who needs you?'

He carefully put the photo under a rock and walked out of the cave. There was no snow, but the sun could not be seen either. Instead, in the horizon and all around him were swirling lights of purple, blue, orange, yellow, and indistinct but vibrant colours that he could not name. They swayed in the air, dancing to the tune of some hidden drum—a carnival of visual delights.

'What is that?' said Kelly, from behind him, 'It can't be, can it? Those can't be the Northern Lights?'

'No,' said Arjun staring at the colours, 'it's not Aurora Borealis, no.'

'I've never seen anything so beautiful in my life,' said Kelly, 'if not the Northern Lights, what are they?'

A tear fell from Arjun's eye. He looked at Kelly and said, 'That's my mother.'

Kelly moved towards him, the blanket covering her tightly. In the freezing cold, she should have been the one feeling the chills, but Arjun—whose body was made for this weather—was the one in need of warmth. She got close and hugged him.

'I don't understand,' she said.

'Where is General Taunque?' he asked her, hugging her back.

'Um, I don't know. Maybe Tawang, if that situation hasn't corrected itself. I've been trekking for weeks, so I can't be sure.'

'Okay,' said Arjun and unhooked himself from her, 'he needs me.'

Kelly pulled the blanket close to her as her teeth chattered in the cold, despite the warming, swirling lights, 'Are you okay? I'm sorry I don't understand what happened.'

Arjun moved further towards the light, trying to grasp his mother, 'I'm not okay, but *we* are more than okay. Get packed. We have to leave. I don't want you to catch a cold.'

After a pause, Kelly moved back into the cave. Arjun passed his hand through the swirling palate of his mother's last remains. She had given her life to make him whole. Tears fell from his eyes and froze into icicles on his cheeks.

He was glad her funeral was an explosion of colours. He wished her life had been the same—more than a recurring dream of grey and black snow, a dreamscape of confusion and despair. A lone warrior fighting enemies within and without, the last carrier of her species, tore down by the depression of a husband who himself had been defeated by his duty. He had to ensure her legacy would paint monumental strokes of brightness. He knew she deserved it. He had to paint for her a masterpiece of hope.

Chapter Fifteen

Legend #95

Lord Hanuman was known for his love for mischief. His sense of humour is something one wishes some of his followers also displayed, but that is neither here nor there.
When he was young, he once tried to swallow the sun. The Lord of the Sun, Surya was so aggravated by a child attempting to eat his sun, he killed him. Lord Vayu, the Lord of the Wind and Hanuman's father was so agitated to have his son killed over the measly sun that he removed all the air from the Earth, asphyxiating every living creature.
The other Gods, realizing their mistake not only brought Hanuman back to life but even granted him immortality. Sometimes, it pays to have an influential father.

General Taunque had to grudgingly admit that the Chinese impressed him. They thought about everything and more, just because they had to sell the China Dream to the people of Tawang. After the reconstruction work in Tawang, India had swept out all Chinese soldiers from their land but that was a mere speed bump for the Chinese.

They used the "No Man's Land" to their advantage and operated out of the gap between the two borders to astonishing effect. The border was tall meshed wire with barb on top and a barricade to allow traffic. Chinese soldiers bypassed this by flinging packages to the townspeople over the barricade.

Hundreds came to receive these packages and Taunque contemplated treating the pamphlets as an act of war but thought better of it. It wouldn't do good to write a cause of war as "Solicitation of citizens". He had once again put himself in a position where his every word mattered and even though Major General Kiran Das had been put in charge of India's battalion, she had acceded her position to General Taunque.

'They are smart,' he told her.

The lady was hard as nails and had replied with a grunt, 'They are shameless.'

But she had picked up a package to see its contents anyway. The package was called, "Welcome to China, Citizen." It included a pamphlet that stated where the new citizens of China would live—a housing society the size of Tawang, with running water, electricity, swimming pool, a playground and no rent for the first five years.

'Is this for a country or Lodha Group's new township in Gurgaon?' she asked the General.

'It is better,' replied the General, 'no rent, no outgoings.

But what happens after five years—who cares?'

Das pulled out an envelope and smirked, 'It's a temporary passport of China. You just fill in your name and you're done.'

'Efficient,' said Taunque, 'a passport takes a fortnight. This takes a second.'

She pulled out the last thing from the package, 'It's a mobile phone,' she cried, 'this is better than the phone I have!'

She held up a sleek android phone called iFone and Taunque inspected it, 'Except your phone probably doesn't have information going back to Beijing. This must have cost them three yuan. It'll probably last till next week. But still, very smart.'

Das groaned but looked across at the people. They looked suitably impressed with the phones, and the other gifts. One gentleman was sitting by a tree, removing his sim-card and putting it in his new phone.

'Thank God we have Lepcha,' said the General, 'though even he cannot compete with free phones, free homes and free passports.'

Over the last few days, Lepcha had been the only thing holding back a majority of the town from leaping over the border. He had been campaigning door to door and Taunque could not help but feel that this was an election campaign—vote for the incumbent Indian government or the hot new favourite, the Chinese Janata Party!

Taunque had joined Lepcha in his "campaigns". At every household, Lepcha made a different emotional pitch, but never forgot to mention three salient points:

His own experiences, 'I saw things in Tibet that have forever convinced me that no matter how assured they appear, the Chinese are kings of deception. Choose whether you want some inefficiencies and rights or human rights violations and progress.'

The deception of this current campaign, 'Look at what's happening here—sixteen Indian soldiers mysteriously dead with the same condition. A mystical robot shows up from nowhere to discredit and destroy our town. We've been systematically aborted from our own country. For lies. Is that what you want to join?'

And, of course, the ever-prevalent emotional Indian dialogue, 'This is your home. You grew up here, played football or kissed your first girl without her father knowing. But the father always knew. I can say this because I too had a daughter. She was killed by the other side. I will never leave. This is my home, my life, I built it over decades. And to start it all anew—I'm sorry, that's just foolish. And it's betrayal. Are you a betrayer?'

Half of the town backed Lepcha and their own sense of patriotism. But India's increasing apathy could not be ignored. And the day Taunque detested was now upon them. It was D-Day, the day of reckoning—28 June, the day of the alleged earthquake when China's offer to Indian citizens began and ended. Taunque beat the sun and was at his post by the border before it arose. A dozen Chinese soldiers stood opposite him. Everyone was curious to see if the plan had worked—Asia's first country election. Scotland had voted years back but this was far less official, much like everything else in Asia.

To Taunque's dismay, people slowly began trudging towards the border, walking, in cars, pushing their cycles on the side and one, even on a pony, with all his family's belongings—hundreds of people that had decided that enough was enough.

'And, so it begins,' muttered Das, sipping on her morning tea, 'I'm glad we did a full media blockade. Or this would be embarrassing.'

'With or without them, this is embarrassing. It is heartbreaking. It's only 6 a.m.'

The people had lined up in an orderly fashion, all of them looking tired and sceptical. China opened their gate and it was now India's turn.

Taunque gestured to Das to go ahead and open the gate and she did so with a heavy heart. She pulled the gate over the mud, towards herself. And then, she turned to the line of people in front of her.

She sat reluctantly at the desk they had set up at the post and finding nothing else to say, she shouted, 'Please keep your passports and visas ready,' and repeated the same in Hindi. She sat down and the first person moved towards her.

However, the first person and his family of three did not make it past Das. As they moved forward, there was a roaring sound in the sky, and in an explosion of wind and dust, something crash-landed a few feet away from where the man stood. All the soldiers kept their weapons ready on both sides of the border and even Das got up with a start.

From the pit that had formed near the wire mesh on the Indian side, Arjun Singh extricated himself and spat out mud, 'Goddamn landings. Stupid flying.'

He pulled himself up and looked at the thirty guns aimed at him from either side of the border and then, at the queues of stunned civilians staring at him. He smiled at them with a full-toothed grin and it made the civilians back away slightly.

'Hi,' he said casually, like the queues were arranged for the water cooler during the office lunch break, 'what's up, mitron?'

'Weapons down,' screamed Taunque, 'he's with us,' and to the Chinese on the opposite side, he added, 'he comes in peace. I think.'

They did not seem convinced and continued aiming at this creature that had fallen from the skies. Taunque looked at Arjun with surprise. Though his frame appeared lither, his muscles still protruded through his ill-fitting pastel shirt. The scar across his face gave him the appearance of a man who had defeated demons and had survived.

Arjun cleared his throat and jumped on a tree stump, addressing the crowd in front of him, 'In 1975', began the rumblings of his voice, reverberating through the crowd, 'yes, Chinese officials predicted an earthquake in Haicheng, China. It is a legend that even the Chinese did not perpetuate until now because of exactly how fluky it was. Their assessment was based on the behaviour of animals. Cats in the region were behaving "unusually". Honestly, using that as proof for future earthquake prediction is about as daft as saying that a tsunami will come because a pigeon is flying diagonally. There can be no earthquake prediction because Mother Earth is as predictable as the weather,' he concluded and smiled.

The crowd still looked at him with suspicious stupefaction. A child started crying in her mother's lap and a baby joined in which led people to start talking to each other. Arjun looked confused and so, Taunque climbed on top of Das' chair and spoke, 'Who are you? Please identify yourself to these people.'

'Oh, right,' said Arjun, picking out a piece of twig from his teeth. 'Hi. I'm Arjun Singh. And I'm with General Taunque. I'm here to protect India, your country.'

Murmurs from the crowd.

He went on, 'Frankly, I think China is great. Really it is. Number 1 nation on Earth. They're good at everything—from sports to infrastructure to manufacturing to everything. Why wouldn't you want to join them?'

More murmurs from the crowd.

'But I serve India because General Taunque serves India. He's the bravest man I know and it is for innumerable men like him that I stick to your side. Now, some of you may find it hard to look for a reason to compliment this country, especially after the indifference of the last six months. But here's the thing, in China, you will be what they want you to be. In India, you can be whatever you want to be. Think about it. This is a nation where the son of a former PM can become PM, where I'm told something called a Tusshar Kapoor is a leading actor, where the world is your oyster.

Where whatever you want is yours. It's your life. Across this border—it's their life.'

The crowd began a group discussion amongst themselves. Even new entrants to the crowd stared at Arjun, trying to understand what was happening.

'India is an open book. You can do whatever you want. You can achieve anything if you're driven. You can even be a criminal and get paid and become CM. Anything is possible. And look, if you have doubts, here's something to convince you. I am on India's side. And I will protect India.'

Air exploded from all parts of him and he flew to the clouds above.

The people stared with wonder and fear at this creature above them as the Chinese cocked their guns ready. They craned their necks to hear the creature give out a deadly roar. He bore his teeth and his tail swirled in the wind. He screamed from above, 'The Chinese gave you a deadline. Well, here's mine—it's 6 a.m. right now, I give you till 4 p.m. to think about it again. Do you want to be on this side or that?'

Ending his aeronautical display in a flourish, he landed beside General Taunque who looked at him with concern, 'Did you just threaten them to stay?' whispered the General.

'No, General. I'm just a good debater,' and he smiled at Taunque as the crowd retreated away from him, as he stood there—not exactly blocking their path, but definitely standing in the way.

Taunque was not sure if he agreed with the tactic but technically this wasn't coercion. He turned to Arjun.

'Where's Kelly?' asked the General.

'She's on a mission,' replied Arjun cryptically, 'for a change, let me brief you.'

⚘

Kelly was not used to improvising missions. She was attuned to following orders. The first time she had made a decision to act independently was when she realized she was in love with Arjun Singh. She had researched the presence of a trident rock in the Himalayas, cashed in a favour for a lift on an IAF chopper, and then trekked for weeks to get to him. It was a foolhardy mission that could have ended with her in a body bag and it was precisely why Taunque would never have ratified it.

But for this new mission, she did not have time to get approval from her superior. It was aimed not to beat the Chinese but to prevent war. She did some basic calculations as she lay, looking at the Chinese gathering.

It was a question of basic math combined with Chinese productivity. There were a total of forty trucks; each could accommodate a hundred people. Presuming that the Chinese were confident of getting at least sixty percent of the Tawang population, this meant they had to transport sixty thousand people. The trucks in the tough terrain could not go more than 40 km/h, and they had an hour to get out of the earthquake epicentre. This meant the location was no more than forty kilometres away. *That is odd*, thought Kelly, as she watched the little Chinese army in the distance. *If an earthquake of the Richter scale they had suggested does strike, the impact would range well beyond that distance.*

Plus, the timing of the earthquake seemed convenient. To allow the people enough time during the day to make their escape. As far as schedules were concerned, this earthquake was quite punctual.

As the glimmer of sun broke through the valley beyond, Kelly looked at the scene again—forty trucks and two cars. Through her binoculars, she saw the first car where Jin, the Defence Minister and of course, the newly drafted Minister of Earthquakes looked impatiently. He looked with trepidation at the second car, leaned into its back window and spoke to the passenger.

What the hell was going on? Everything seemed amiss. And then the real fact of the matter struck Kelly. She could not believe it had taken her this long to figure it out. This changed everything. She got up from the ground, only to find a gun at the back of her head.

A man screamed something to her in what she assumed was Mandarin. Another man behind her translated, 'Chinese territory. What you do here? We shoot at sight.'

She heard them deflate both the wheels of her motorcycle, as if the guns weren't enough.

⁂

Down below, Jin's hopes were deflating as the day wore on. At first, his soldiers at the border had told him that over a thousand Tawangese were expected and that too, the first batch. But nobody had come. At one stage, a civet or Indian raccoon had popped in, but he wasn't sure of the raccoon's nationality. It came to him, looking like a bandit and Jin felt as though someone had stolen something from him.

Towards the latter half of the day, he got his first glimmer of hope. A tiny car made its way towards them, one of those annoying Japanese cars that were sold in India. It stopped right next to him, slowing as it approached the soldiers. There was a family of four inside it. One of them came out of the car.

'Welcome,' said Jin, 'welcome home,' with a little too much enthusiasm.

'My name is Meiyang,' said the man as he approached him, 'where are we going?'

'To safety,' said Jin, 'in Tibet. And then, beyond.'

The man shuffled. He looked back at the car where his family was waiting, their luggage oozing from the boot, their life squeezed into one tiny vehicle, their aspirations dependent on this precipitous plan. His son's face was caked with tears because his football friends were left behind. His daughter was trying to snub her parents by refusing to cry. His wife was surprised that her tame husband had been so decisive about leaving.

But now, indecision surfaced at the vagueness of his future plans. Would he be able to find a job in Tibet? What would he do with his life?

'Four minutes to the earthquake,' said Jin, 'or you could go back to your torn down home.'

Meiyang sighed and nodded his head. He walked back to his car.

'Are there...are there any more coming?' asked Jin, in desperation.

'He came out of the skies,' said Meiyang, 'that turned the tide.'

'Who came out of the skies? What are you talking about?' said Jin, confused.

'He's an accountant, they say,' said Meiyang, 'but, he can fly.'

'What are you going on about? A flying accountant? Are you insane?' asked Jin, doubting if it was actually worth getting these crazy people to China.

Meiyang shook his head as he walked back to his car, too lost in his own thoughts to even realize that Jin was more lost than he was. After Jin assigned one soldier to lead Meiyang towards his new life, he waited till the four minutes to the earthquake passed, and then told his men to take their buses back. Obviously, no one was coming. He stood in the dust and fumes as the buses rode off, till all that was left was his car and the SUV. He walked to the tinted SUV, and knocked. The window of the passenger seat opened slightly.

'This is a complete disaster, Ling. We got four people instead of forty thousand. Your plan is a failure.'

Ling's disfigured face peeked through the tinted window, 'Our plan, Jin. Your entire future was riding on this. Once again, it's that flying idiot. But it's okay.'

'What flying idiot? What do you mean it's okay? It's been almost a year of planning and we've lost.'

'No,' growled Ling, 'they have lost,' and he pointed

towards Tawang, 'they have lost a chance to be a part of the victors. And, now, they are officially a part of the losing side—which makes them the enemy. It's time for Phase 4.'

'No!' cried Jin, 'No Phase 4. The Chinese Government does not approve this plan. I'd rather have my reputation tarnished than have the blood of so many on my hands, it's inhumane and...'

'It would be an embarrassment to China—not you, you egotistical oaf. This is about a larger picture. It's time for Phase 4.'

'You're missing the larger picture, Ling. This is not the way of the new China, I'll have you imprisoned...' began Jin. A hefty arm swung out from the car and wrapped around his neck. He tried to pull it off, but it was too strong for him. The hand crushed him till it cracked his neck and then dropped him to die by his own car. The hand retreated, 'Take me to Tawang,' said Ling to Sun.

Sun, in the driver's seat, was about to argue when she saw the dying man struggle on the side of the car. She began to drive the car slowly. Maybe this way she could hold off her mentor/psychopath from committing genocide.

∞

Kelly sighed as she turned to look at the two soldiers. They were young men. One had a badge that said "Chang" and the other's badge said "Lee". She had met her Jackie Chan and Bruce Lee—what were the odds of that? Or was she being racist?

Jackie made a rumble in his Bronx and spoke to her in

broken English, 'You doing what here? You sniper?'

Bruce entered the dragon and added, 'You spy?'

Kelly shook her head and felt sadness at what she was about to do. Both men had their lives ahead of them—their fists of fury, police stories and even their rush hours to deal with. They had made the mistake of being at the wrong place at the wrong time, and of assuming that she was an ordinary woman.

'Both,' she replied and the two hands beneath her jumper shot two bullets into both men's shoulder and thigh. They fell to the ground clutching their respective injuries and she kicked their guns away. She tied both of them against each other as they groaned in protest and surprise.

'Sorry, but it's loose, so you'll eventually be free,' she said, 'also, I'm going to have to borrow your bike.' She pulled out the keys from one of them.

She pointed her binoculars towards where Jin and the tinted SUV stood, just in time to see a hand reach out from inside the SUV, grab Jin by the neck and crush him. He lay thrashing on the ground like a goldfish out of water.

'Ling!' she exclaimed. Grabbing her backpack, she jumped on to the Chinese motorcycle that had been so hospitably provided to her. As assurance, she took a cloth with petrol and set it ablaze on her own motorbike.

'The flames,' she told the tied kung fu masters, 'should bring help. Cheers.'

She put the bike in top gear and raced towards the Indian border, hoping they wouldn't shoot her down. She could beat Ling and his vile plan with a vehicle from his own country.

～

The alarm on Arjun's watch went off. It was zero hour—6:47 p.m.—and he heard the alarm with panic. Like the twelve soldiers stationed at the border, he looked back at the town, expecting the worst, but nothing happened. It was an odd thing for soldiers who waited for an attack from people to be now waiting for an attack from Mother Nature. Even if the earthquake came, it was not as if any of them could do much to respond. They couldn't exactly fire AK-47s into the Earth and kill the tectonic plates.

In the distance, he could hear Lepcha screaming instructions, ensuring everyone's safety if the earthquake did come. The man was a dynamo; he had put people in the safest place in town—Tawang Monastery. With its hard stone and deep foundation, the monastery was the least likely place to cave in. The remaining people had been herded around the town square or under sturdy beds. It was the pre-emptive rescue operation of a lakh people shepherded by one man. He was telling people that it was better to be safe than sorry. His assessment was mixed with a combination of patriarchy and warmth.

Now all that was irrelevant and the moment of reckoning was closing. The minute passed and nothing happened. Smiles broke on the soldier's faces but General Taunque held up a hand and waited for an extra minute. Arjun was delighted to be near his guiding light. They waited for two extra minutes, but nothing happened. Finally, Taunque put his hand down and smiled.

'It's 6:51 p.m. Four minutes gone. Nothing,' he said, 'not even a fart from below the surface.'

The soldiers laughed. Arjun smiled. Suddenly, one of the soldiers with his binoculars towards the Chinese side screamed, 'Incoming, Sir. Incoming. Coming fast! Sir, please advise.'

Arjun could see a whirr of dust in the distance as a Chinese motorcycle sped quickly towards them. All the soldiers cocked their guns into position and aimed for the fast-moving two-wheeler.

'Chinese motorcycle, Sir. Unidentified, Sir. Please advise.'

'Hold your fire,' screamed Taunque. The Chinese soldiers had retreated, so what was this act of aggression?

'Waving an India flag, Sir. Waving an India flag. Three hundred meters!'

Arjun used his binoculars which happened to be his sharp eyes, and saw Kelly waving the India flag on a Chinese motorcycle. It made no sense. 'It's Kelly,' he told Taunque, 'alone. No hostage situation. Kelly alone. Don't fire.'

'Confirmed. Confirmed. Hold your positions and your fire, men,' screamed the General.

With her hair flying in the freezing breeze, Kelly skidded to a halt in front of the Indian border, still waving the Indian flag as a precaution. She got off the bike and started running towards Arjun. Her face was blue because of the cold. Arjun ran towards her and put an arm around her. She almost resisted but his warmth filled her. He rubbed his hands and placed them on her face.

'Did you eat onions?' she said, between chattering teeth, 'Your breath stinks!'

'Kelly,' said Taunque, interrupting the tender scene, 'if you're done trying to kill yourself, the Chinese prediction of the earthquake was wrong.'

'Yes,' said Kelly, 'it was wrong because they haven't done it yet.'

'What do you mean?' asked Taunque.

'I mean, they haven't triggered the earthquake yet. But something tells me they will.'

'They won't trigger anything. But he will,' said Arjun, looking at the valley.

'Who?' said Taunque.

As if in response, one of the soldiers screamed, 'Man in the valley! A lone man approaching the valley.'

Another added, 'Black SUV in the distance.'

Arjun stared at the figure of Dr Ling treading confidently towards Tawang. A lone man walking into a hostile country with the audacious confidence of someone who knew that nothing could touch him.

'Instructions, Sir,' screamed the soldiers.

'Something coming out of the SUV, Sir. Confirmed, Sir. They've released drones. 1, 2, 3... I can count up to seven drones, Sir.'

Kelly looked at Arjun and then, at Taunque, 'They predicted it because they were planning to cause it,' she said. 'He killed the Defence Minister, Arjun. He's not what we remember. He's...he's...mutated.'

'Fire at the drones,' screamed Taunque, but the drones

split into seven different directions, whirring at a speed that was impossible to lock down.

They fired, but they all missed.

'They're flying at over a hundred miles an hour, Sir. How is this possible?'

'You guys take care of this. I'm taking care of him,' said Arjun and took off in an explosion of wind in the direction of his Number 1 threat—a solitary, old man walking from the valley, in the peak of the day.

∞

Kelly led the team of soldiers to where the drones were about to come. It was abundantly clear that the drones were supposed to cause the earthquake. As one blazed through the air, she saw glittering cones of metal at their fronts, which made them automated moles. They'd bore through Earth until they were deep enough to cause an explosion.

The drones flew off towards the town to avoid the gunfire but Kelly knew this was a distraction. She knew their final objective and saw through the subterfuge. She knew they'd take a U-turn and come back.

She took charge from Taunque and divided the twelve men into two groups—four to stay with her and eight in separate directions to locate the drones. She *knew* where the drones would land up—the cricket field. It stood bang in the centre of the town and every earthquake needs its epicentre.

She stood on the cricket field, wondering how they would come. The four soldiers stood near her, awaiting instructions.

'I need you to get me as many gas cylinders as you can,' she said.

The soldiers looked confused, 'Gas cylinders, Ma'am?'

'Yes. It's hard to bring them down with ammunition but maybe they aren't immune to fire. Run, now!'

As the soldiers implemented her confounding instructions, she removed her backpack and laid it on the ground. Decades as a solo spy had prepared her for the worst. She thought about what Taunque said to her regularly, 'Panic is adrenaline. Adrenaline is your friend. Ride it, let it be your stallion, and you'll race through.'

She assembled the kit for what she was planning and quickly laid out four improvised flamethrowers. The drones buzzed from the distance and as she had predicted, seven drones descended from seven different directions towards the cricket pitch.

Behind her, she could hear gasps from the people within the monastery. They knew something was up and if they lost, they would not be alive to tell the tale. The four soldiers materialized almost as quickly as the drones themselves with their cylinders in hand. Using that innate Indian skill for jugaad, she placed four gas cylinders beside her. She took their pipes and shoved her gadgetry into the cylinders. The drones' sounds grew louder—buzzing bees of technological massacre. They swooped towards the spot near her.

'The drones are not impenetrable. Enough gunfire should bring them down. Divert them towards me. Fire at will. Go, go. Now!' she screamed.

The men took their positions and fired at the drones. The

drones took the bait; the gunfire drove them towards Kelly. One drone collapsed in a heap a few meters away from her, but the other six kept coming. Just as they got within firing range, she let loose. Her four hands unleashed a rage of fire; she was a juggler of a brutal inferno. The gas cylinders were emptied into the metallic birds of death. Unprepared for the onslaught, three drones smoked in protest and crashed.

The soldiers looked at her extra limbs, mollified.

'Four down, three to go,' she screamed, 'this is the worst Quidditch match. Every ball is the snitch!'

She knew that even one drone could do the job because the haphazard town rested on a mountain. The poorly constructed homes would crash down like a house of cards. The three drones diverted from the gunfire and came towards her, just as her last gas cylinder gave up. Short of diving in front of the drones and futilely killing herself, Kelly didn't know what to do.

Both drones almost beheaded her—guided relentlessly by their target—and then broke through the ground in the middle of the cricket pitch with shocking rapidity. Kelly whipped out her gun and along with the rest of the soldiers, fired at the swiftly descending drones. But it was futile. Their best efforts had not been enough and the drones bore through the ground, sounding like the harbingers of death, banshees in metal form. Then, just as their ammunition ran out, the sounds stopped. The drones had stopped cold.

Kelly raced to the mouth of the hole the two had dug. Around twenty feet deep, the drones lay stalled, upside down, pointed towards the core of the Earth.

'Fire,' said Kelly and all the soldiers reloaded and fired at the stalled drones, taking no chances, till their ammo was exhausted. Soon, the drones were stagnant pieces of shining uselessness.

'That was close,' said one of the soldiers.

'We averted the earthquake,' said Kelly, affording herself a relieved smile. As soon as she said this, there was a loud boom. It shook the entire town and shrieks rang out from the monastery behind—the inaugural rumblings of Earth caving in.

∞

Drones had been banned in times of war. The explanation was that they were devious; drones could come out of nowhere and deal in death without responsibility, even on innocents. General Taunque had never understood that logic. As a soldier, he would have preferred a drone doing the job, rather than his men dying in a battle initiated by some fat politician with little understanding of ground realities.

But today, he understood the real problem with drones—a complete lack of accountability. They could have come from anywhere—China, Pakistan, Narnia—and nobody would ever know who sent them and why. Taunque knew one thing though, the drones were being controlled from somewhere nearby because of the way they darted about, it was as if they had a 3D view and improvised their movement. Satellites wouldn't allow such improvisation. It had to be that SUV. He searched the enemy territory and finally, found it hidden crudely behind some bushes.

He pulled out his gun and saw a diminutive figure next to the SUV. She stood with a large tablet in her hands, operating the drones like she was piloting toy helicopters and not weapons of destruction that could smite over a lakh people. Sun alternated between looking at the screen and the view, through her attached binoculars. Taunque saw the drones' POV—them racing past Kelly whose four hands blazed fire with the fury of an enraged Phoenix.

Meanwhile, Sun was so engrossed in her task that she did not hear Taunque sneak up. He put a gun to her head and said, 'Stop the drones now!'

She was startled and hesitated. Then, she did something Taunque had not expected—she began to cry. She said something in Mandarin but it was too fast for Taunque. Between sobs, she explained in English, 'I never wanted to do it. Never. This is massacre. It is culling.'

His surprise at her tears had given the drones time and he watched as the drones raced past Kelly and began to bore into the ground.

'Stop the drones now!' he said, 'Or I will blow your head off.'

After more sobs, she did. The drones came to a halt in the middle of mud, which was all he could see from their POV.

'Drop the tablet and slowly move away from it.'

She cried again and said, 'I can't. It's a new Apple iPad Diamond. Only four are available in the market. I spent my whole salary on it. I can't drop it.'

'Fine, just hand it to me,' he said.

'Don't break it,' she said and held it out to him.

He reached out for it with his right hand, his left still holding a gun to her temple. As soon as he held the tablet, an electric shock soared through his body. The tablet pulsed and smoked and Taunque dropped the gun. After decades of service, the General had been foiled by a tweeny Chinese civilian.

'Electric Shock App, asshole,' screamed Sun at his vibrating figure on the ground, 'available for only twenty-three yuan on App Store. Death installation is free. See you later, sucker.'

She sprang for her car to hasten her escape when there was a loud boom. The Earth shook. She fell backward, on top of a palpitating Taunque, and felt electricity course through her back.

∞

From a distance, Dr Ling appeared about the same but as he walked towards Arjun, he noticed the mutations. He had grown a few inches, and it was definitely not because of Complan. He wore a black vest and camouflage pants. His biceps, shoulders and chest muscles protruded unnaturally from his previously lithe frame. It was as if his body could not accommodate the metamorphosis of muscle. But it was his face that screamed loudest of the aberration—his jaw protruded outward. Not as prominently as Arjun's, but it looked more like Dr Ling had eaten a rasgulla and had forgotten to swallow.

Sinews and blue nerves stood out from bare skin and the parts that were not muscle were covered with robotic levers on his elbows, arms, legs and even his chest. He looked like a robot had mutated with a vanara's foetus. Arjun cringed and then he saw Dr Ling's blazing, red eyes. They burned with anger, insomnia and frustration. They narrated a story of a genius whose humanity had been swallowed by his disappointments.

Dr Ling moved towards Arjun with a grimace, 'Thank you,' he said, 'thank you, Arjun Singh.'

The confidence of the man was unnerving. Even though Arjun towered over him, he felt doubtful.

'You're not a soldier anymore, Ling. You're an assassin, a mutant and a genocidal maniac. Turn back to where you left your humanity,' said Arjun.

Ling pretended he hadn't heard him, 'Thank you, Arjun Singh', he said and bowed, 'for giving me parts of you—your blood, your DNA, your genome and your vanara's exoskeleton.'

'What the hell have you become, Ling?' said Arjun, seeing the pulsing veins on Ling's shoulders.

'In 2015, German scientists created robotic arms that allowed men to lift thirty times their weight. And well, before that, in some ancient civilization in the Roman calendar, before Christ, the vanaras existed. A race of beings that were so strong that each one was considered equal to a hundred humans,' said Ling, his lava eyes boring holes into Arjun, 'Can you imagine if some man, some genius figured out a way to combine ancient power with modern initiative?'

'You're not a vanara, Ling. Look at you, you're an abomination. You're a bad genetic remix.'

'I'm a robotic vanara, Arjun Singh, and nothing can beat me. Your father humiliated me, your mother shamed me and now you took Tawang away from me. They had a chance and they made the wrong decision. We predicted an earthquake and we predicted annihilation, and it shall be delivered. For I am you, Arjun Singh—only better.' With that, the doctor smashed his right fist into Arjun's face.

The vanara keeled over at the punch, it was a blow harder than he had ever felt. His head throbbed after the unexpected attack. But months in a cave had conquered his mind. He shook his head and with all his strength, took Ling down in a rugby tackle. The older man didn't see it coming and both of them smashed into the ground, rolling.

Arjun sat on top of Ling's torso and with devastating power, he punched the man's face. He hit him with all his fury—once, twice and then, thrice. It was a blow that would have smashed a normal person's face into pulp but the blows were greeted by a quiet laugh from the older man.

He spat out blood from his mouth and threw Arjun off him. The vanara went flying in the opposite direction.

'Why would you hurt yourself, Mr Singh? Why would you harm that which you helped create?' With another jump, the doctor was on Arjun. He delivered swift blows—a left hook to the nose and a right kick to Arjun's ribs. The swift fury threw Arjun off his feet. All his healed injuries resurfaced with more pain.

From somewhere behind him, gunfire exploded on Ling's torso. The doctor looked surprised and then laughed as the bullets ricocheted off him like peas fired at a brick wall.

'First, I will destroy this wretched town. I will kill all the survivors. Then, I will go deep into your country. Nothing can take me down, Mr Singh. Because, nothing could take you down. I can do anything you can do, except fly.'

Arjun struggled to his knees. At least he had one thing the doctor didn't. With a concentrated explosion, he took off close to the ground and picked up the stunned doctor.

He raced toward the skies, grabbing the doctor with his right hand. The doctor did not struggle and as they rose higher, he screamed over the velocity.

'When I said I can't fly,' he said, 'I lied. Blowholes,' and Arjun felt himself flung mid-air in the opposite direction with the doctor now grabbing on to him. Wind enveloped the doctor and he reversed in the opposite direction that Arjun had taken—towards the ground below.

Like a meteor plummeting towards its certain death on to the valley below, the two figures sped through air and smashed into the ground, creating chaos in their wake. A loud boom echoed across the valley as Ling crumpled Arjun on to the ground below—two immortals causing the earthquake by themselves.

He was dying. This time he knew it was a certainty. His ribs poked into his lungs. He lay in the crater, unable to breathe. Arjun opened his eyes slightly to see Ling's frame tower over him. The man wheezed as if the effort had taken the wind out of his sails.

'Say hello to your parents for me, Mr Singh,' said Ling, as he lifted a big rock from inside the crater and slammed it on Arjun's torso, head and legs.

Each blow crumpled his life force and his old wounds bled out. *What had been the point of any of this?* He had spent months trying to get better and now his entire recovery had been extinguished in moments.

'Killing you has been exhausting, Mr Singh!' said Ling, 'Happy dying!'

Fatigued by the futility of two invincible creatures fighting to death, he flew out of the crater and left Arjun to die. Despite Arjun's heavy breathing, he felt the Earth move as Ling proceeded towards conquering the land. Alexander, the Great, with an army of one. A few minutes later, Arjun heard more gunfire. And the arrogant guffaws of Ling—he had chosen this moment in his life to finally have a sense of humour, as the bullets failed to harm him at all.

It will all be over soon, thought Arjun, *and I will become a memory.*

He closed his eyes and snow filled his vision. In the snow, he saw his mother looking at him with a determined expression. Despite the blanket of snow around her, he could make out the words on her lips, 'Who needs you?'

His eyes opened suddenly and despite his physical body being mauled beyond comprehension, he began to rise. He tried to pull his consciousness beyond his physicality. With groans, he dragged himself to the mouth of the crater and looked ahead at the battlefield.

The sun was setting and in the twilight, Dr Ling continued walking. Bullets exploded all around him. A missile seared towards him but he swatted it as if it was a mosquito—it detonated with no effect at his advance. Another missile fired and Ling punched it with his bionic arm. The missile flew back to where it had come from—dangerously close to Tawang. His walking silhouette lit up with orange and red ammunition ineffectively exploding all around him—a black hole of war.

The source of this last attack stood far from him, screaming her head off. Arjun saw Kelly with her four hands holding four long-range weapons in each hand. She shouted instructions to her soldiers who followed their leader despite the futility of it all. Kelly did not stall even once in the face of the immortal that approached them. She did not hesitate despite the screams from the town behind her.

That's when Arjun realized it. For months, he had thought his compass, his guiding light, his Gandhi had been General Taunque. He had been wrong. It had always been her—this survivor, this being of fire and light who existed despite nature commanding her to never have been born in the first place. He saw her then as a Goddess—four arms akimbo and firing with all the rage that drove her against all the wrongs of the world. She was his reason. She had always been his reason.

Who needs you the most?

She didn't need him.

He needed her.

∞

Dr Ling had had enough of this firework display and with a growl of rage, he began charging towards her. She didn't flinch and replaced her ammunition as if Ling was part of a tricky training exercise at her garden in Ooty.

Her curse at Ling echoed over the gunfire in the valley, 'Kill me now, Ling! I dare you. I may pass on, but you will burn forever in the depths of hell, you vile demon goat!'

The screams infuriated Ling. He raced towards her with murder in his eyes. She watched him with a wrath of her own. Arjun didn't care what he believed in but if she believed in something with such unfettering certainty, he had to believe in it too.

He took a deep breath and prepared himself. He kneeled in the starter's position waiting for his mental gun to go off. With one enormous broken intake of breath, he exploded towards Ling. He became a living missile, flying at the speed of light, shattering the very essence of time and space—a moving portrait of the wind's glory.

Just as Ling was about to grab Kelly by the throat, he was lifted off his feet by the missile that was Arjun. They took off in the air together in an eruption of air and blood—bounding towards the sliver of the setting sun above the valley.

Arjun gripped Ling from the back, his hands around the man's neck and his legs wrapped around his torso like a baby monkey on the back of his mother. Ling struggled and screamed but Arjun was determined to not let go.

'I will have your skin, Singh,' screamed Ling as their velocity tore the skies, 'again!'

'You should have just used your lasers, you egoist,' screamed Arjun.

As they reached a few hundred meters above the air, Arjun stalled. He floated above Tawang Town and looked below—it looked like a toy town, a Lego set that represented more than residence of a lakh. It personified the very concept of a nation, twisted as it may be.

'Let me go,' howled Ling, trying to fly on his own but held back by the iron grip of the vanara behind him.

'You may fly like me or be impenetrable like me, Ling. But there's something you don't know about being a vanara. You cannot defeat me, Ling. And I cannot defeat you. But I can defeat myself,' said Arjun.

'What are you talking about?' screamed the doctor, amidst his struggles.

'Humans carry the energy potential of thirty hydrogen bombs within them. Imagine how much a vanara carries,' screamed Arjun as wind exploded from inside him, 'I cannot defeat you from the outside, but I can defeat you from within.'

'I will crush you, Singh. I will bathe in a fountain of your blood and ashes,' screamed Ling as the two figures floated in the pale orange sky.

'Call me Pawan,' said Arjun and he concentrated hard on his third eye, harder than he had ever meditated in his life. He focused on every cell of his body, till they all aligned as one—till every pore, every minor proton, each little atom and strand of his body was combined as one and then, with one final breath, he imploded, taking every cell inside Dr Ling with him.

They burst above Tawang Town in an explosion of life that had existed moments before, but would never exist again—the last mahasamadhi of the last vanara over the town at the edge of an ancient civilization; atoms that would carry on for generations, but never as one whole being.

Every citizen of Tawang looked up at the blinding radiance that mushroomed like a solar eclipse where the sun swallowed itself, a supernova of orange light. Then, there was a canvas of colours none of them had ever seen before, colours that humankind would never see again. Tawang witnessed Aurora Borealis' first and last visit to the eastern edge of India.

Kelly collapsed to her knees. She could not look at the lights above. Those lights were the last expression of the love of her life—his final attempt to commit suicide was his ultimate sacrifice to her. She stared at the ground and could feel his atoms fall all around her, the last molecules of her soulmate trying desperately to touch her again, to be breathed by her, to be consumed by her. She touched her stomach with a sense of grief and wondered if any of the people he had saved even knew what or who he was. Did he die for his own beliefs or hers?

He had immolated himself for a land that would probably never know him. Her tears fell to the ground he had fought for. The townsfolk stared in wonder as the Northern Lights enveloped her till she was a part of the myriad colours of an ancient world—covered by the tales of mythology.

She would trade all of it to have him back. But the lights reminded her with their buoyant glow that she would always be a part of him—a physical manifestation of his memory and his last light, shining brighter than the colours that coated her.

It was his masterpiece of hope, his final expression of himself.

Acknowledgements

I've never written acknowledgements. Nothing I've worked on has ever warranted one. But for *Pawan*, I have to make an exception. Writing a book is only half the job and the other half is rarely done by a writer.

This story has been jumping at the back of my subconscious mind, desperately trying to get my attention since 2012. It took a considerable amount of research—both mental and otherwise—to get it finished.

The first draft was a bloated blue whale double the size of this and thanks to my agent Mita Kapur from Siyahi, it is not beached at the banks of rejection.

Then, of course, there is my sister Meghna Pant—an author of far more repute than me who went through this book—as she did with my previous books *Under Delhi* and *The Wednesday Soul*—with a fine toothcomb despite it being out of her genre. Her grouse is that I haven't returned the favour for her novels but my excuse is that she doesn't need my help.

My friend Nitin Parmar gave some terrific plot suggestions and character motivations that would have otherwise slipped my mind and I'm glad he didn't let them.

Thanks also to Kapish Mehra from Rupa for supporting my words. And Shambhu Sahu and Aparna Kumar for their insightful edits. I hope they don't edit this part out.

If you bought this book, then I must thank Vasundhra Raj for her marketing that probably induced you to do so. Kudos to Mugdha Sadwani and her design team that managed to encapsulate my 70,000+ words into one cover!

And of course, my wonderful wife Iva Bagchi, who holds the fort while I'm out trying to build forts in my head.

The biggest thanks is to you. Thanks for reading my stories or supporting my comedy. Or if you're truly patient, doing both. It means a lot to me. I'm constantly surprised to see that I'm able to pursue both my passions and always end up finding people who care.

Arjun Singh may not believe in countries but thanks for believing in me.

Follow me:
Twitter & Snapchat @hankypanty
Facebook & Instagram @SorabhPant
YouTube @PantOnFire